SUPER TURBO

VS. THE FLYING NINJA SQUIRRELS

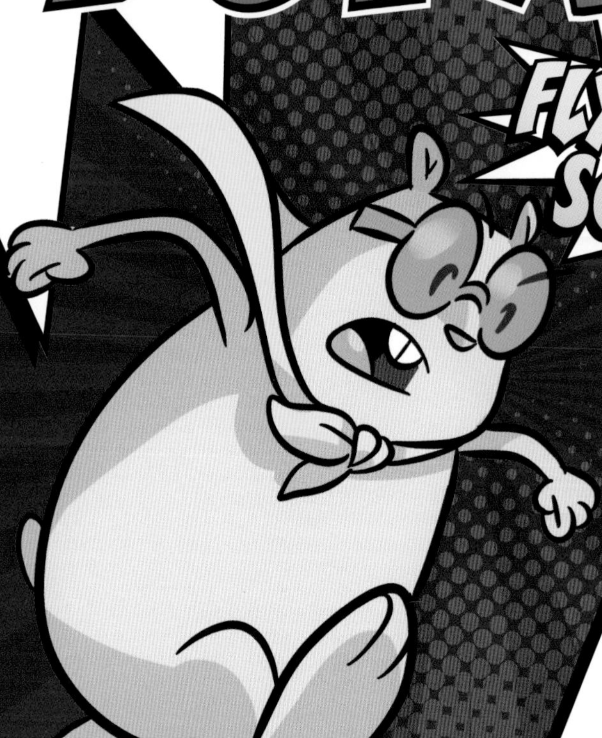

WRITTEN BY EDGAR POWERS
ILLUSTRATED BY SALVATORE COSTANZA
AT GLASS HOUSE GRAPHICS

LITTLE SIMON
NEW YORK LONDON TORONTO SYDNEY NEW DELHI

LITTLE SIMON
AN IMPRINT OF SIMON & SCHUSTER CHILDREN'S PUBLISHING DIVISION
1230 AVENUE OF THE AMERICAS, NEW YORK, NEW YORK 10020
FIRST LITTLE SIMON EDITION FEBRUARY 2021 * COPYRIGHT © 2021 BY SIMON & SCHUSTER, INC. ALL RIGHTS RESERVED, INCLUDING THE RIGHT OF REPRODUCTION IN WHOLE OR IN PART IN ANY FORM. LITTLE SIMON IS A REGISTERED TRADEMARK OF SIMON & SCHUSTER, INC., AND ASSOCIATED COLOPHON IS A TRADEMARK OF SIMON & SCHUSTER, INC. FOR INFORMATION ABOUT SPECIAL DISCOUNTS FOR BULK PURCHASES, PLEASE CONTACT SIMON & SCHUSTER SPECIAL SALES AT 1-866-506-1949 OR BUSINESS@SIMONANDSCHUSTER.COM. THE SIMON & SCHUSTER SPEAKERS BUREAU CAN BRING AUTHORS TO YOUR LIVE EVENT. FOR MORE INFORMATION OR TO BOOK AN EVENT CONTACT THE SIMON & SCHUSTER SPEAKERS BUREAU AT 1-866-248-3049 OR VISIT OUR WEBSITE AT WWW.SIMONSPEAKERS.COM. DESIGNED BY NICHOLAS SCIACCA * ART SERVICES BY GLASS HOUSE GRAPHICS * ART, COLORS, AND COVER BY SALVATORE COSTANZA * COLOR ASSISTANT: FRANCESCA INGRASSIA * LETTERING BY GIOVANNI SPATARO/GRAFIMATED CARTOON * SUPERVISION BY SALVATORE DI MARCO/GRAFIMATED CARTOON * MANUFACTURED IN CHINA 1120 SCP * 2 4 6 8 10 9 7 5 3 1 * LIBRARY OF CONGRESS CATALOGING-IN-PUBLICATION DATA NAMES: POWERS, EDGAR J., AUTHOR. | GLASS HOUSE GRAPHICS, ILLUSTRATOR. TITLE: SUPER TURBO VS. THE FLYING NINJA SQUIRRELS / BY EDGAR POWERS ; ILLUSTRATED BY GLASS HOUSE GRAPHICS. DESCRIPTION: FIRST LITTLE SIMON EDITION. | NEW YORK : LITTLE SIMON, 2021. | SERIES: SUPER TURBO, THE GRAPHIC NOVEL ; BOOK 2 | AUDIENCE: AGES 5-9 | AUDIENCE: GRADES 2-3 | SUMMARY: "FRESH OFF THEIR VICTORY AGAINST WHISKERFACE, THE SUPERHERO PETS OF SUNNYVIEW ELEMENTARY FACE OFF AGAINST A FIERCE NEW FOE: FLYING NINJA SQUIRRELS!"— PROVIDED BY PUBLISHER. IDENTIFIERS: LCCN 2020024907 (PRINT) | LCCN 2020024908 (EBOOK) | ISBN 9781534474499 (PAPERBACK) | ISBN 9781534474505 (HARDCOVER) | ISBN 9781534474512 (EBOOK) SUBJECTS: LCSH: GRAPHIC NOVELS. | CYAC: GRAPHIC NOVELS. | SUPERHEROES—FICTION. | HAMSTERS—FICTION. | PETS—FICTION. | NINJA—FICTION. | ELEMENTARY SCHOOLS—FICTION. | SCHOOLS—FICTION. CLASSIFICATION: LCC PZ7.7.P7 SV 2021 (PRINT) | LCC PZ7.7.P7 (EBOOK) | DDC 741.5/973—DC23 LC RECORD AVAILABLE AT HTTPS://LCCN.LOC.GOV/2020024907   LC EBOOK RECORD AVAILABLE AT HTTPS://LCCN.LOC.GOV/2020024908

CONTENTS

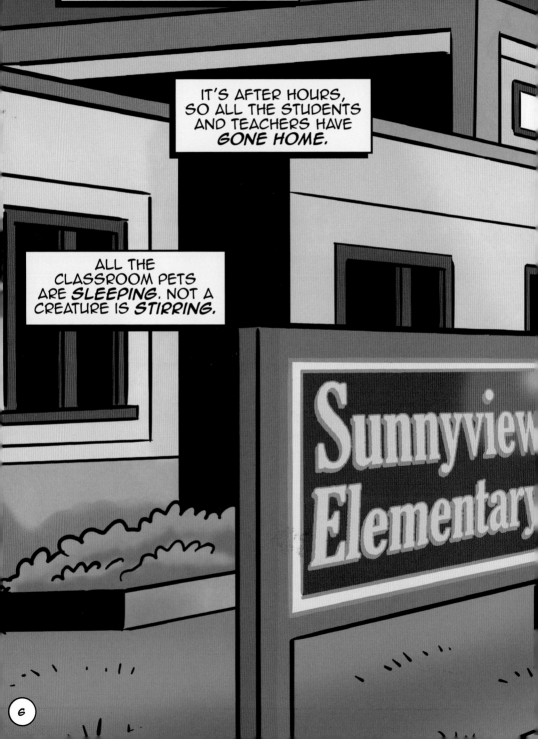

CHAPTER 1

WELCOME BACK TO *SUNNYVIEW ELEMENTARY!*

IT'S AFTER HOURS, SO ALL THE STUDENTS AND TEACHERS HAVE *GONE HOME.*

ALL THE CLASSROOM PETS ARE *SLEEPING.* NOT A CREATURE IS *STIRRING.*

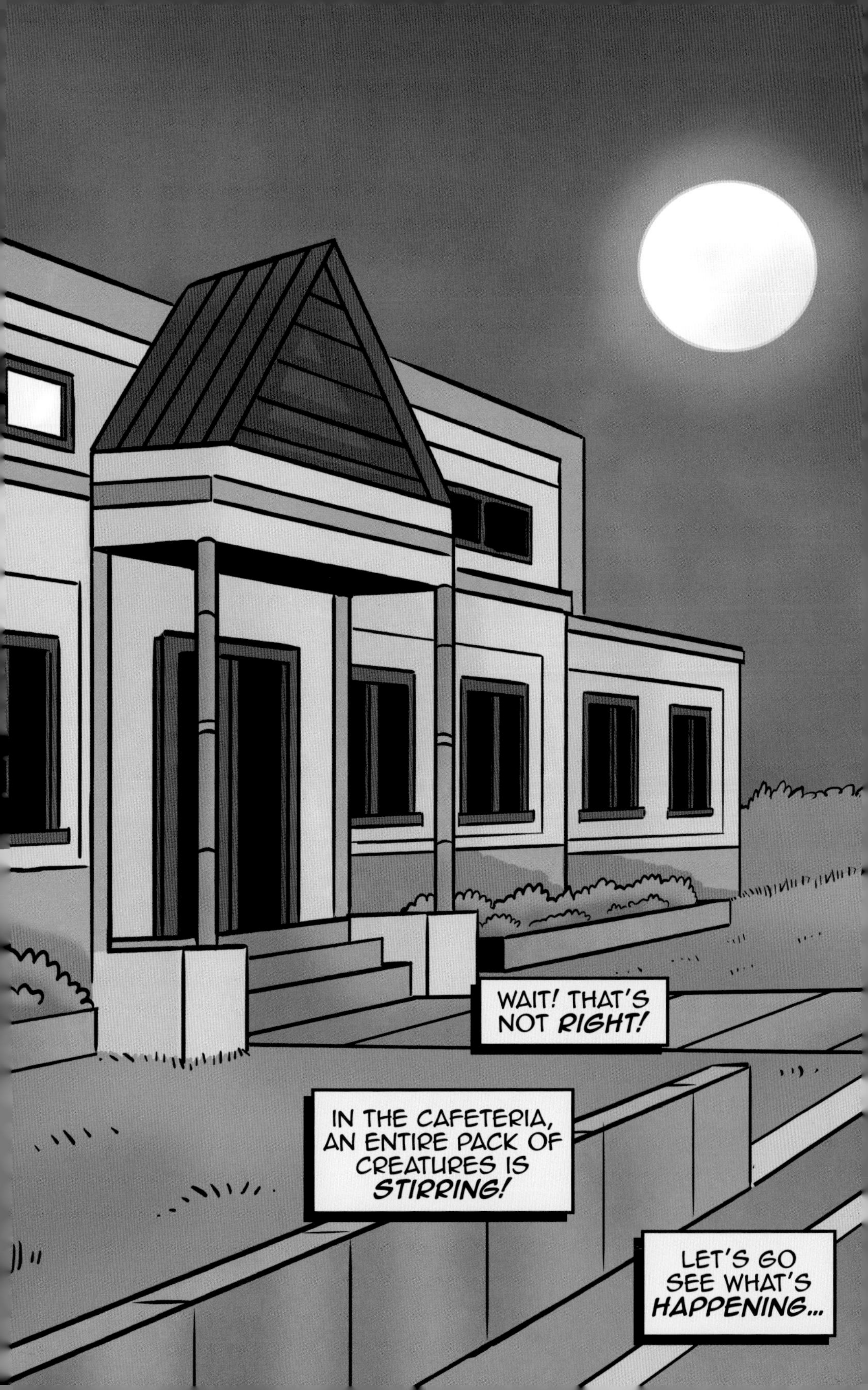
WAIT! THAT'S NOT RIGHT!
IN THE CAFETERIA, AN ENTIRE PACK OF CREATURES IS STIRRING!
LET'S GO SEE WHAT'S HAPPENING...

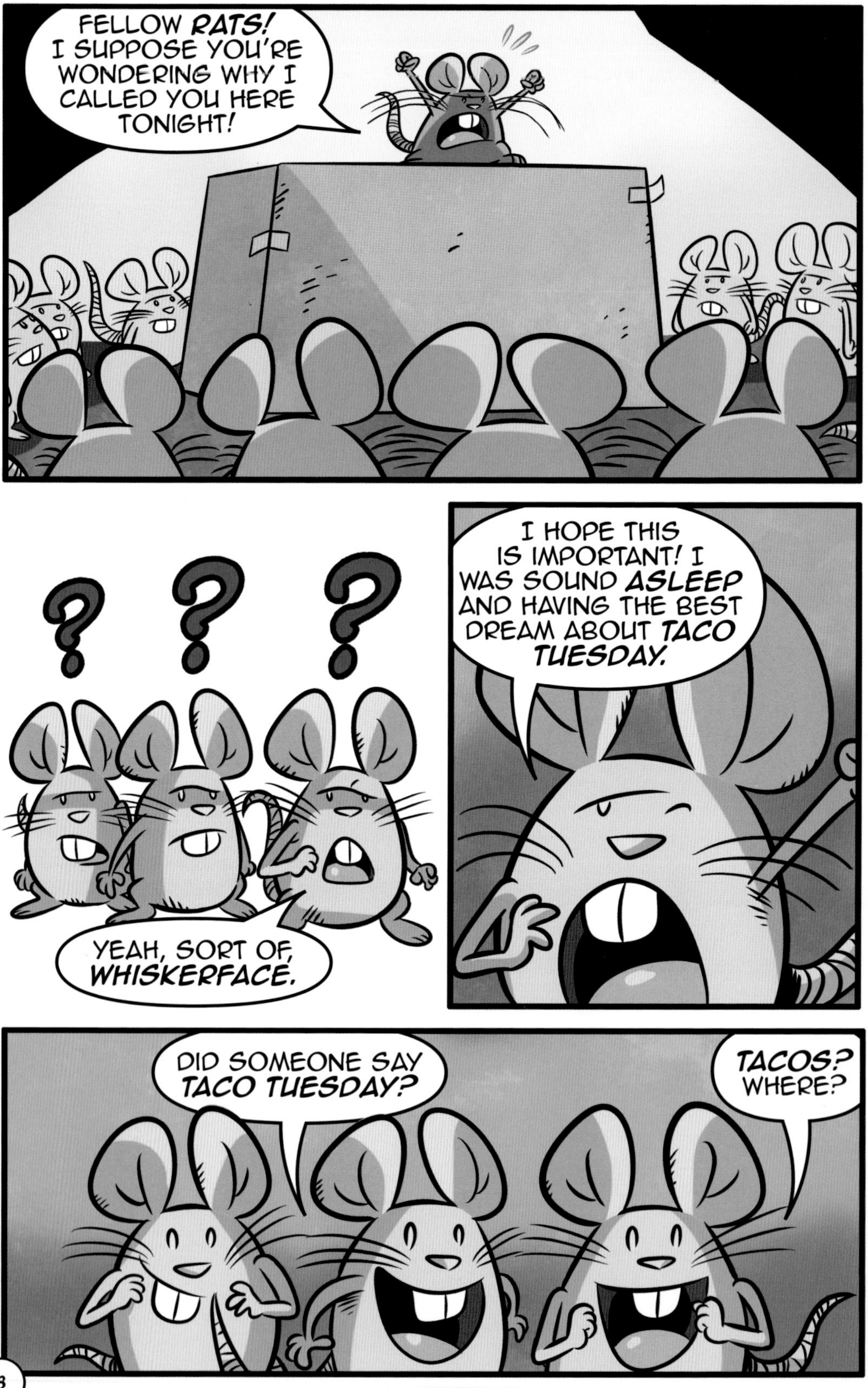
FELLOW RATS! I SUPPOSE YOU'RE WONDERING WHY I CALLED YOU HERE TONIGHT!
YEAH, SORT OF, WHISKERFACE.
I HOPE THIS IS IMPORTANT! I WAS SOUND ASLEEP AND HAVING THE BEST DREAM ABOUT TACO TUESDAY.
DID SOMEONE SAY TACO TUESDAY?
TACOS? WHERE?

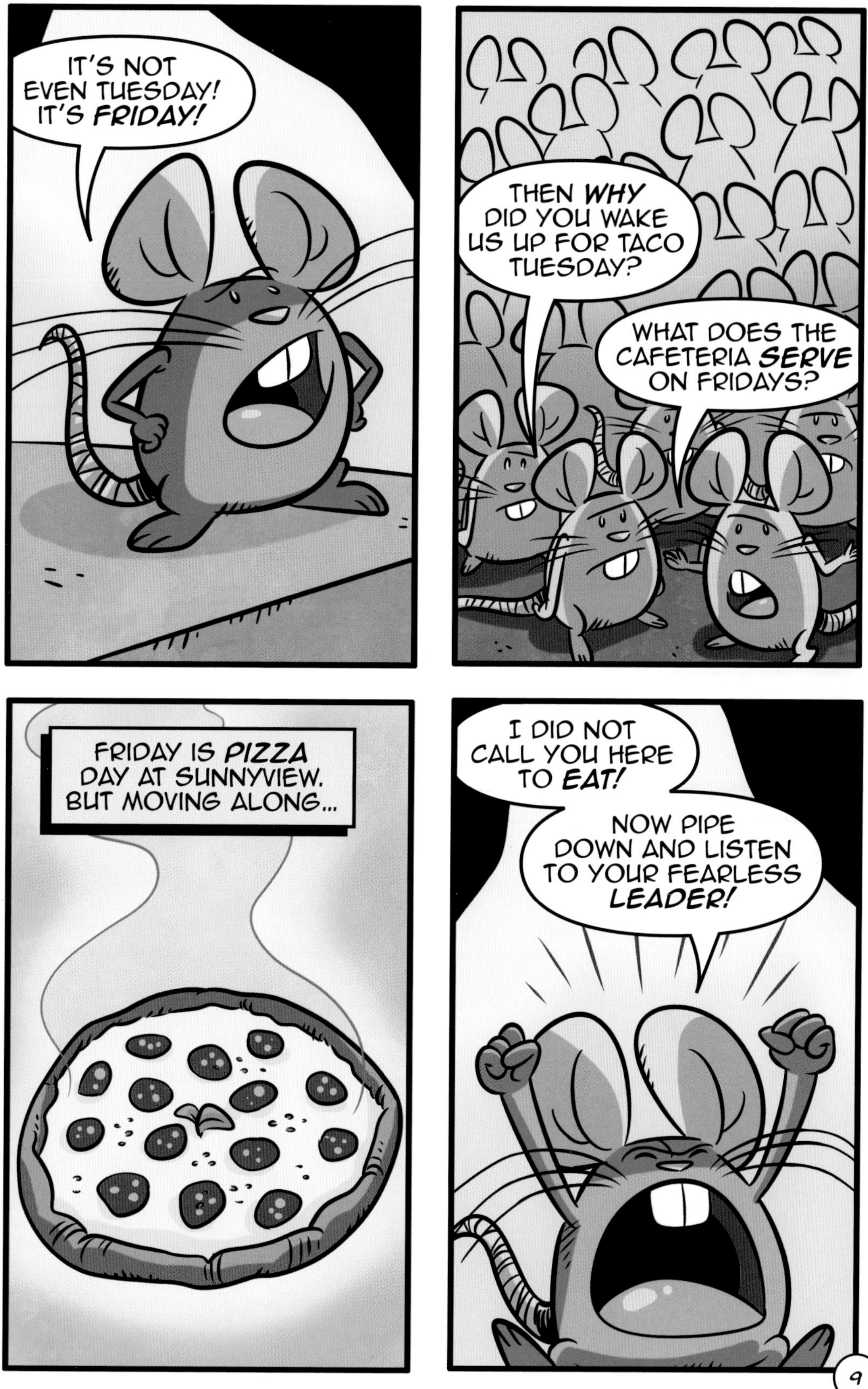
IT'S NOT EVEN TUESDAY! IT'S *FRIDAY!*
THEN *WHY* DID YOU WAKE US UP FOR TACO TUESDAY?
WHAT DOES THE CAFETERIA *SERVE* ON FRIDAYS?
FRIDAY IS *PIZZA* DAY AT SUNNYVIEW. BUT MOVING ALONG...
I DID NOT CALL YOU HERE TO *EAT!*
NOW PIPE DOWN AND LISTEN TO YOUR FEARLESS *LEADER!*

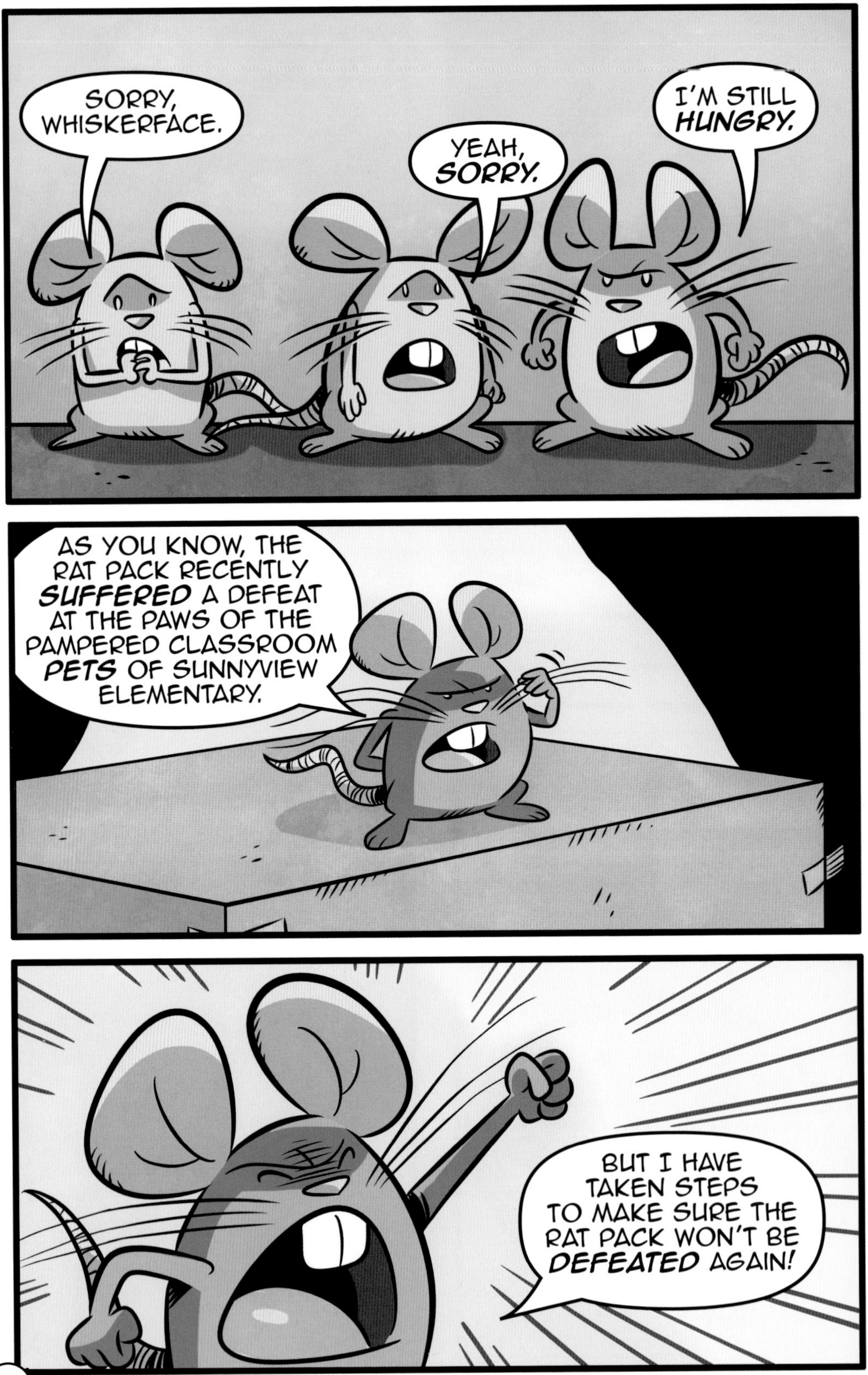
SORRY, WHISKERFACE.
YEAH, *SORRY.*
I'M STILL *HUNGRY.*
AS YOU KNOW, THE RAT PACK RECENTLY *SUFFERED* A DEFEAT AT THE PAWS OF THE PAMPERED CLASSROOM *PETS* OF SUNNYVIEW ELEMENTARY.
BUT I HAVE TAKEN STEPS TO MAKE SURE THE RAT PACK WON'T BE *DEFEATED* AGAIN!

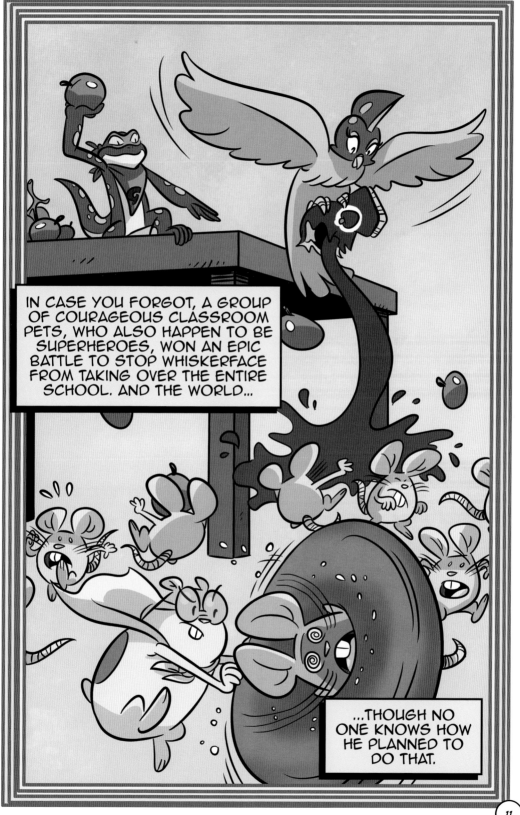

IN CASE YOU FORGOT, A GROUP OF COURAGEOUS CLASSROOM PETS, WHO ALSO HAPPEN TO BE SUPERHEROES, WON AN EPIC BATTLE TO STOP WHISKERFACE FROM TAKING OVER THE ENTIRE SCHOOL. AND THE WORLD...

...THOUGH NO ONE KNOWS HOW HE PLANNED TO DO THAT.

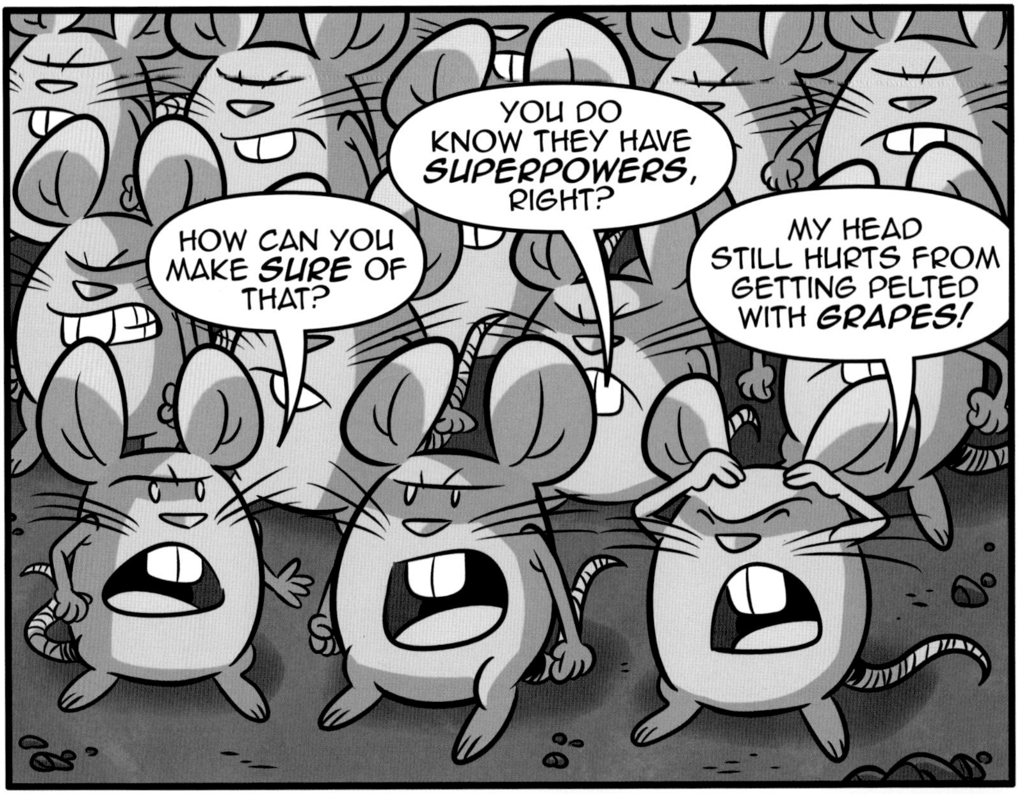
HOW CAN YOU MAKE SURE OF THAT?
YOU DO KNOW THEY HAVE SUPERPOWERS, RIGHT?
MY HEAD STILL HURTS FROM GETTING PELTED WITH GRAPES!

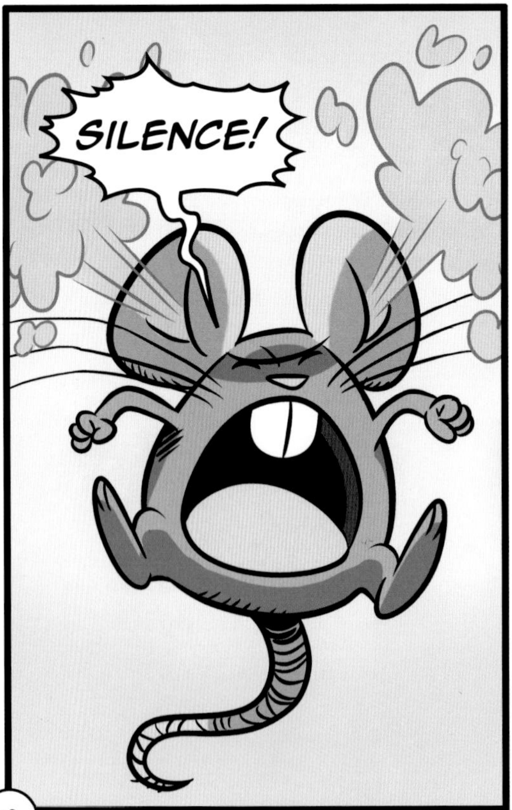
SILENCE!

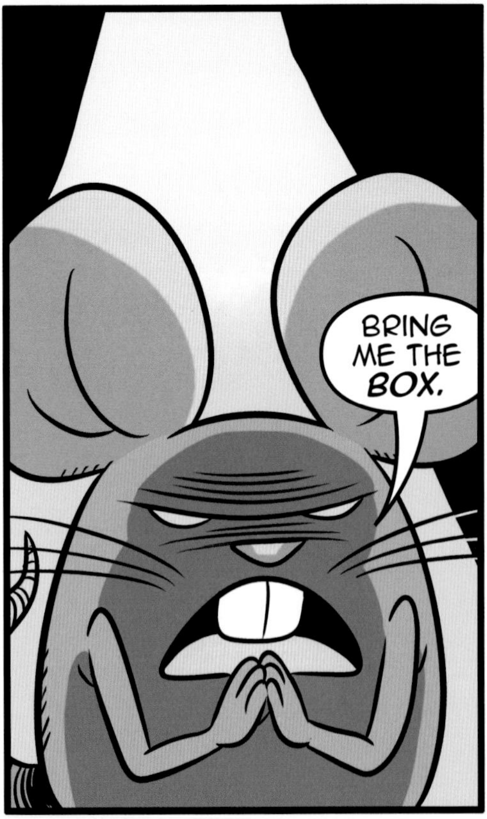
BRING ME THE BOX.

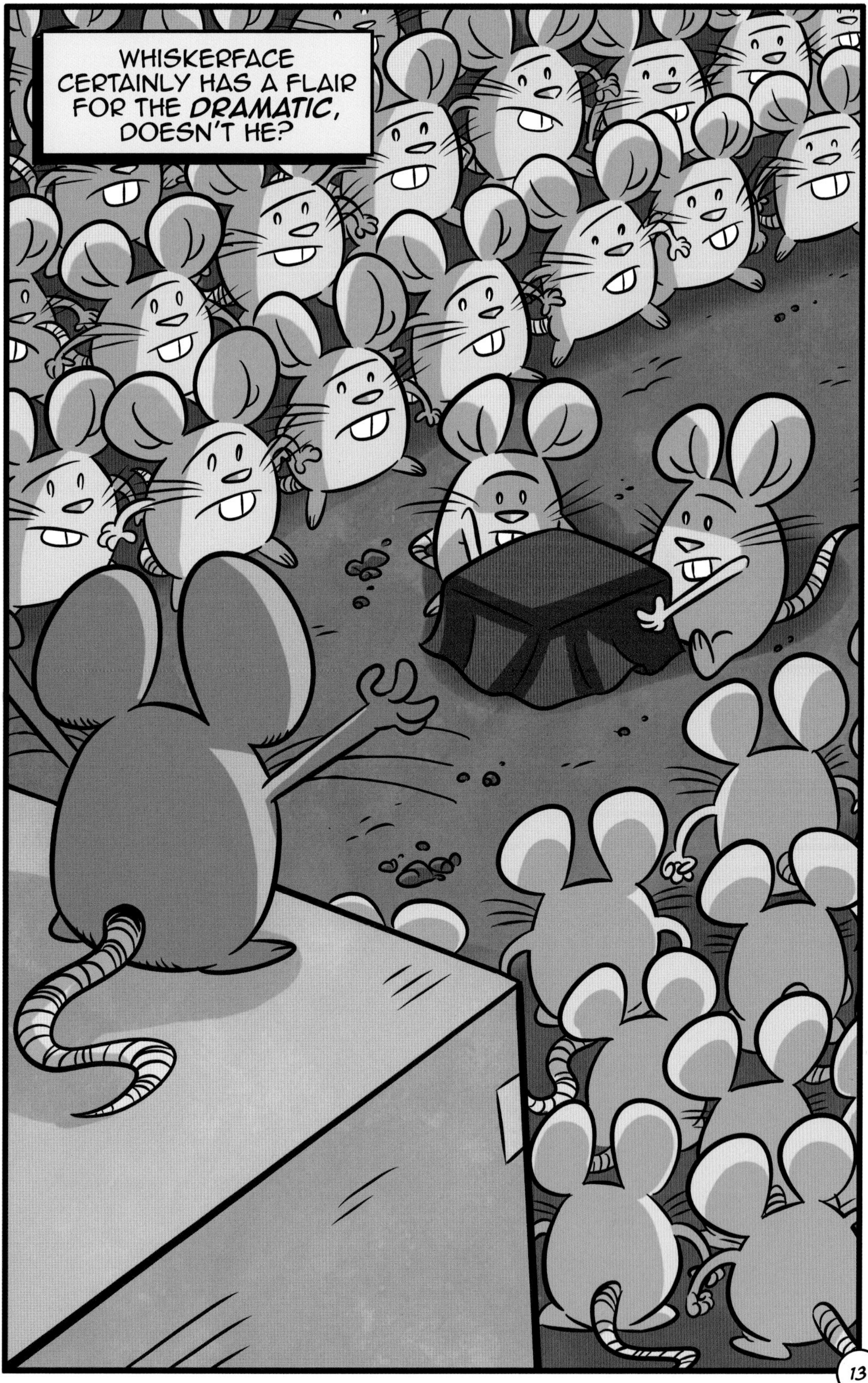
WHISKERFACE CERTAINLY HAS A FLAIR FOR THE *DRAMATIC*, DOESN'T HE?

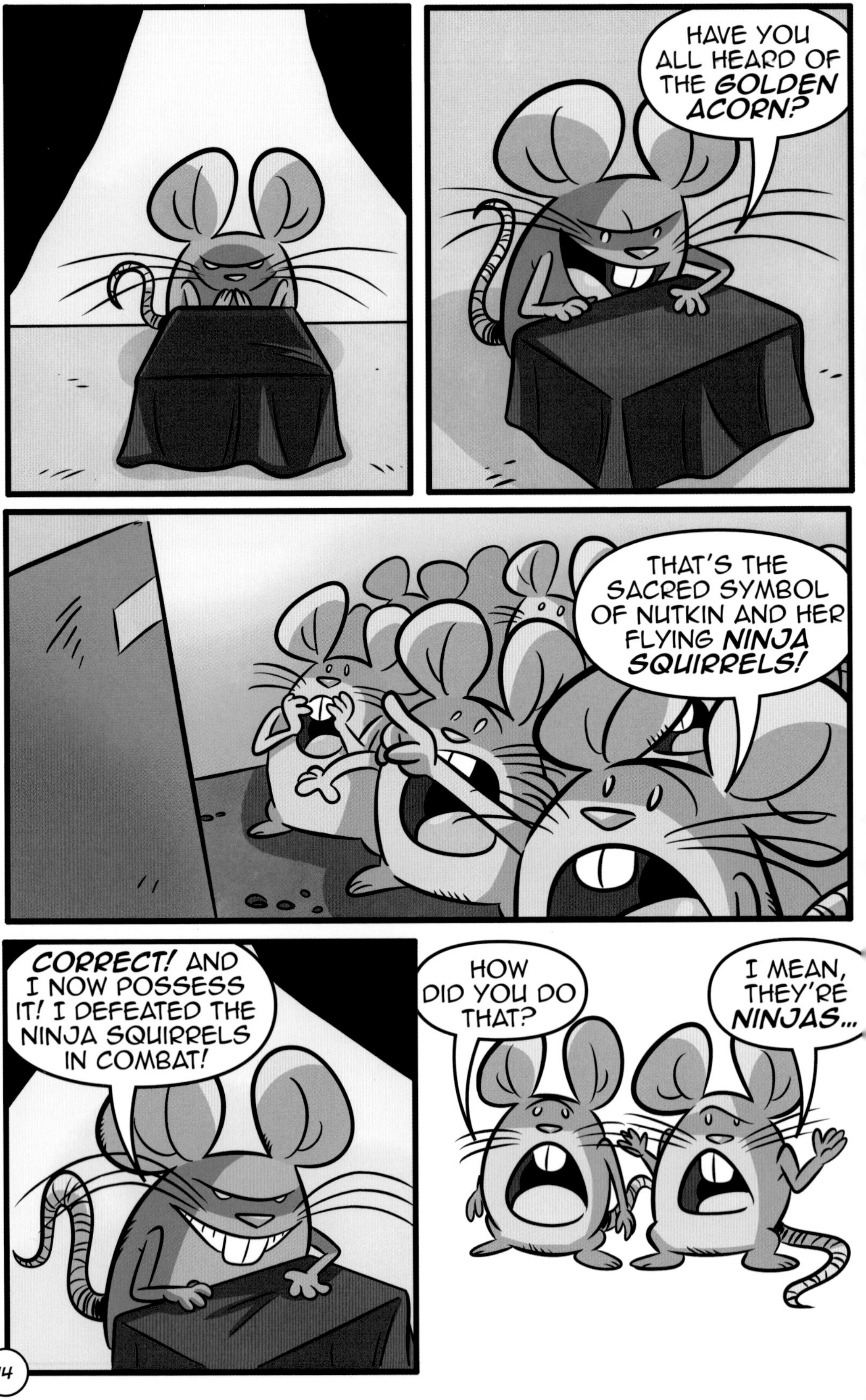
HAVE YOU ALL HEARD OF THE *GOLDEN ACORN?*
THAT'S THE SACRED SYMBOL OF NUTKIN AND HER FLYING ***NINJA SQUIRRELS!***
CORRECT! AND I NOW POSSESS IT! I DEFEATED THE NINJA SQUIRRELS IN COMBAT!
HOW DID YOU DO THAT?
I MEAN, THEY'RE ***NINJAS...***

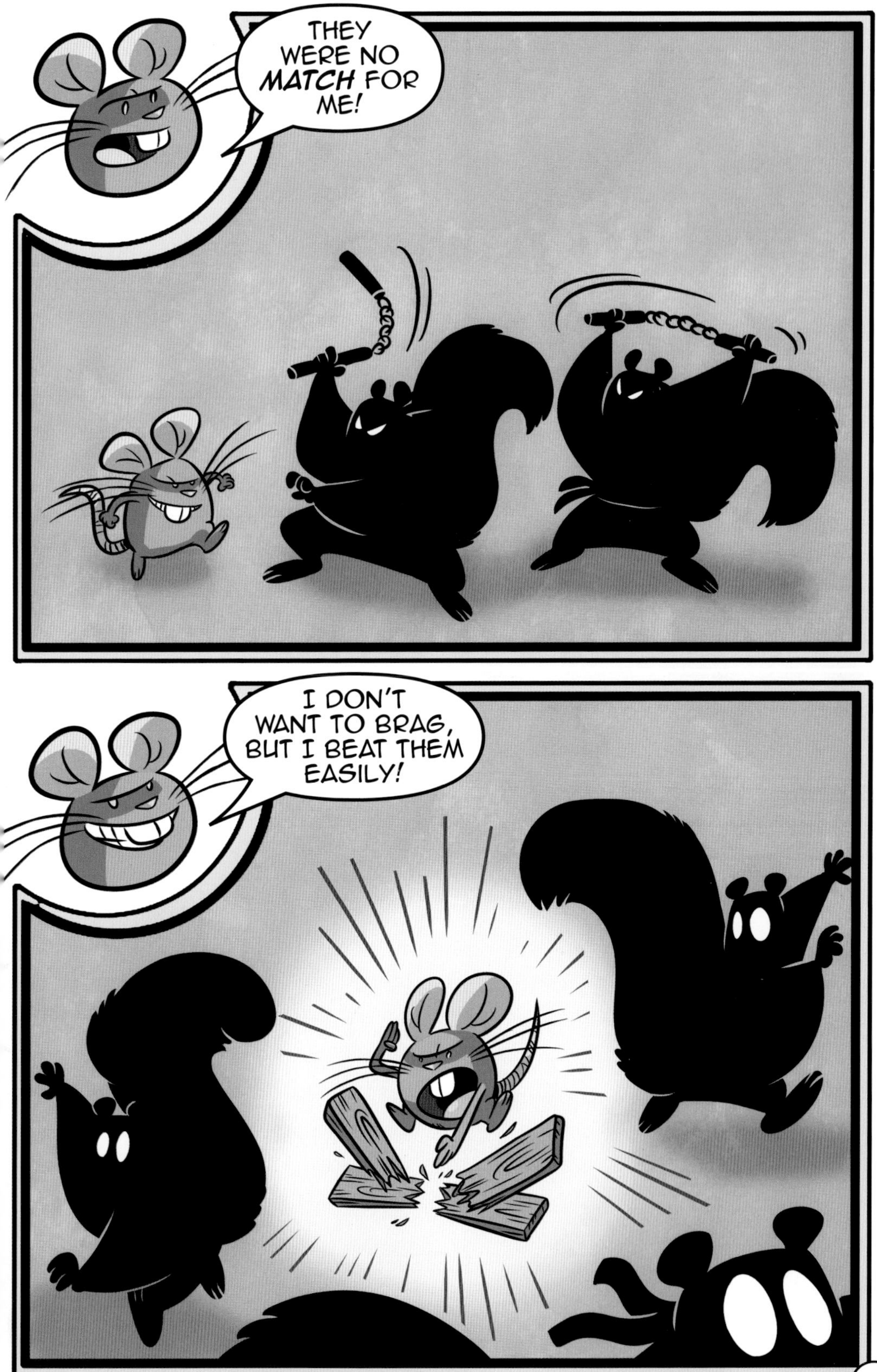
THEY WERE NO MATCH FOR ME!
I DON'T WANT TO BRAG, BUT I BEAT THEM EASILY!

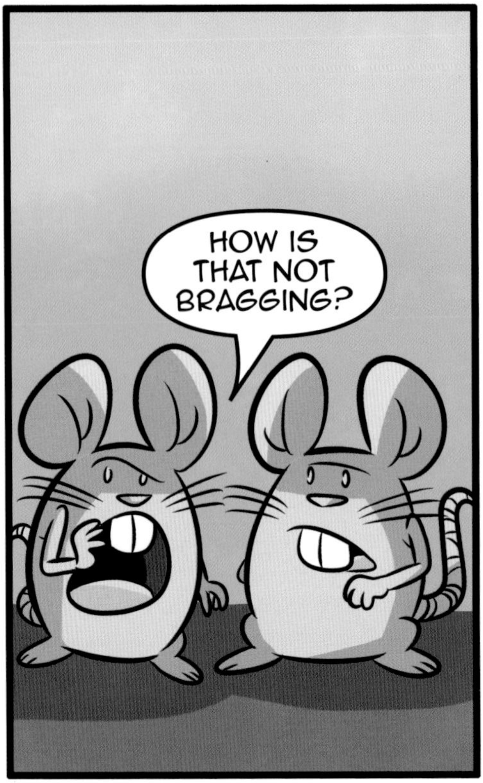
HOW IS THAT NOT BRAGGING?

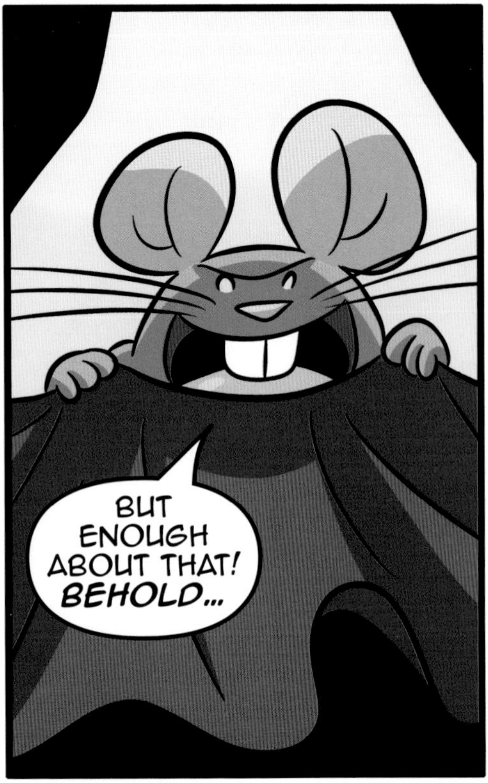
BUT ENOUGH ABOUT THAT! *BEHOLD...*

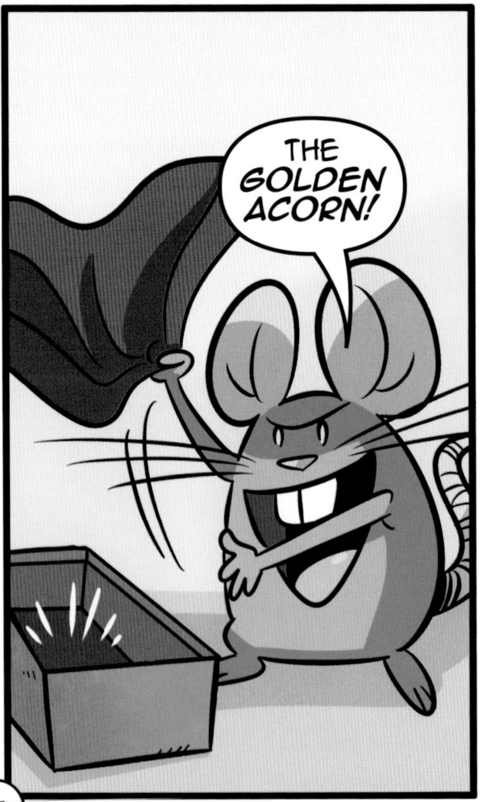
THE *GOLDEN ACORN!*

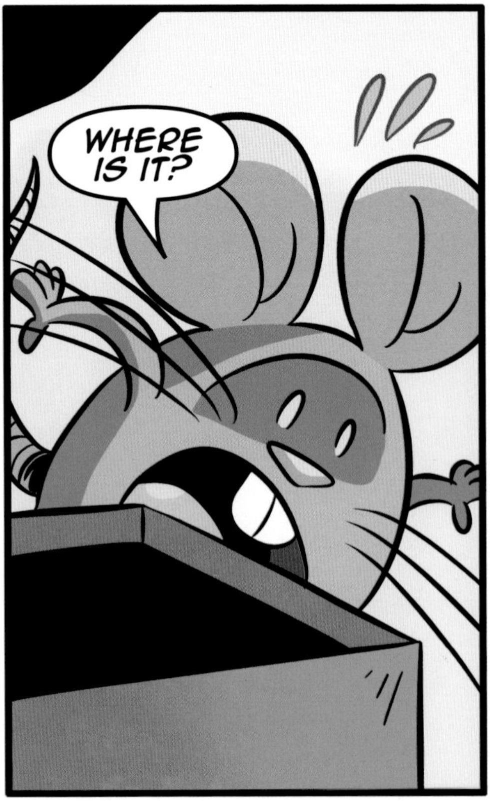
WHERE IS IT?

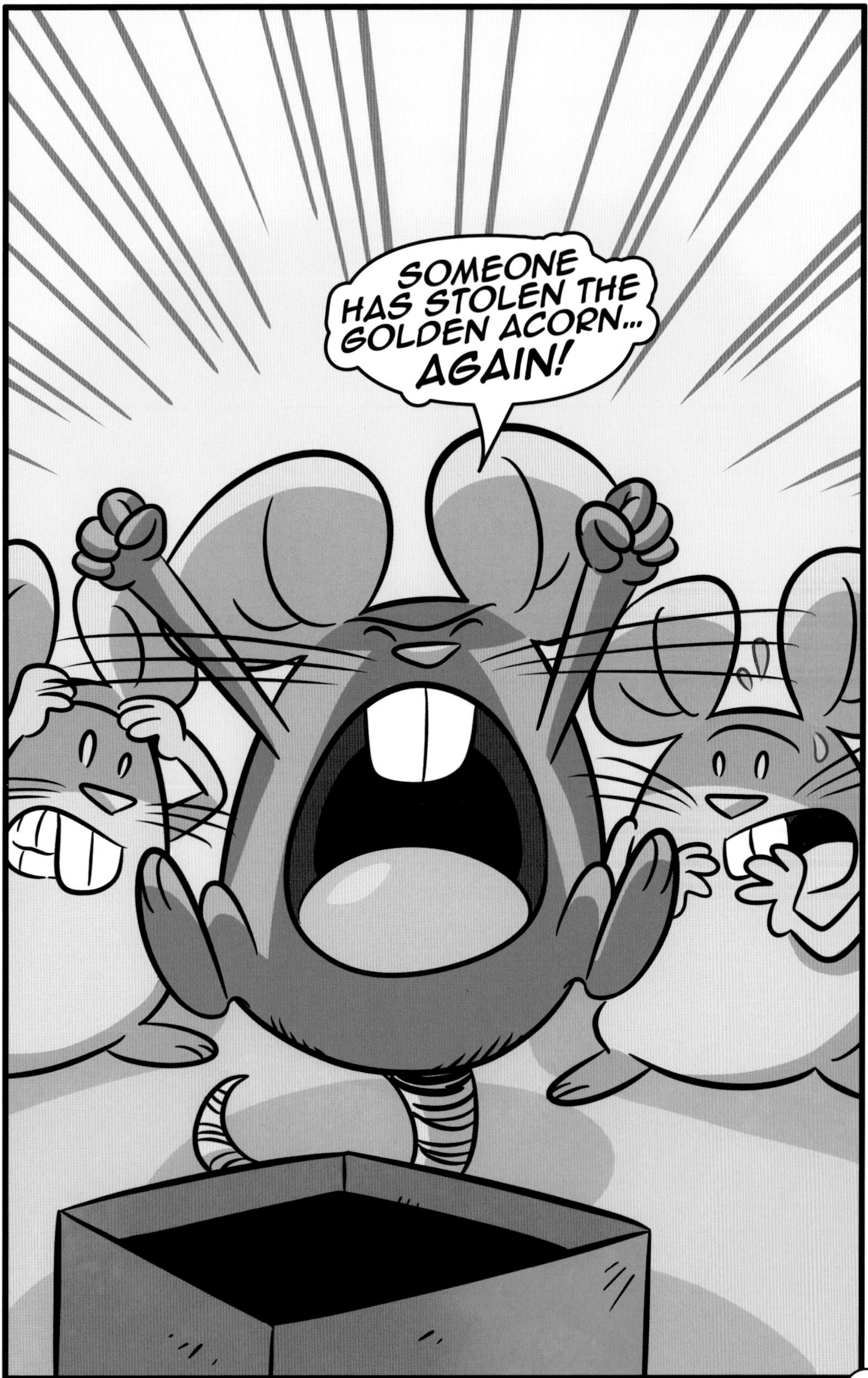
SOMEONE HAS STOLEN THE GOLDEN ACORN... AGAIN!

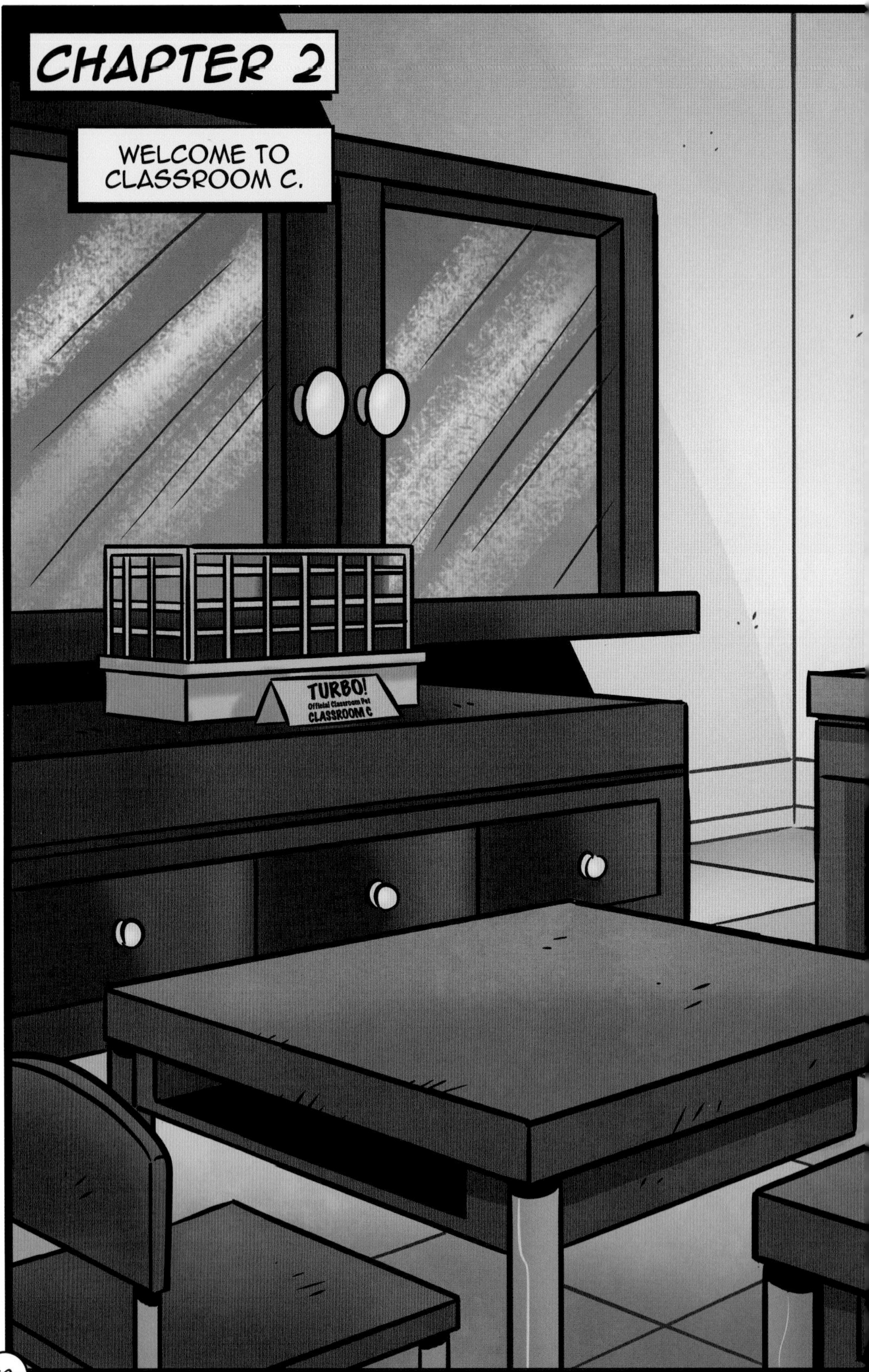
CHAPTER 2
WELCOME TO CLASSROOM C.
TURBO!
Official Classroom Pet
CLASSROOM C

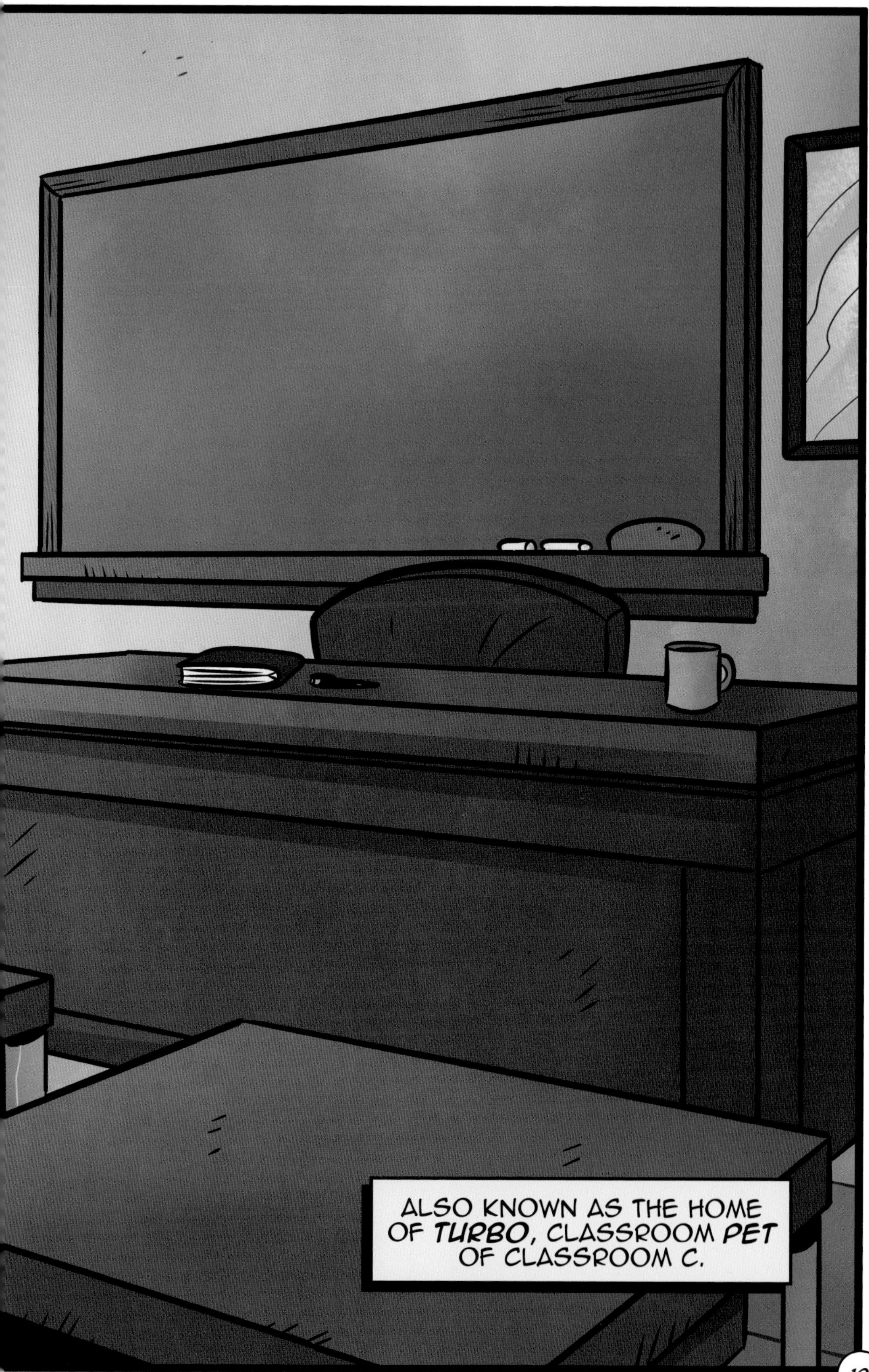
ALSO KNOWN AS THE HOME OF TURBO, CLASSROOM PET OF CLASSROOM C.

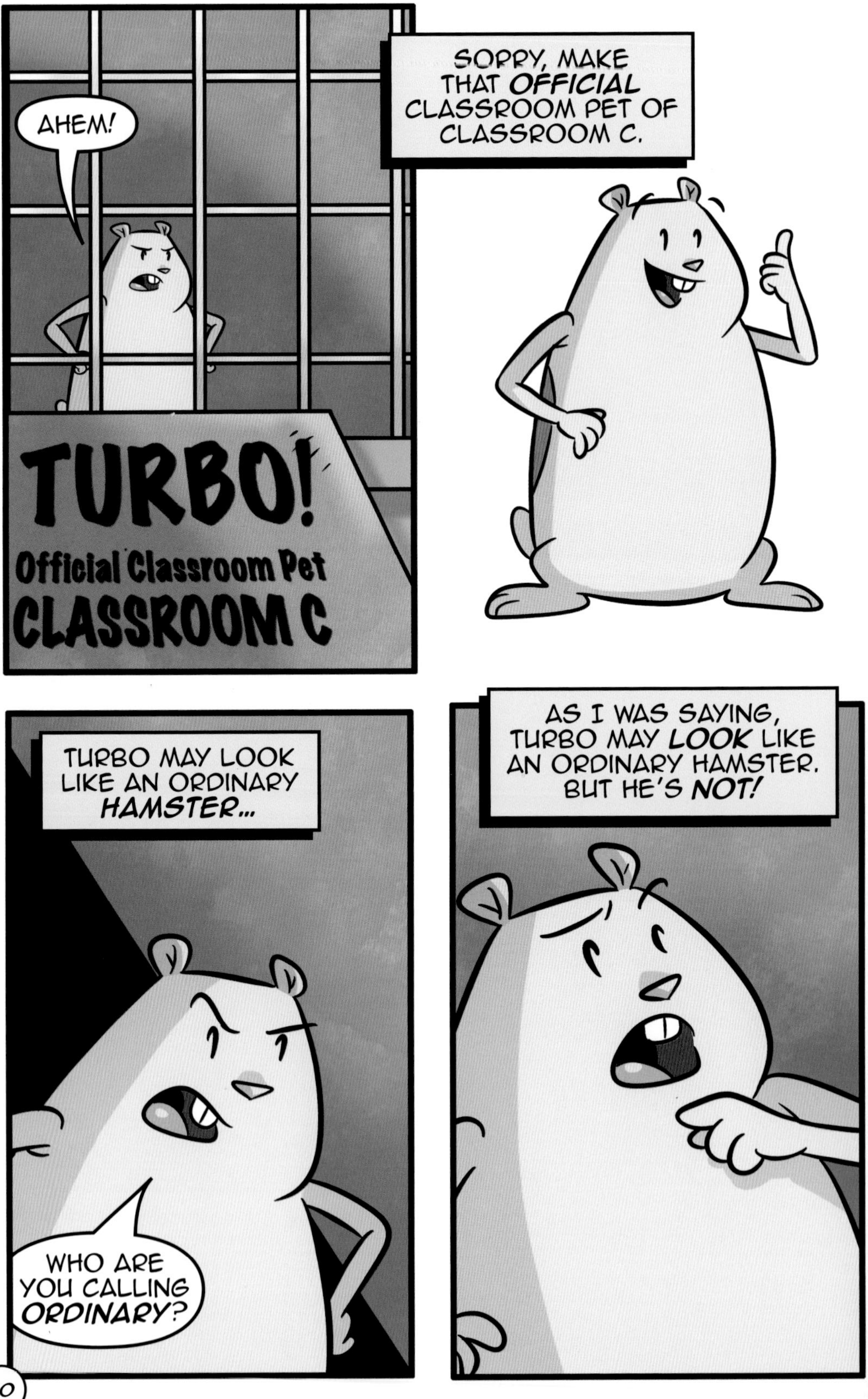
AHEM!
TURBO!
Official Classroom Pet
CLASSROOM C
SORRY, MAKE THAT OFFICIAL CLASSROOM PET OF CLASSROOM C.
TURBO MAY LOOK LIKE AN ORDINARY HAMSTER...
WHO ARE YOU CALLING ORDINARY?
AS I WAS SAYING, TURBO MAY LOOK LIKE AN ORDINARY HAMSTER. BUT HE'S NOT!

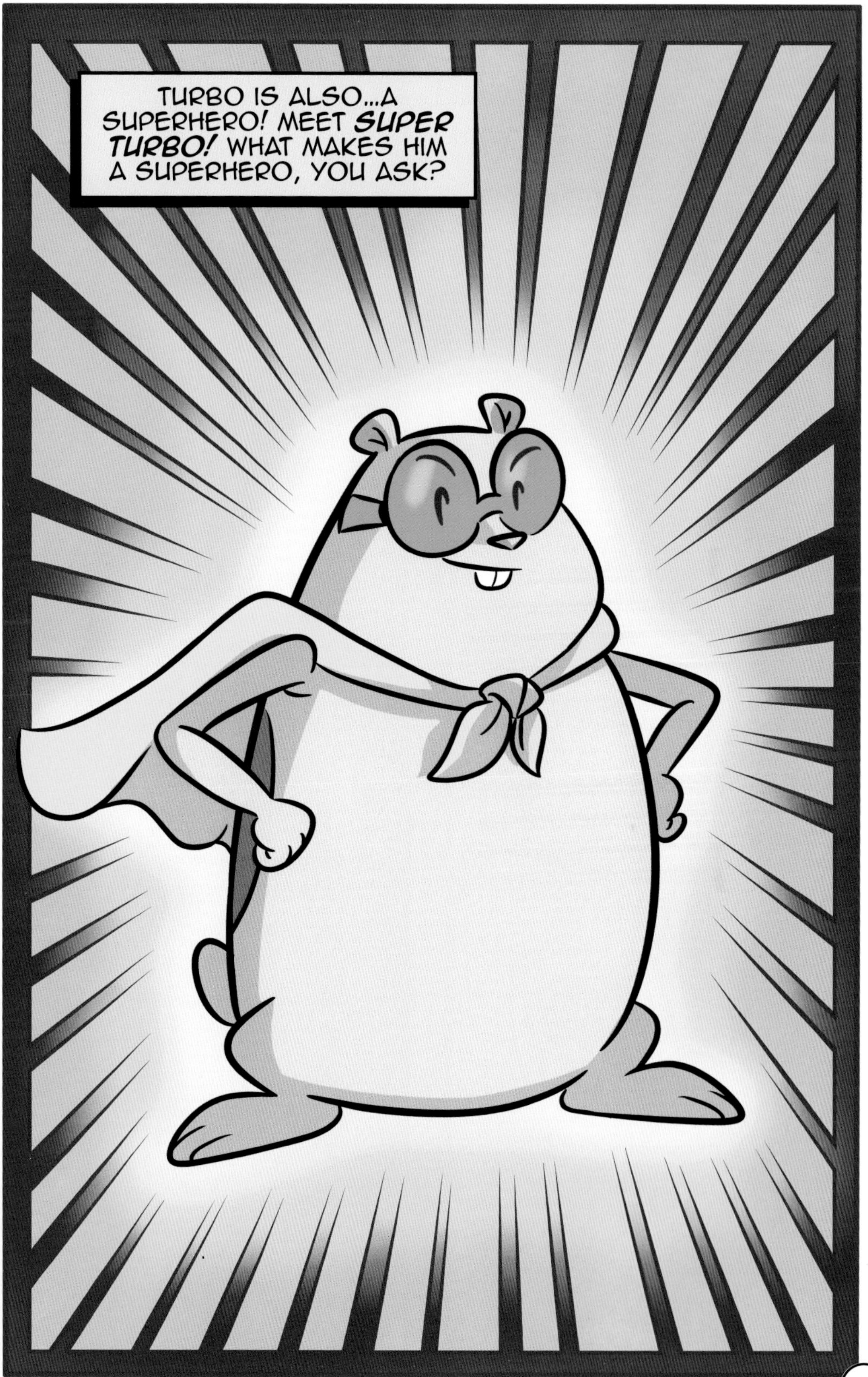
TURBO IS ALSO...A SUPERHERO! MEET *SUPER TURBO!* WHAT MAKES HIM A SUPERHERO, YOU ASK?

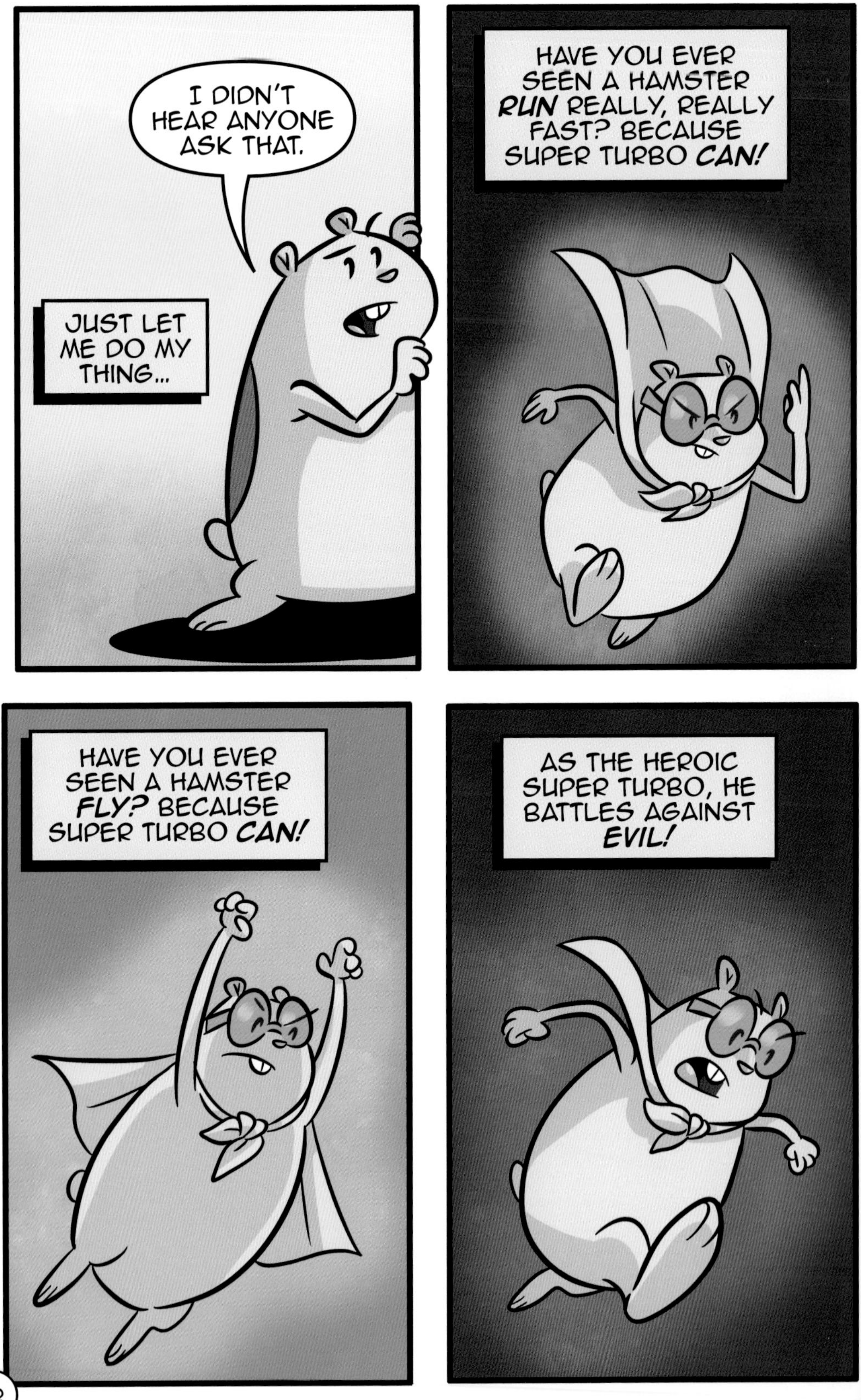
I DIDN'T HEAR ANYONE ASK THAT.
JUST LET ME DO MY THING...
HAVE YOU EVER SEEN A HAMSTER **RUN** REALLY, REALLY FAST? BECAUSE SUPER TURBO **CAN!**
HAVE YOU EVER SEEN A HAMSTER **FLY?** BECAUSE SUPER TURBO **CAN!**
AS THE HEROIC SUPER TURBO, HE BATTLES AGAINST **EVIL!**

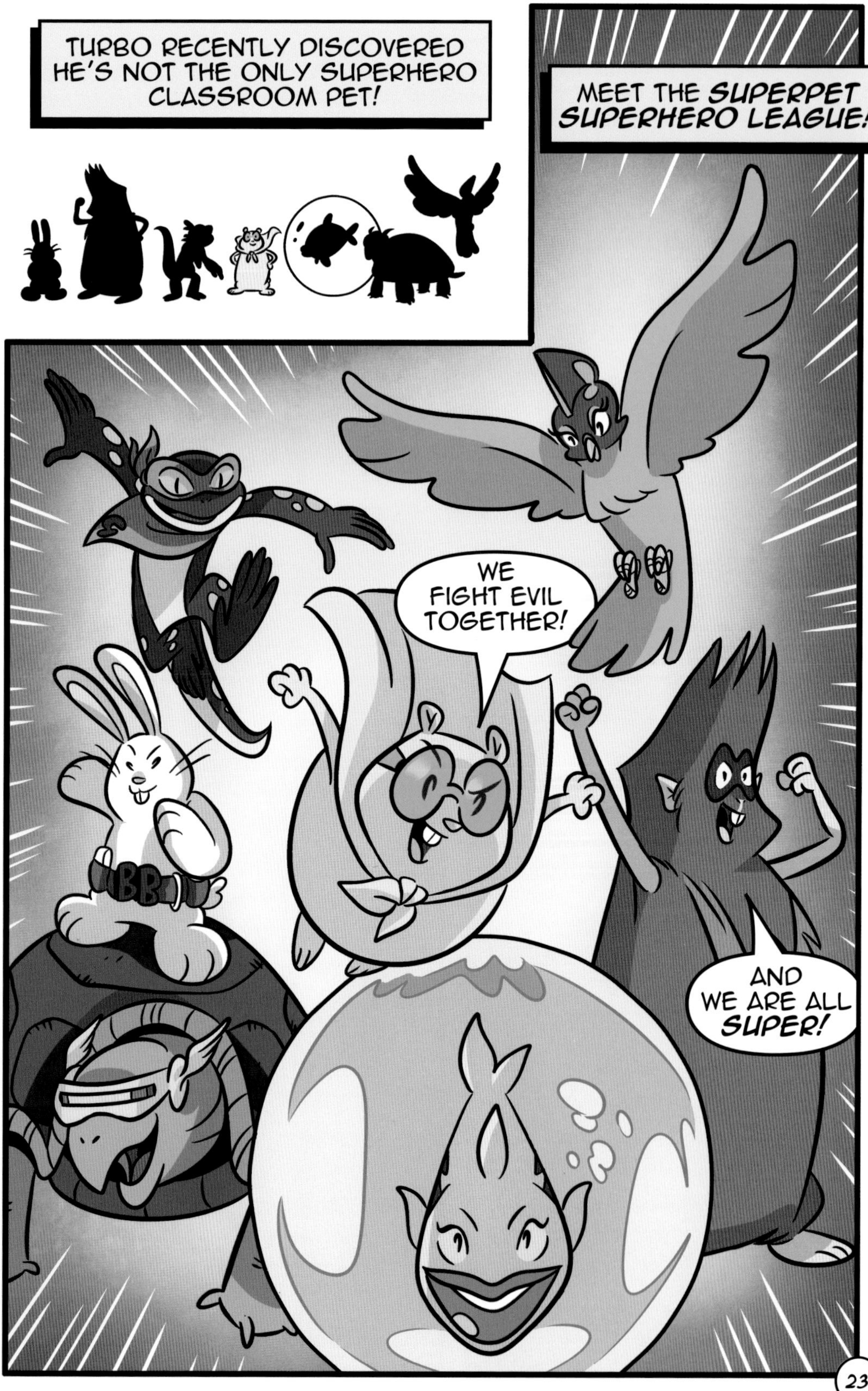
TURBO RECENTLY DISCOVERED HE'S NOT THE ONLY SUPERHERO CLASSROOM PET!
MEET THE SUPERPET SUPERHERO LEAGUE!
WE FIGHT EVIL TOGETHER!
AND WE ARE ALL SUPER!
BB

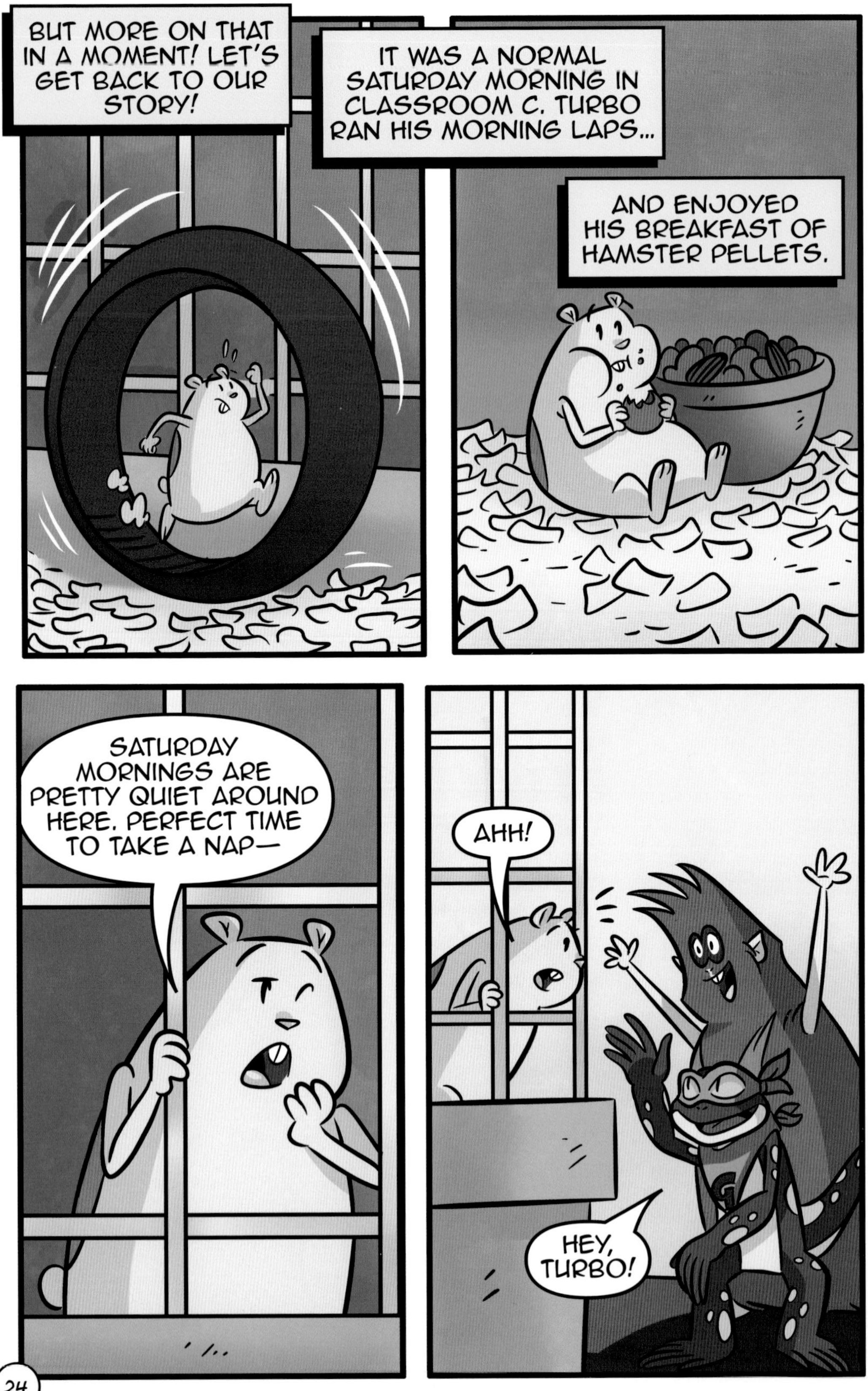
BUT MORE ON THAT IN A MOMENT! LET'S GET BACK TO OUR STORY!
IT WAS A NORMAL SATURDAY MORNING IN CLASSROOM C. TURBO RAN HIS MORNING LAPS...
AND ENJOYED HIS BREAKFAST OF HAMSTER PELLETS.
SATURDAY MORNINGS ARE PRETTY QUIET AROUND HERE. PERFECT TIME TO TAKE A NAP—
AHH!
HEY, TURBO!

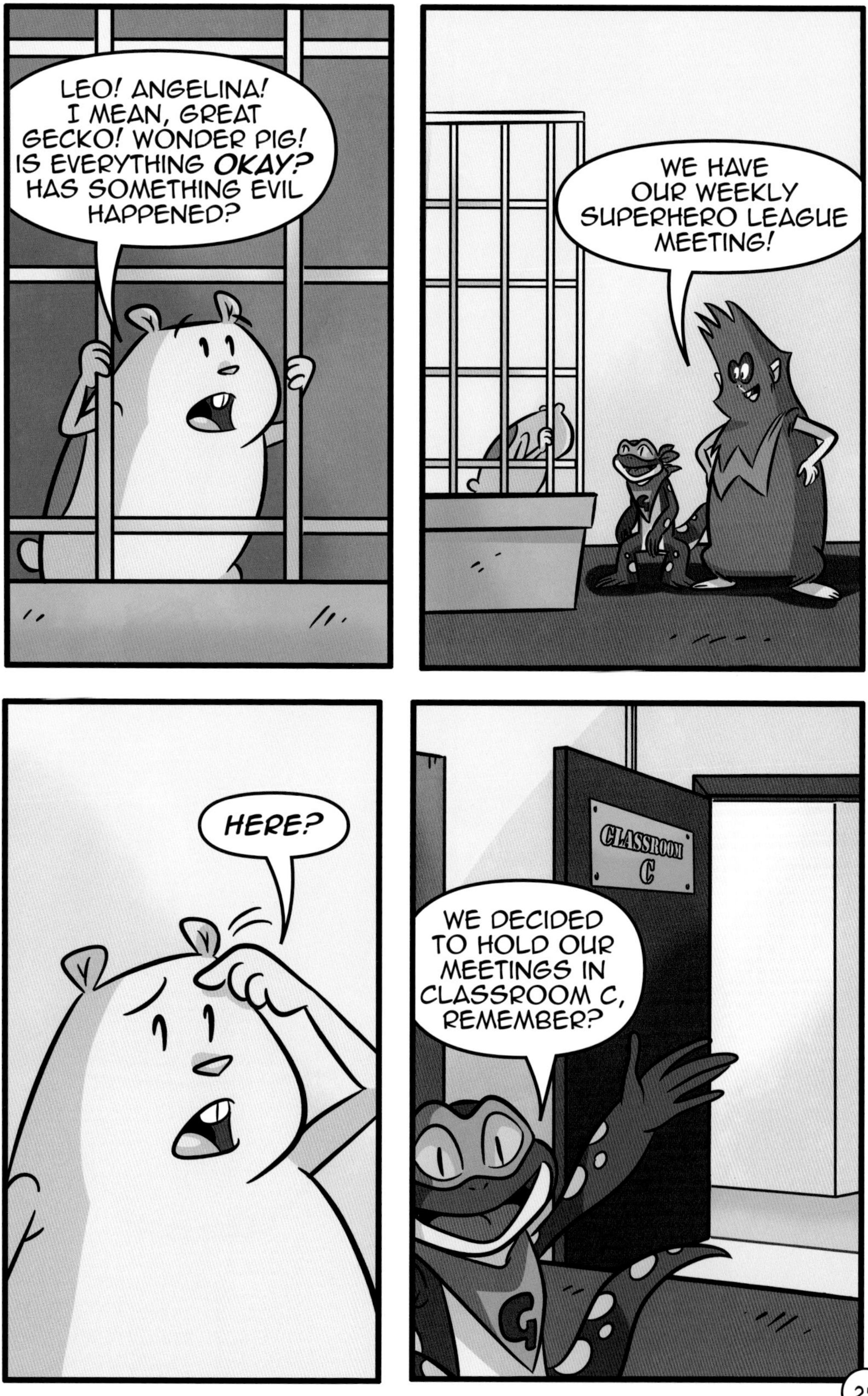
LEO! ANGELINA! I MEAN, GREAT GECKO! WONDER PIG! IS EVERYTHING *OKAY?* HAS SOMETHING EVIL HAPPENED?
WE HAVE OUR WEEKLY SUPERHERO LEAGUE MEETING!
HERE?
CLASSROOM C
WE DECIDED TO HOLD OUR MEETINGS IN CLASSROOM C, REMEMBER?

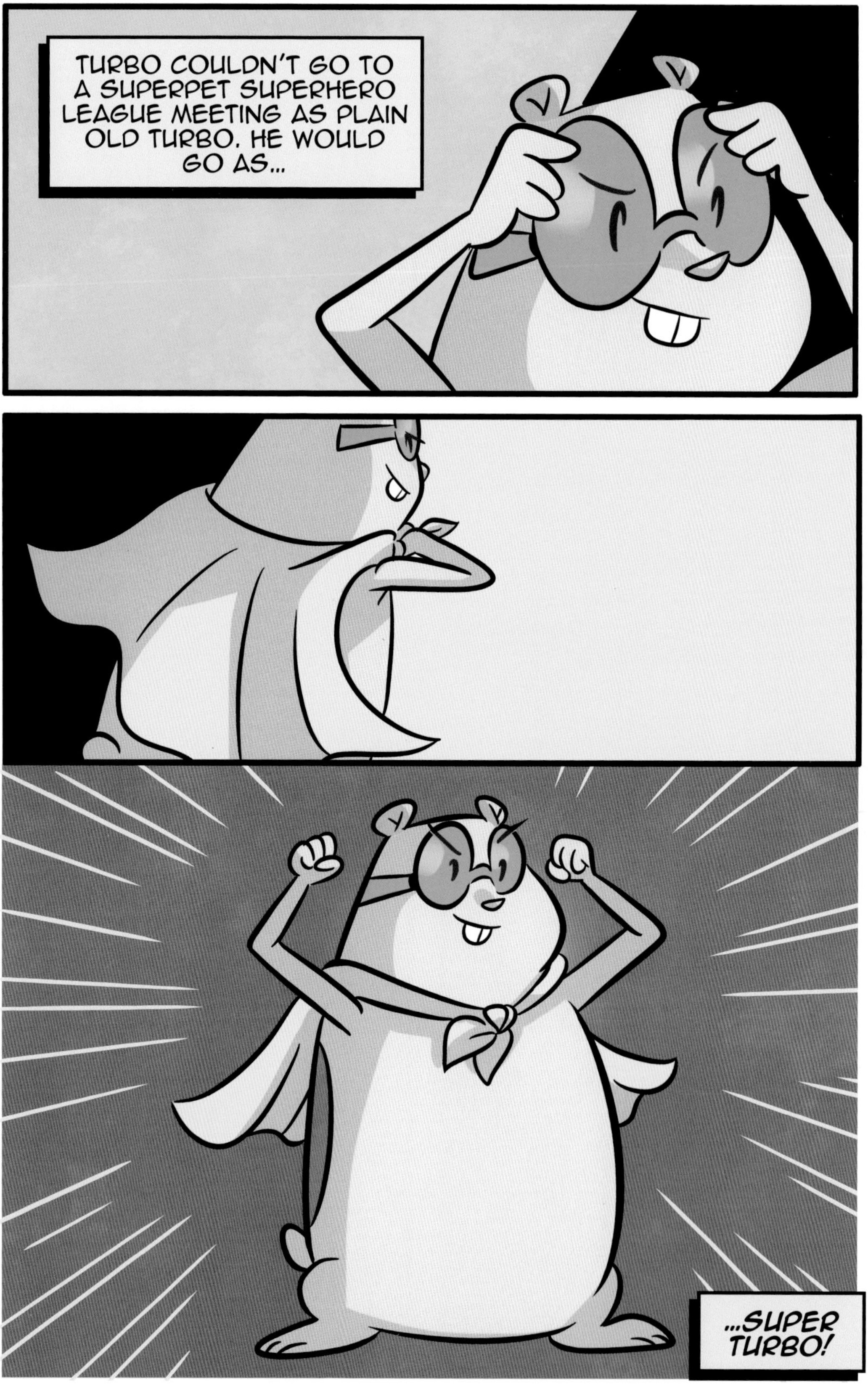
TURBO COULDN'T GO TO A SUPERPET SUPERHERO LEAGUE MEETING AS PLAIN OLD TURBO. HE WOULD GO AS...
...SUPER TURBO!

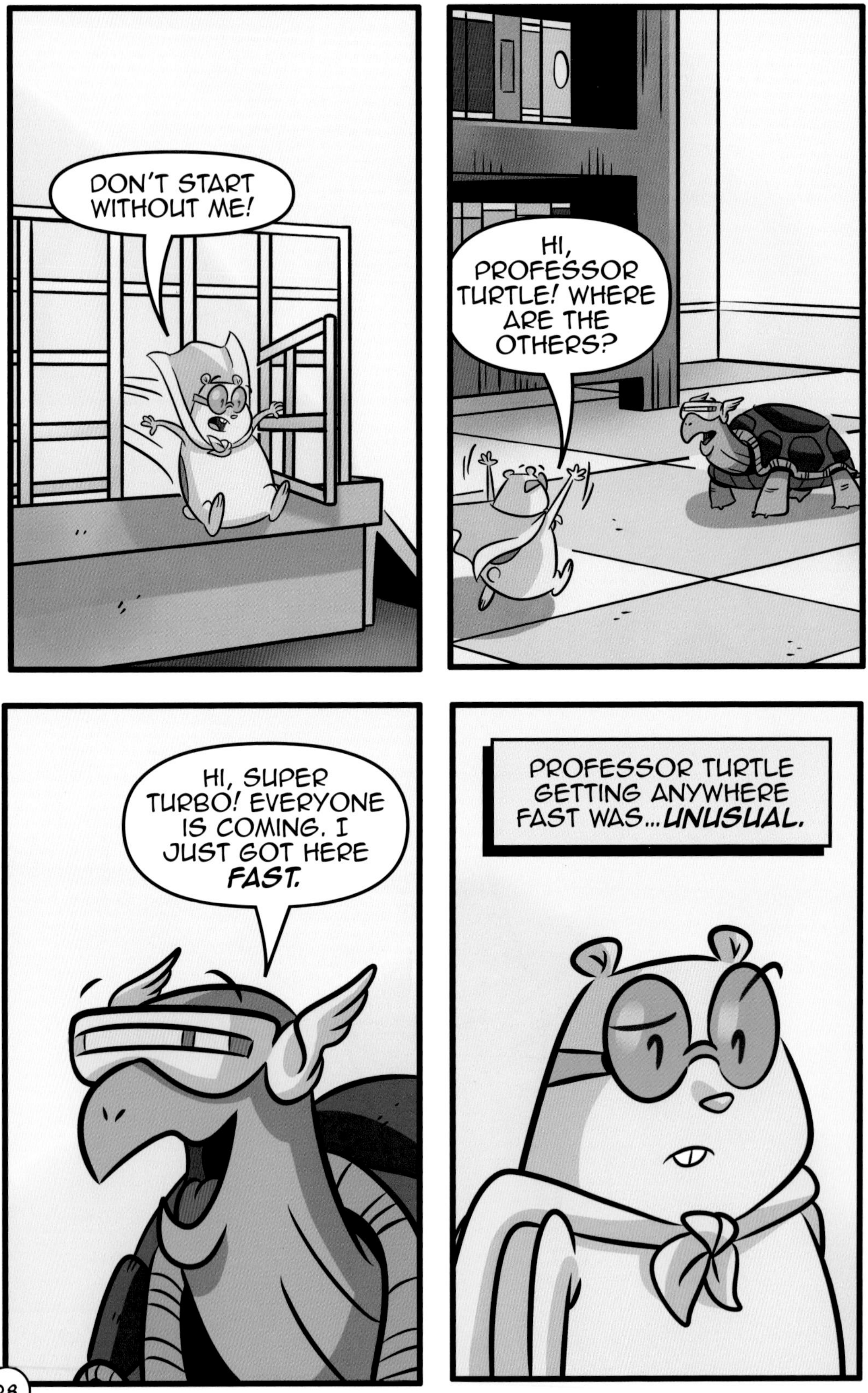
DON'T START WITHOUT ME!
HI, PROFESSOR TURTLE! WHERE ARE THE OTHERS?
HI, SUPER TURBO! EVERYONE IS COMING. I JUST GOT HERE FAST.
PROFESSOR TURTLE GETTING ANYWHERE FAST WAS...UNUSUAL.

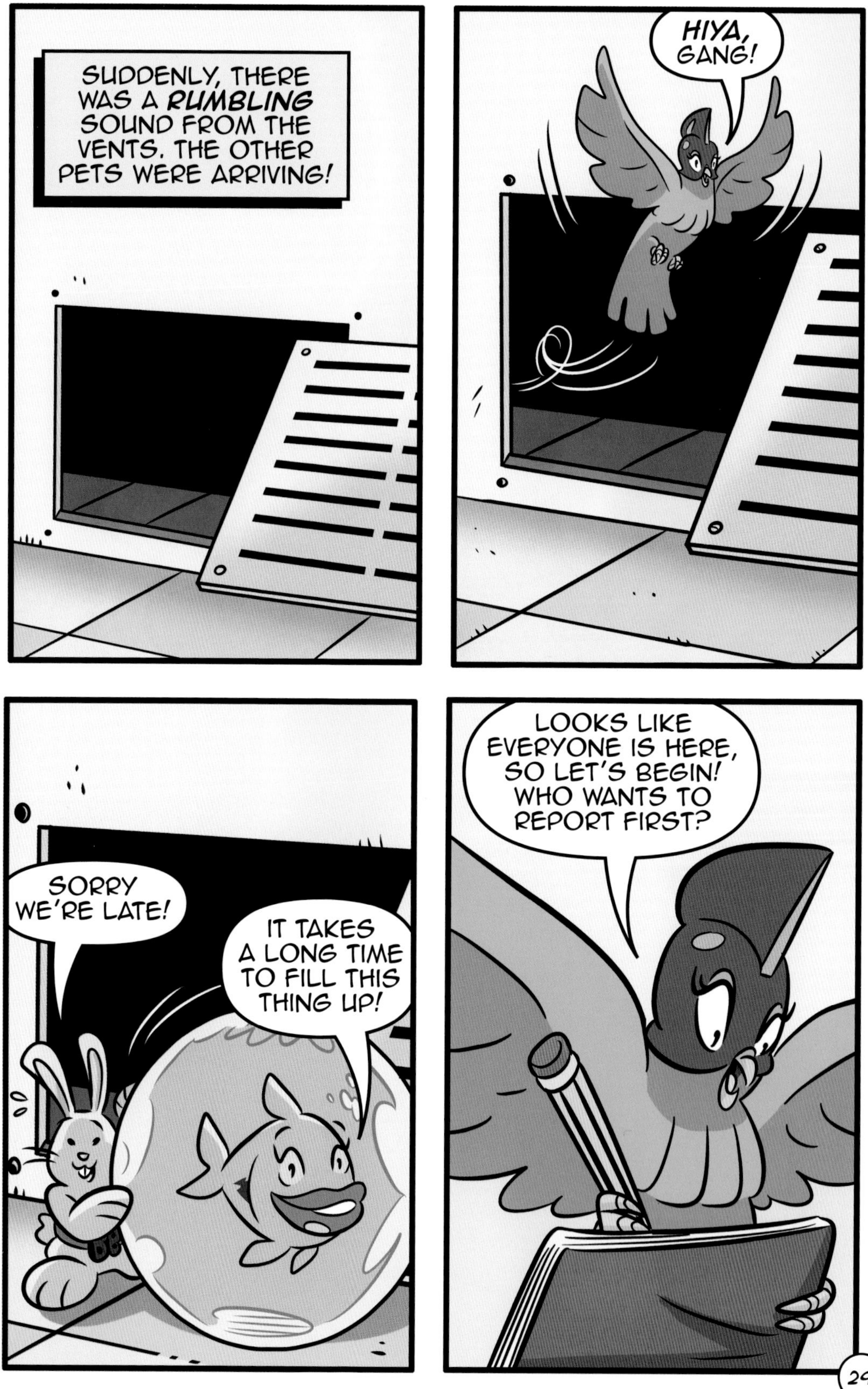
SUDDENLY, THERE WAS A RUMBLING SOUND FROM THE VENTS. THE OTHER PETS WERE ARRIVING!
HIYA, GANG!
SORRY WE'RE LATE!
IT TAKES A LONG TIME TO FILL THIS THING UP!
LOOKS LIKE EVERYONE IS HERE, SO LET'S BEGIN! WHO WANTS TO REPORT FIRST?

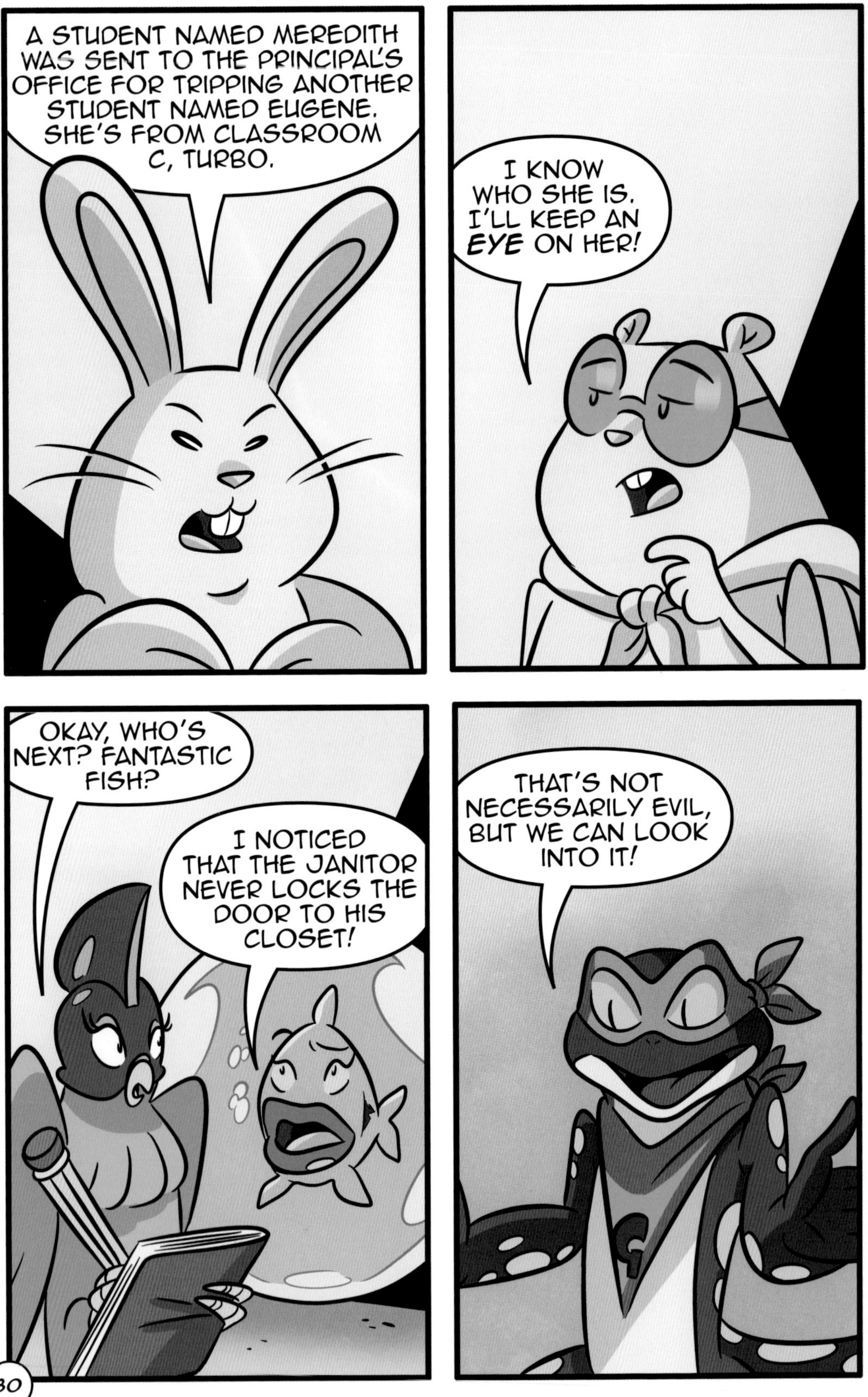
A STUDENT NAMED MEREDITH WAS SENT TO THE PRINCIPAL'S OFFICE FOR TRIPPING ANOTHER STUDENT NAMED EUGENE. SHE'S FROM CLASSROOM C, TURBO.
I KNOW WHO SHE IS. I'LL KEEP AN *EYE* ON HER!
OKAY, WHO'S NEXT? FANTASTIC FISH?
I NOTICED THAT THE JANITOR NEVER LOCKS THE DOOR TO HIS CLOSET!
THAT'S NOT NECESSARILY EVIL, BUT WE CAN LOOK INTO IT!

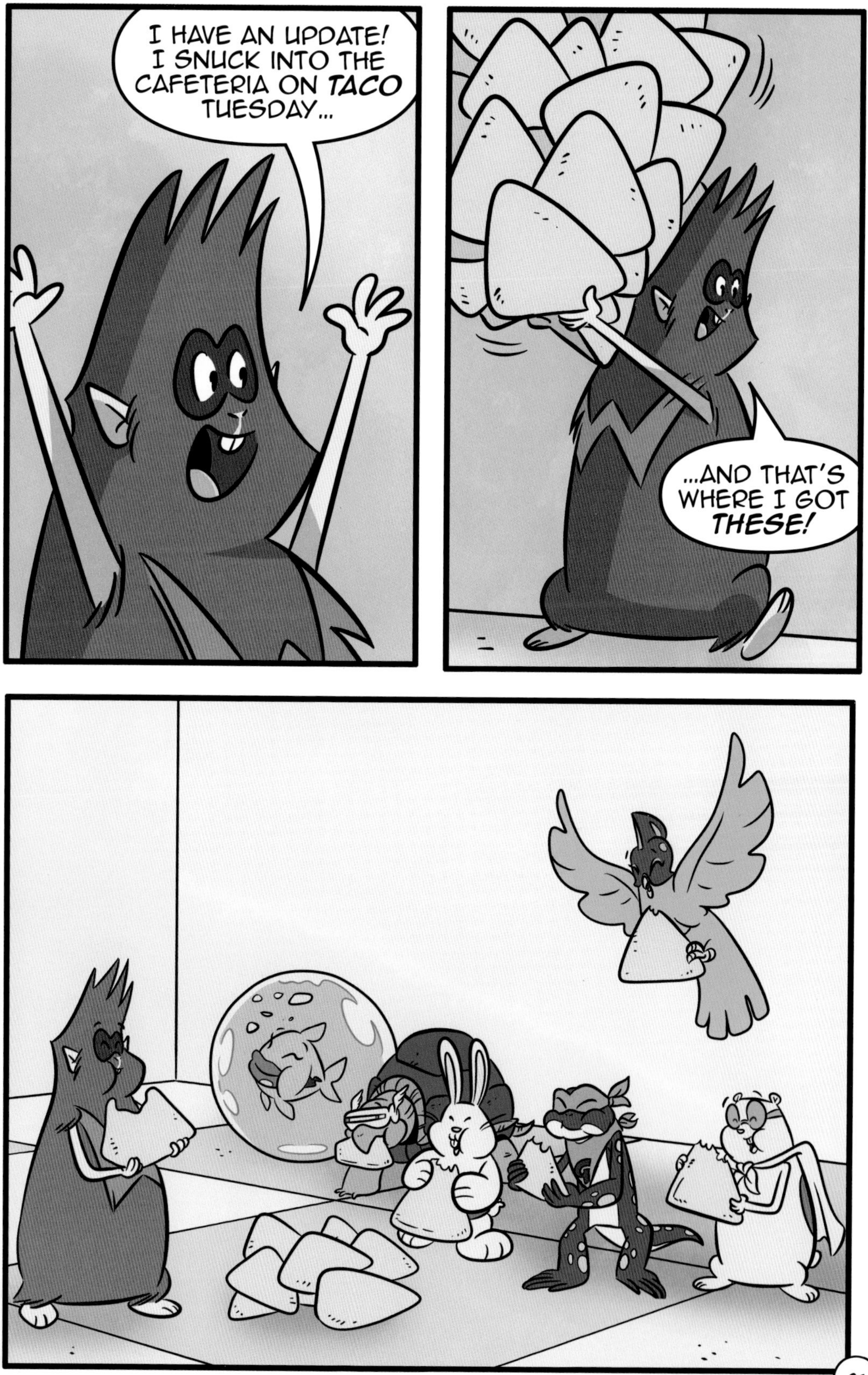
I HAVE AN UPDATE! I SNUCK INTO THE CAFETERIA ON *TACO* TUESDAY...
...AND THAT'S WHERE I GOT *THESE!*

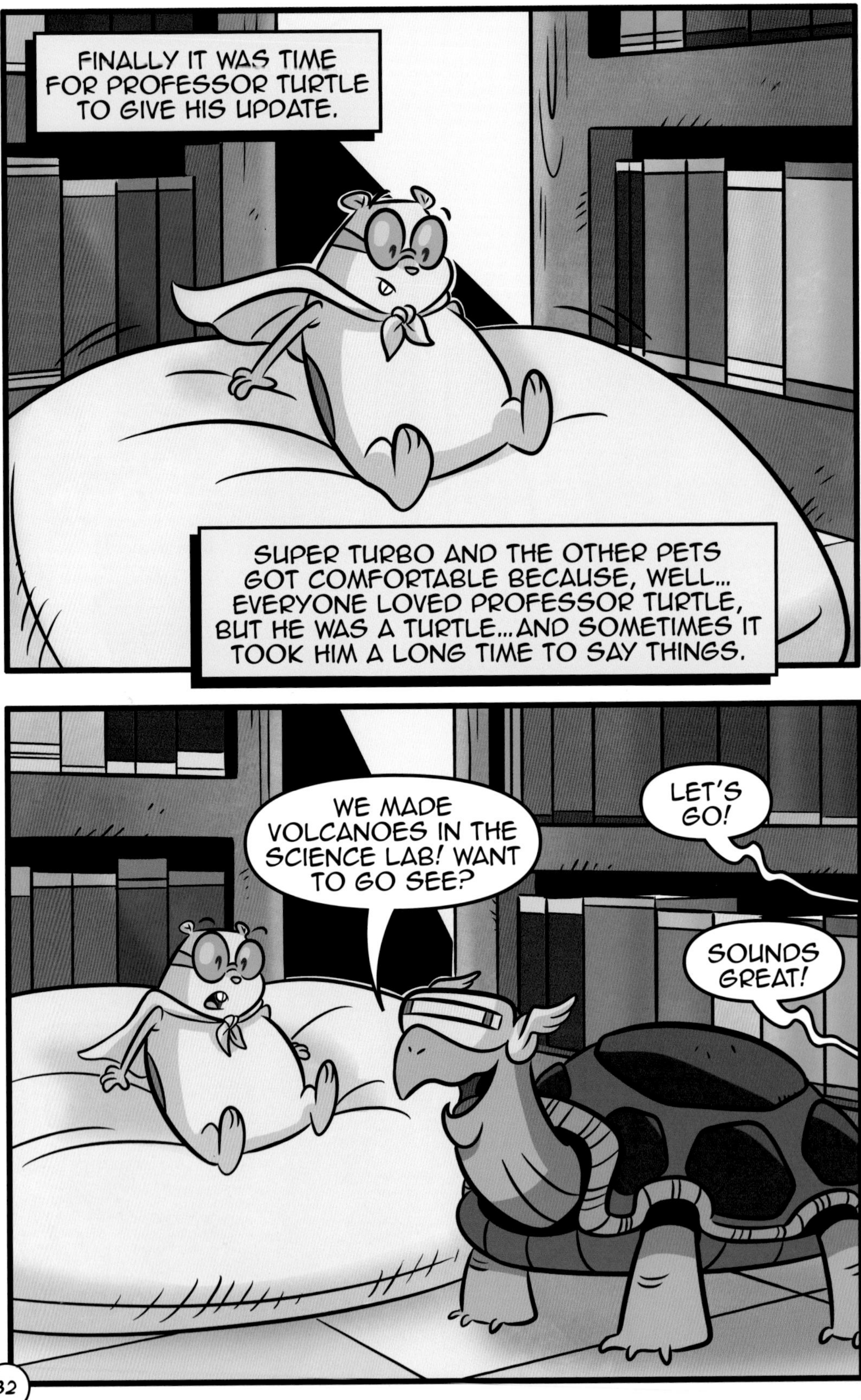
FINALLY IT WAS TIME FOR PROFESSOR TURTLE TO GIVE HIS UPDATE.
SUPER TURBO AND THE OTHER PETS GOT COMFORTABLE BECAUSE, WELL... EVERYONE LOVED PROFESSOR TURTLE, BUT HE WAS A TURTLE...AND SOMETIMES IT TOOK HIM A LONG TIME TO SAY THINGS.
WE MADE VOLCANOES IN THE SCIENCE LAB! WANT TO GO SEE?
LET'S GO!
SOUNDS GREAT!

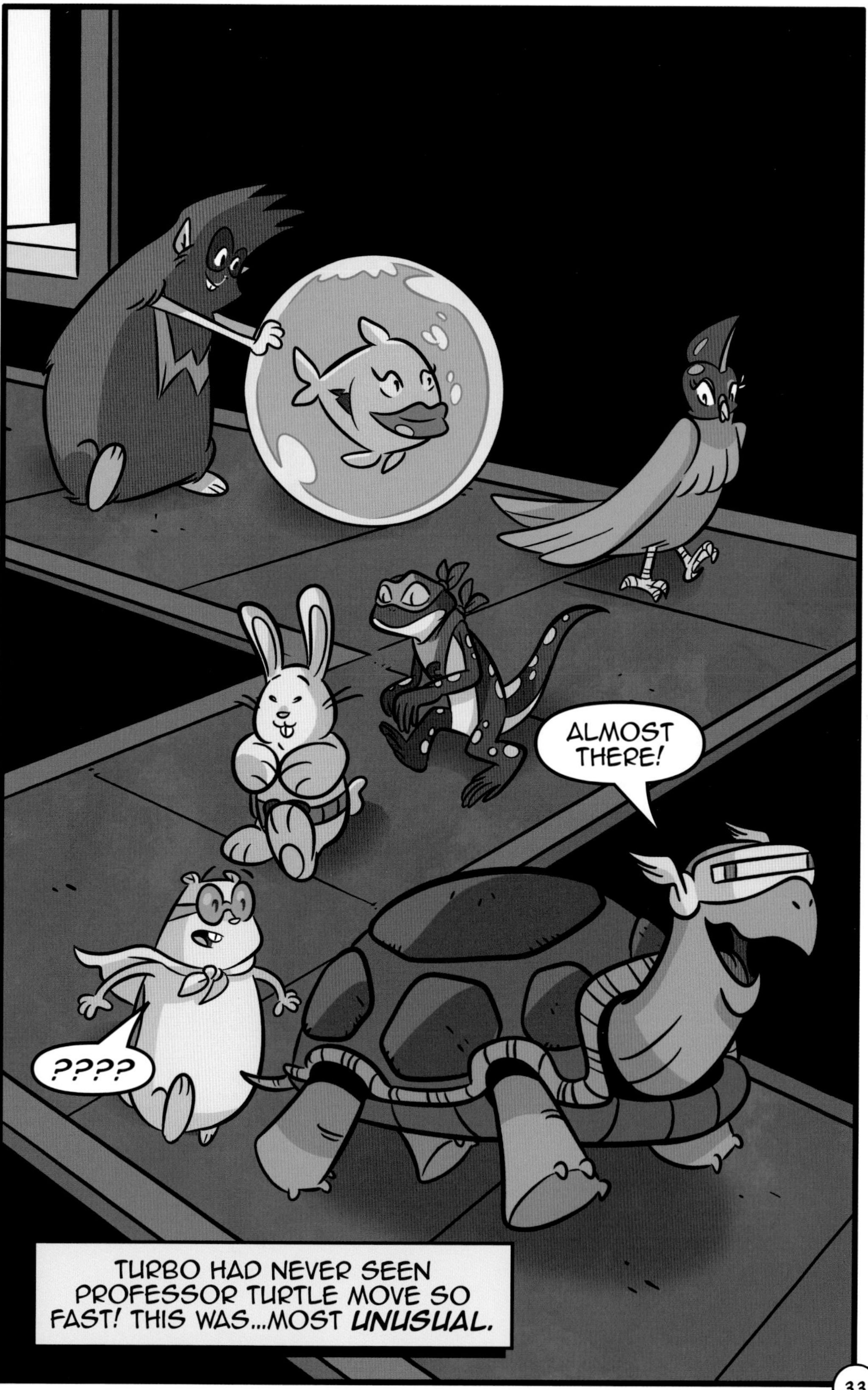
ALMOST THERE!
????
TURBO HAD NEVER SEEN PROFESSOR TURTLE MOVE SO FAST! THIS WAS...MOST *UNUSUAL.*

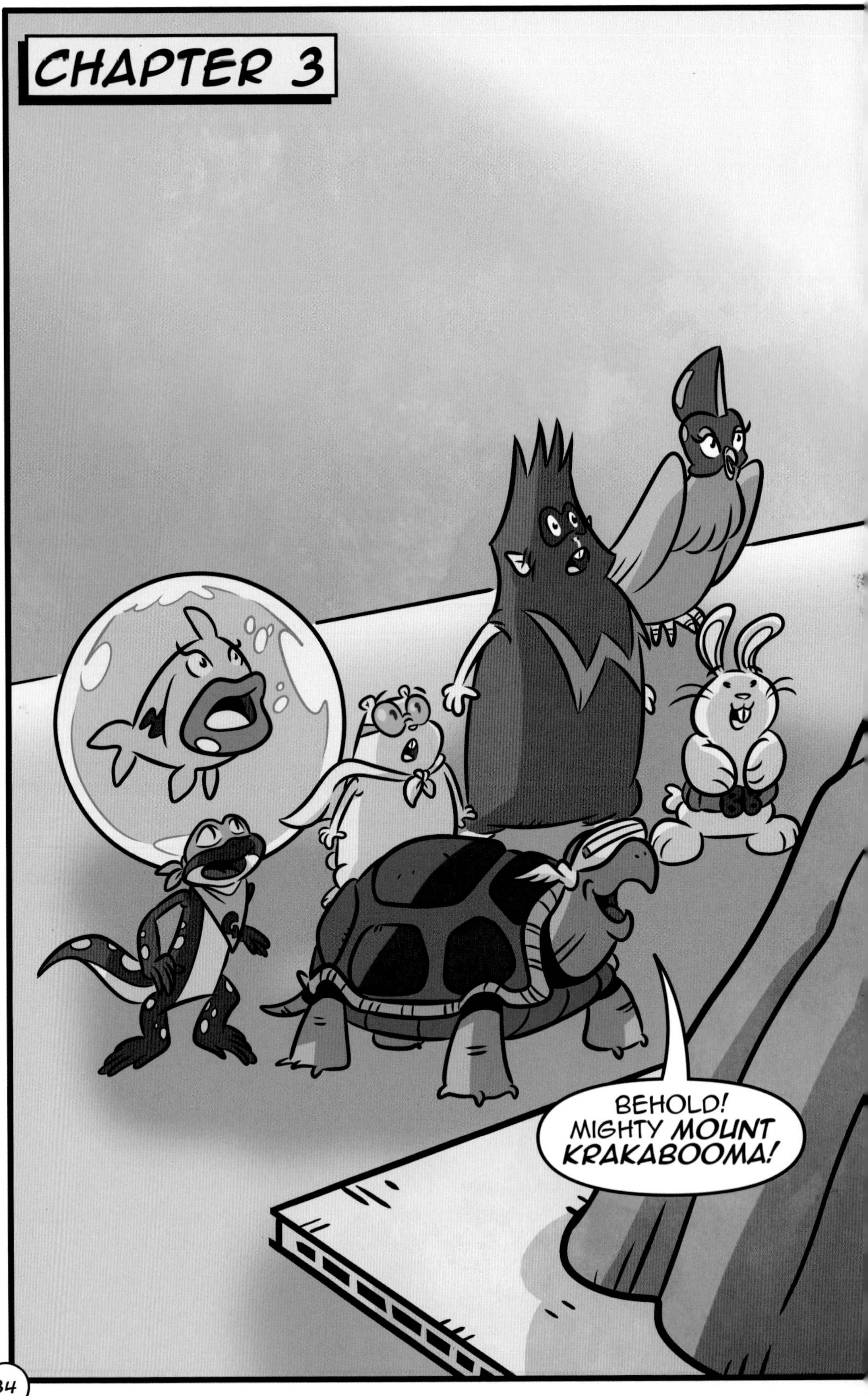
CHAPTER 3
BEHOLD! MIGHTY MOUNT KRAKABOOMA!

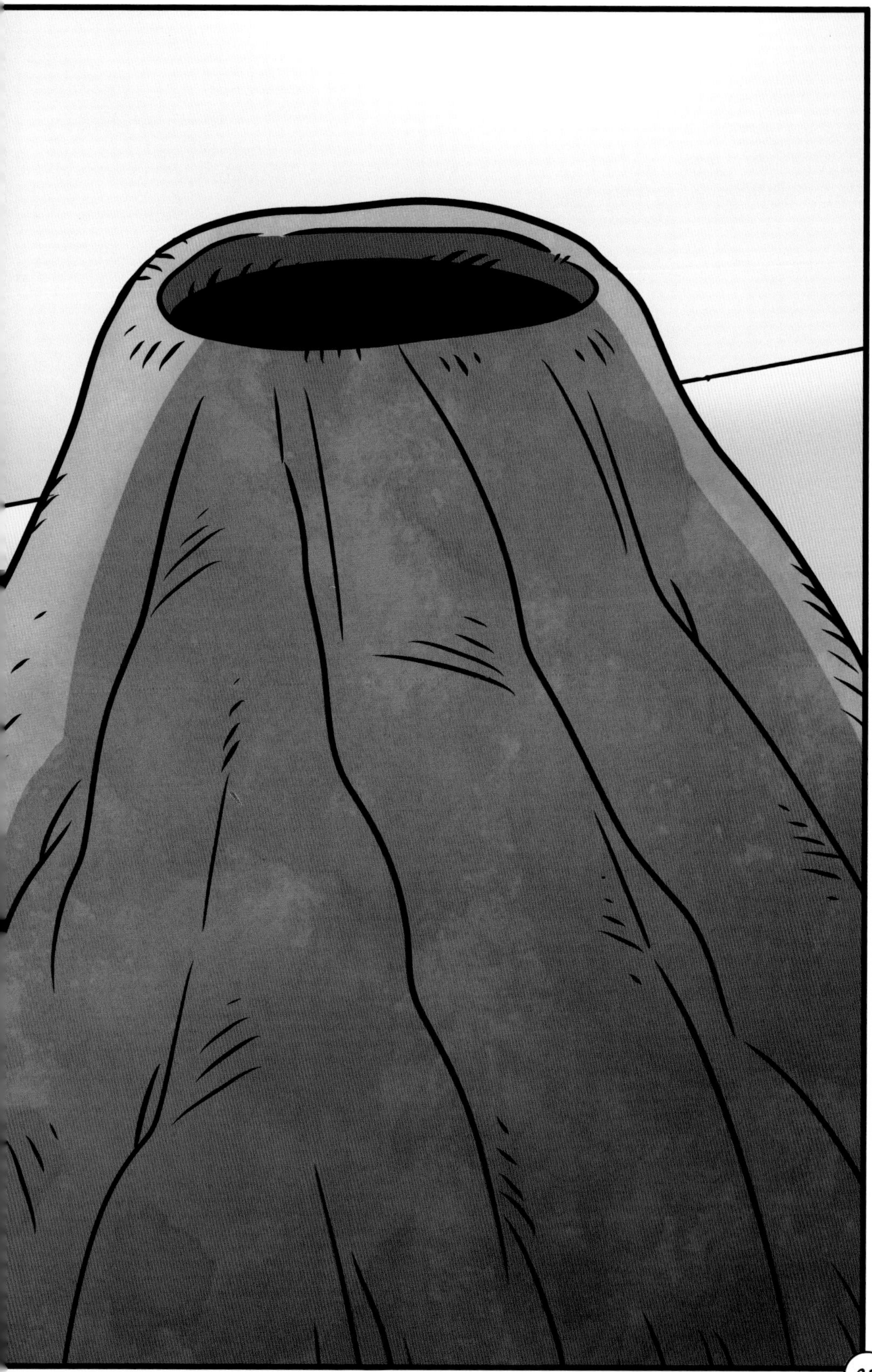

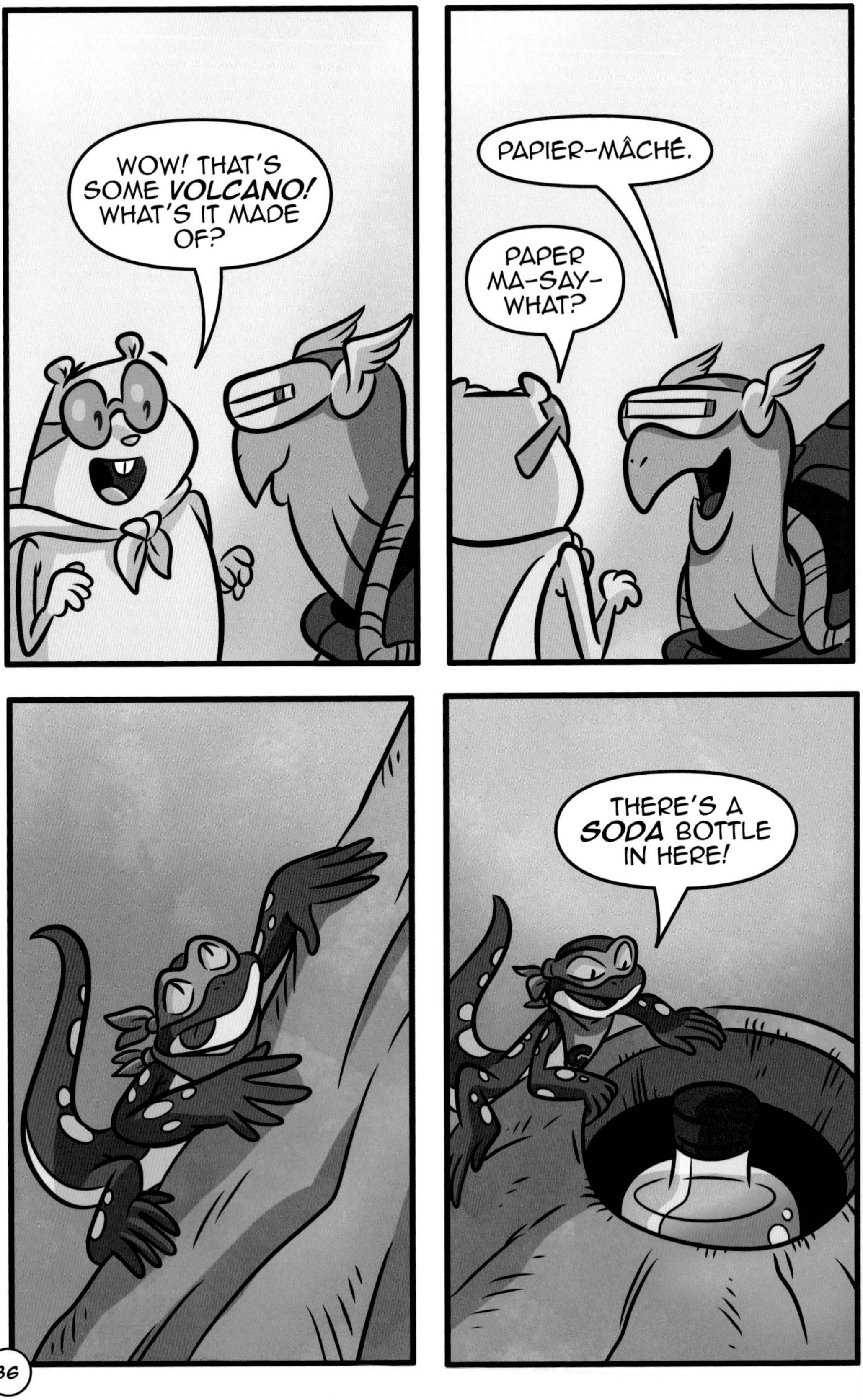
WOW! THAT'S SOME VOLCANO! WHAT'S IT MADE OF?
PAPIER-MÂCHÉ.
PAPER MA-SAY-WHAT?
THERE'S A SODA BOTTLE IN HERE!

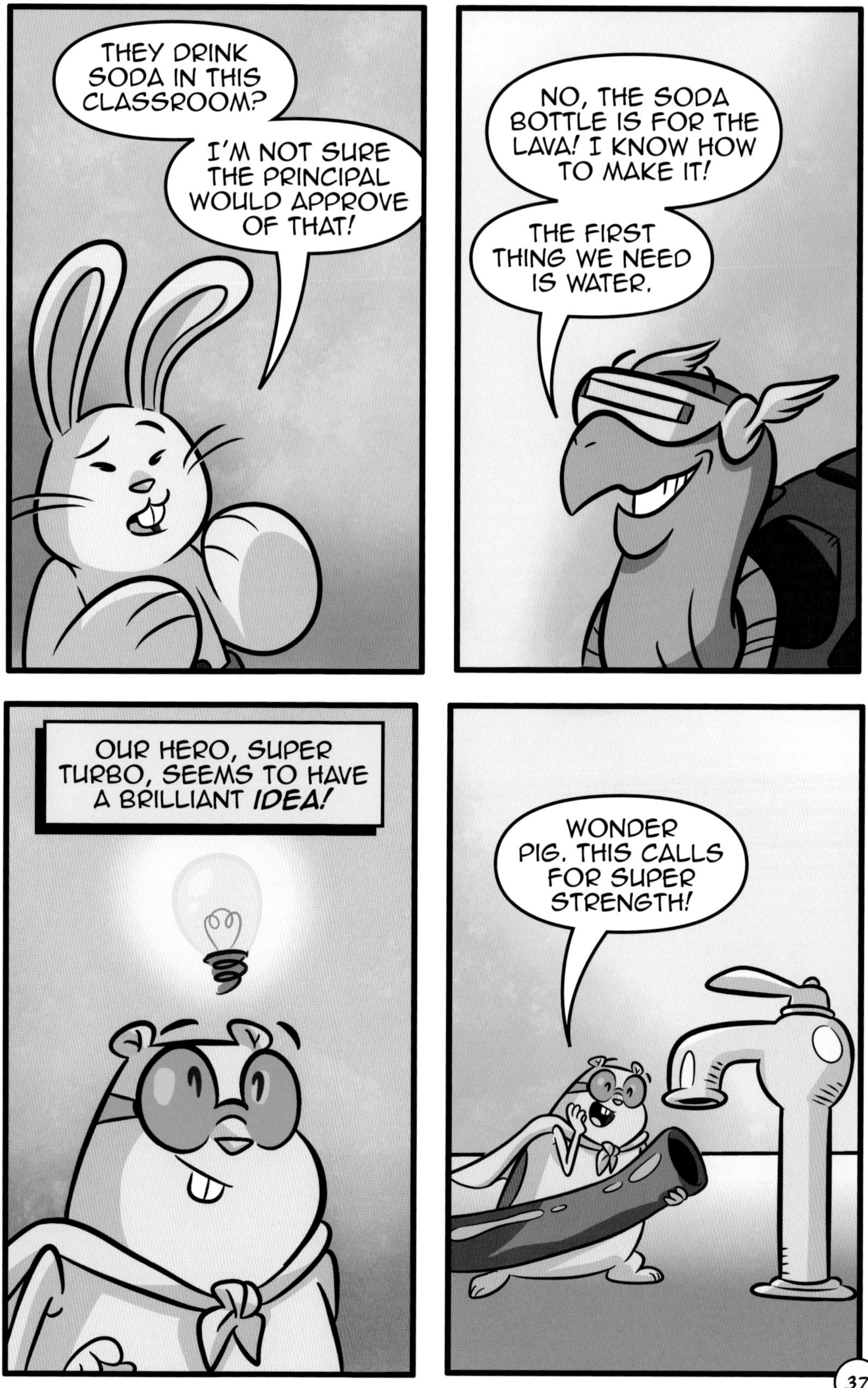
THEY DRINK SODA IN THIS CLASSROOM?
I'M NOT SURE THE PRINCIPAL WOULD APPROVE OF THAT!
NO, THE SODA BOTTLE IS FOR THE LAVA! I KNOW HOW TO MAKE IT!
THE FIRST THING WE NEED IS WATER.
OUR HERO, SUPER TURBO, SEEMS TO HAVE A BRILLIANT *IDEA!*
WONDER PIG. THIS CALLS FOR SUPER STRENGTH!

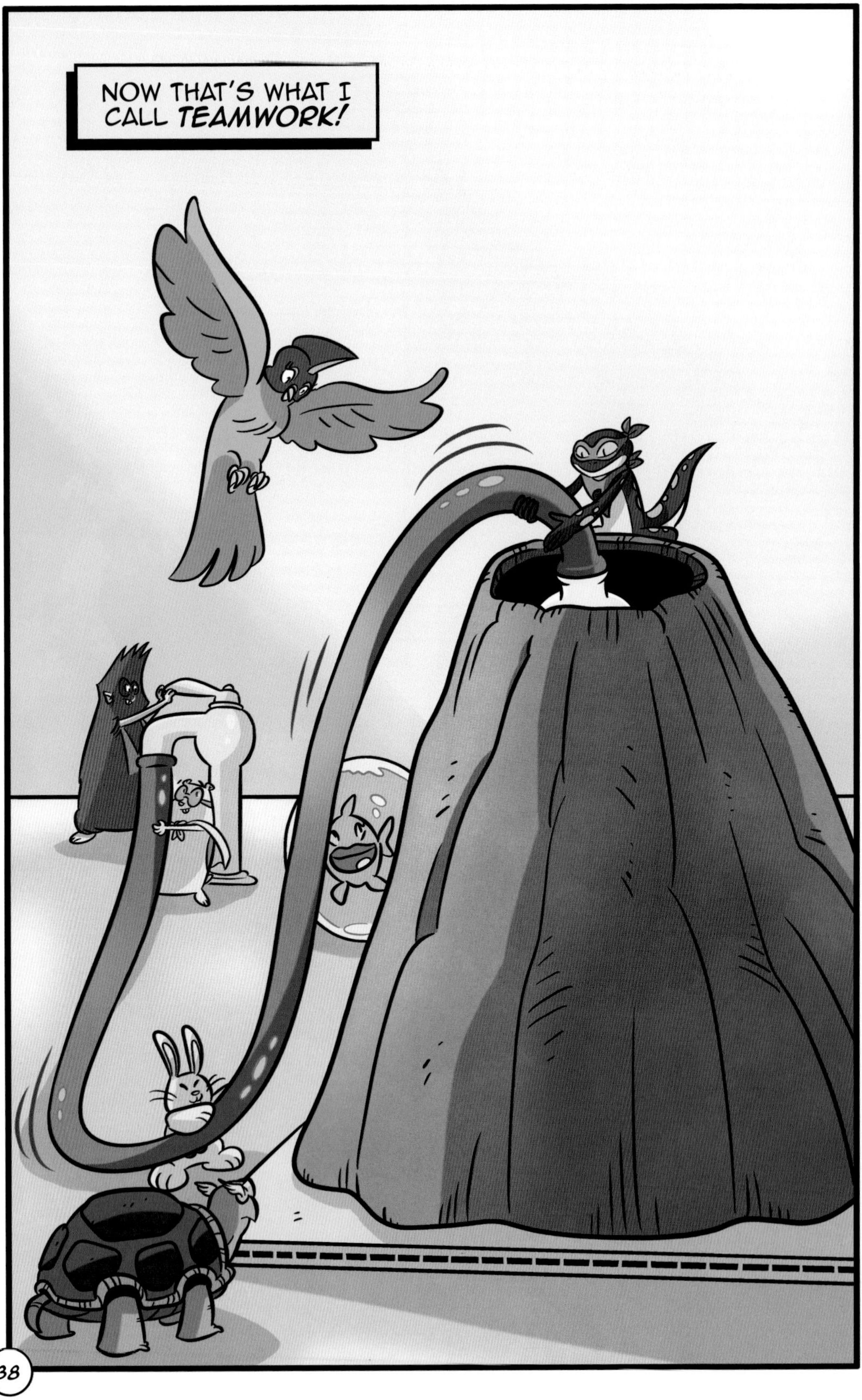
NOW THAT'S WHAT I CALL *TEAMWORK!*

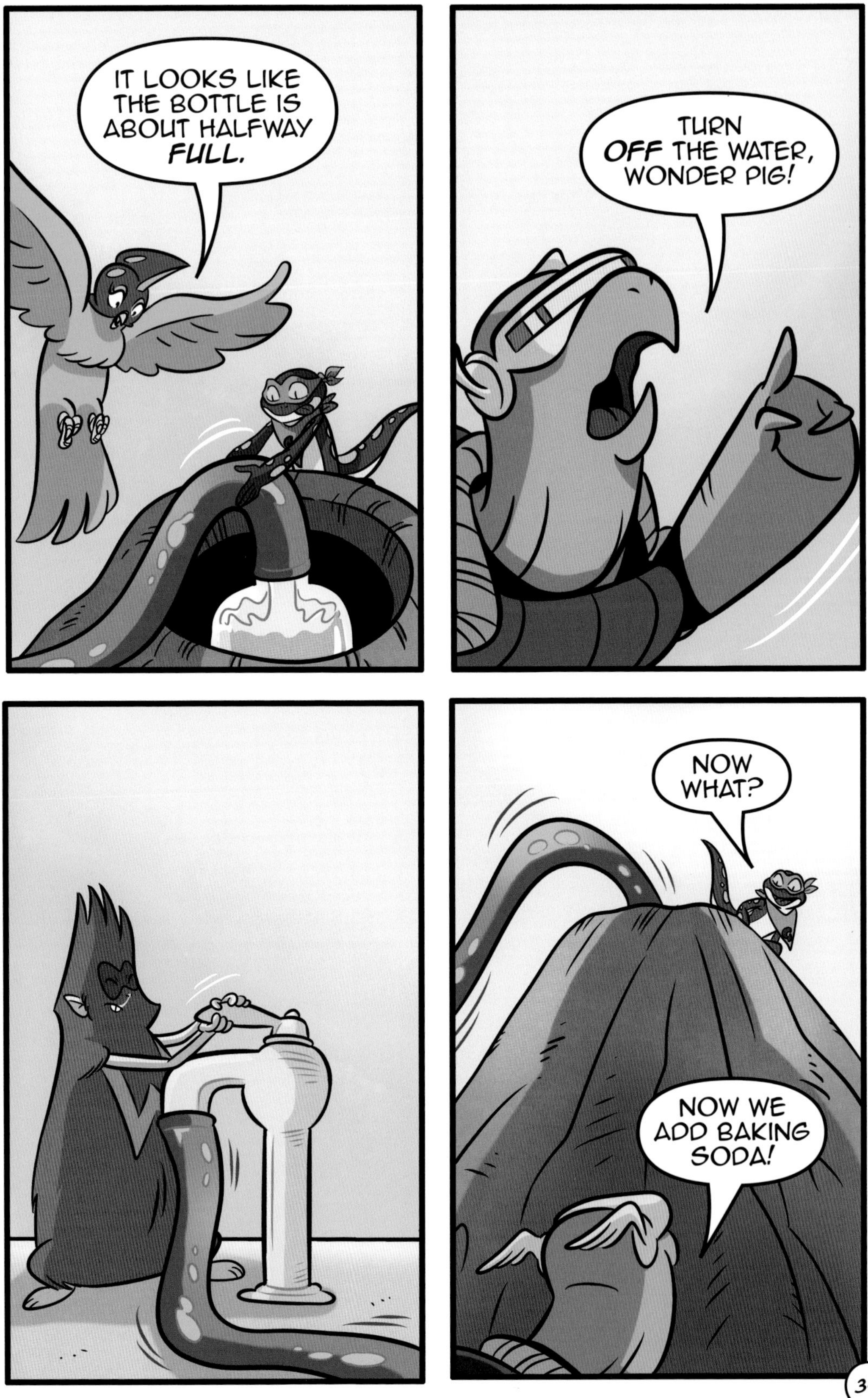
IT LOOKS LIKE THE BOTTLE IS ABOUT HALFWAY **FULL.**
TURN **OFF** THE WATER, WONDER PIG!
NOW WHAT?
NOW WE ADD BAKING SODA!

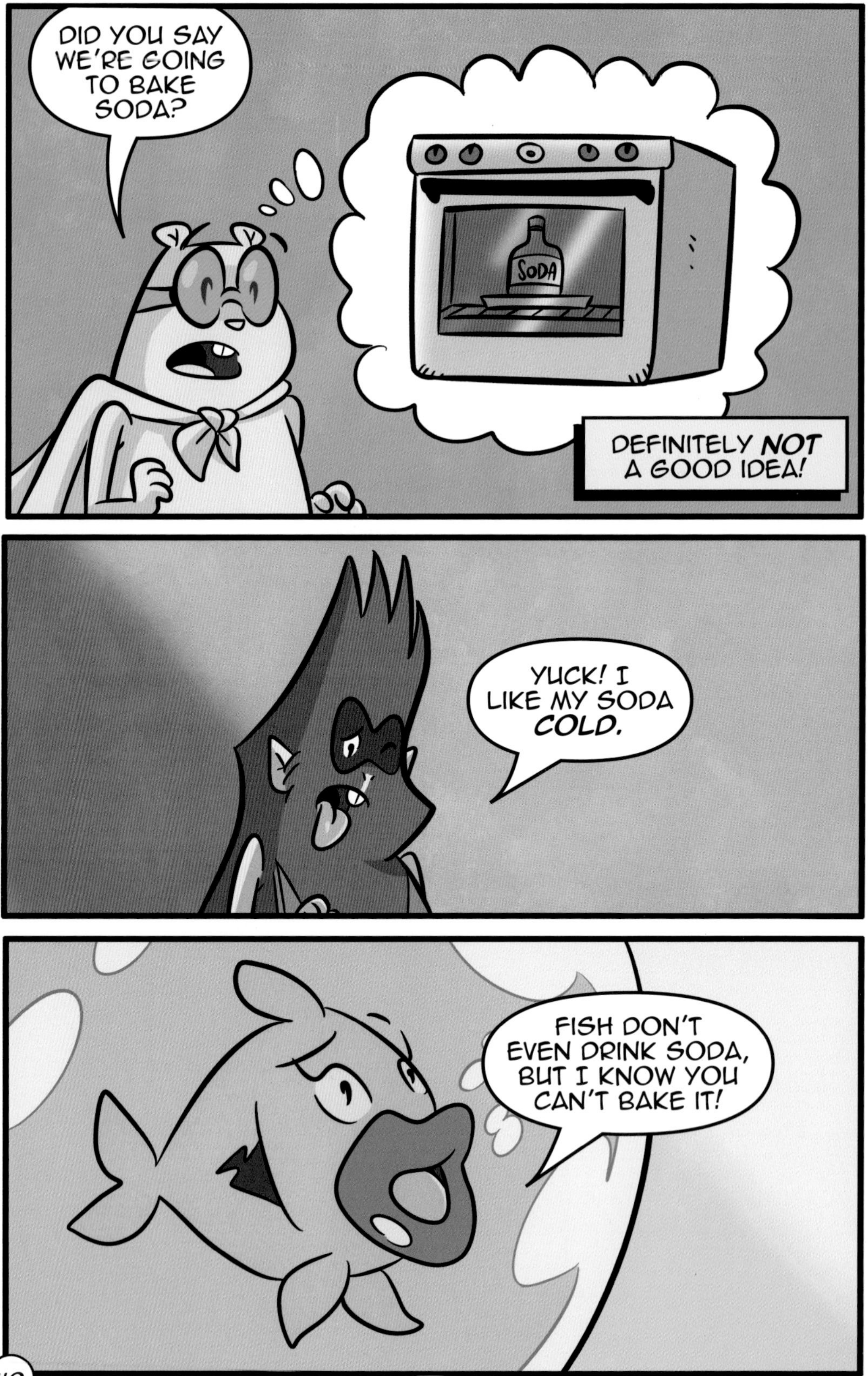
DID YOU SAY WE'RE GOING TO BAKE SODA?
SODA
DEFINITELY **NOT** A GOOD IDEA!
YUCK! I LIKE MY SODA **COLD.**
FISH DON'T EVEN DRINK SODA, BUT I KNOW YOU CAN'T BAKE IT!

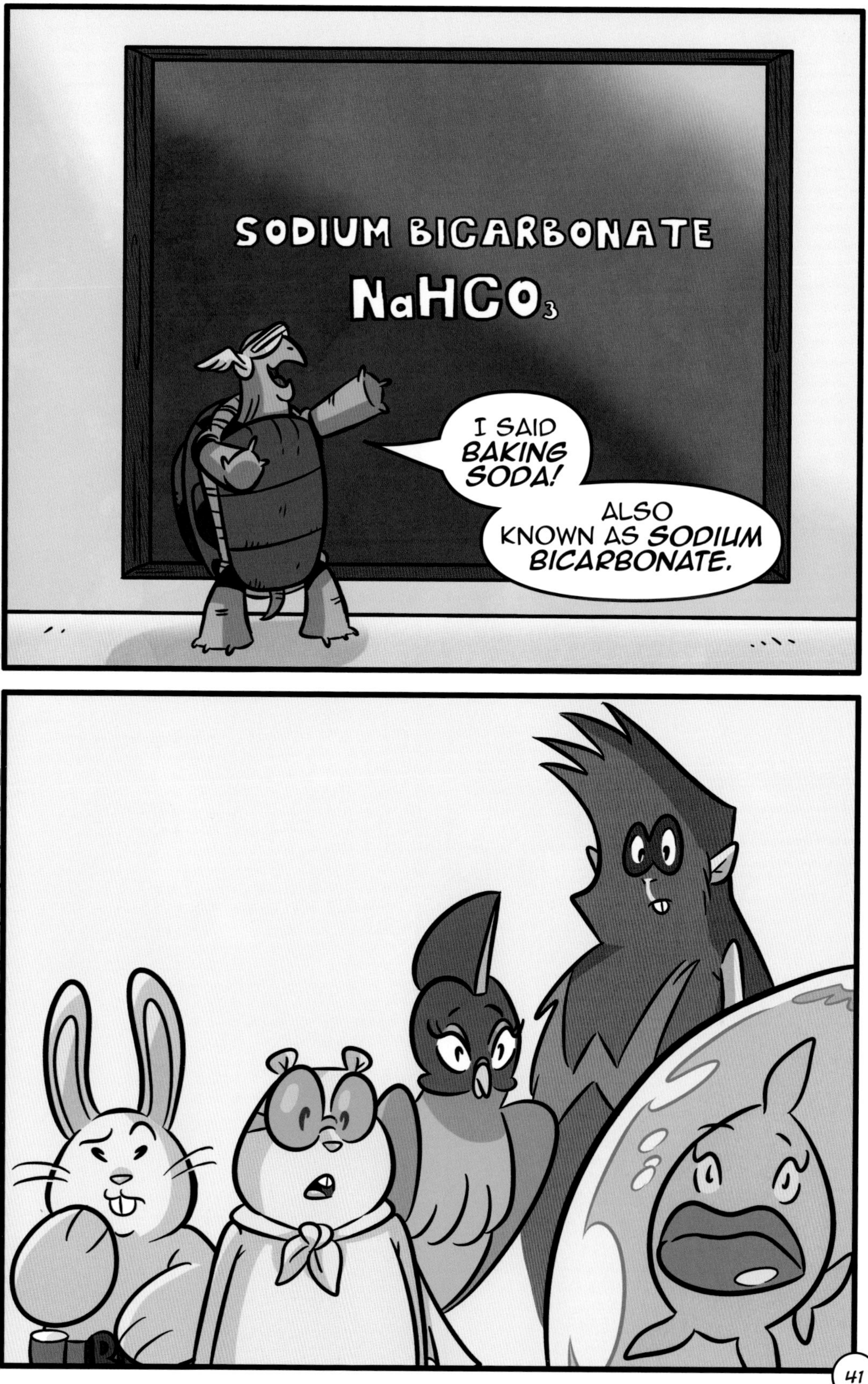

SODIUM BICARBONATE
$NaHCO_3$
I SAID *BAKING SODA!*
ALSO KNOWN AS *SODIUM BICARBONATE.*

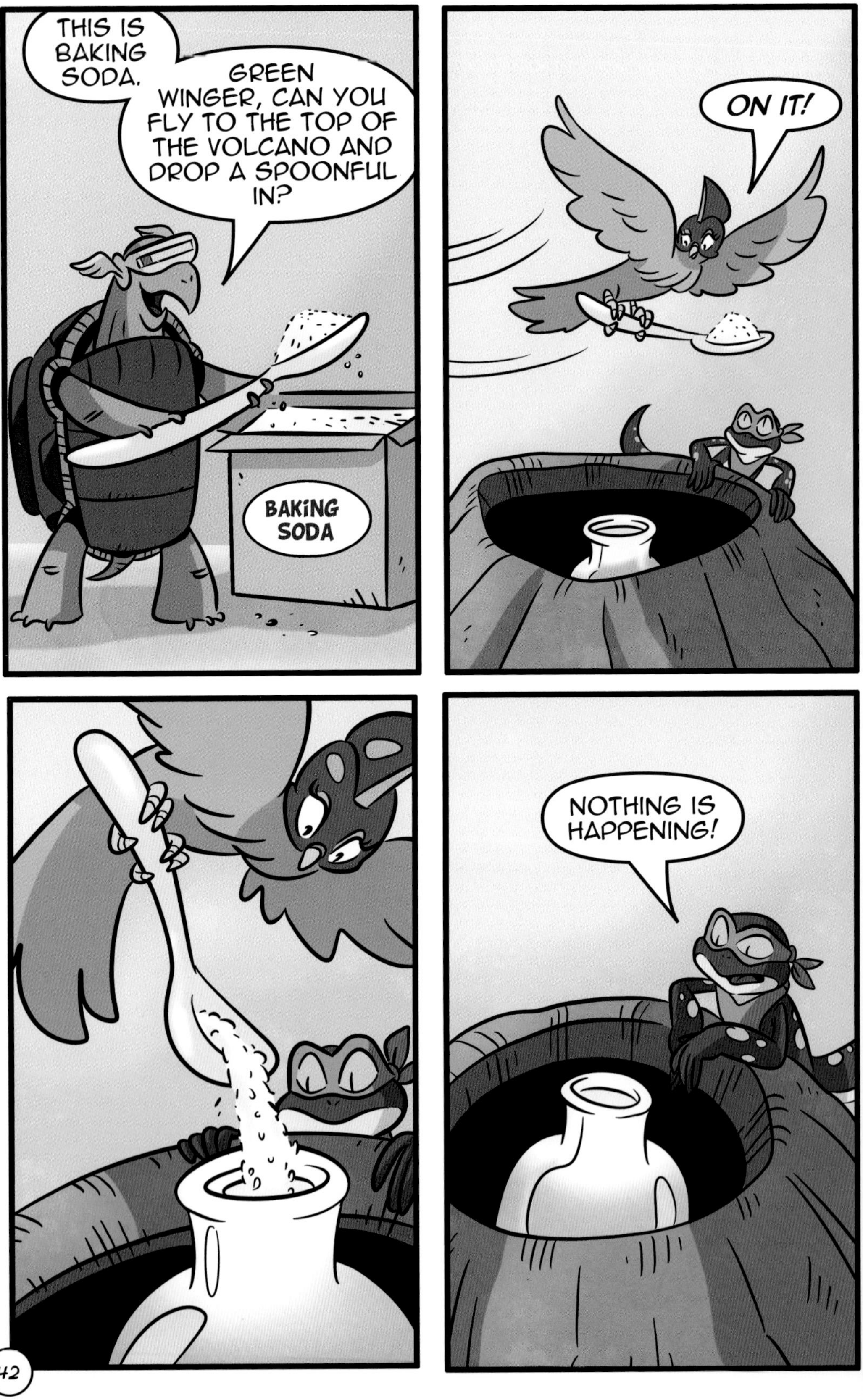
THIS IS BAKING SODA.
GREEN WINGER, CAN YOU FLY TO THE TOP OF THE VOLCANO AND DROP A SPOONFUL IN?
BAKING SODA
ON IT!
NOTHING IS HAPPENING!

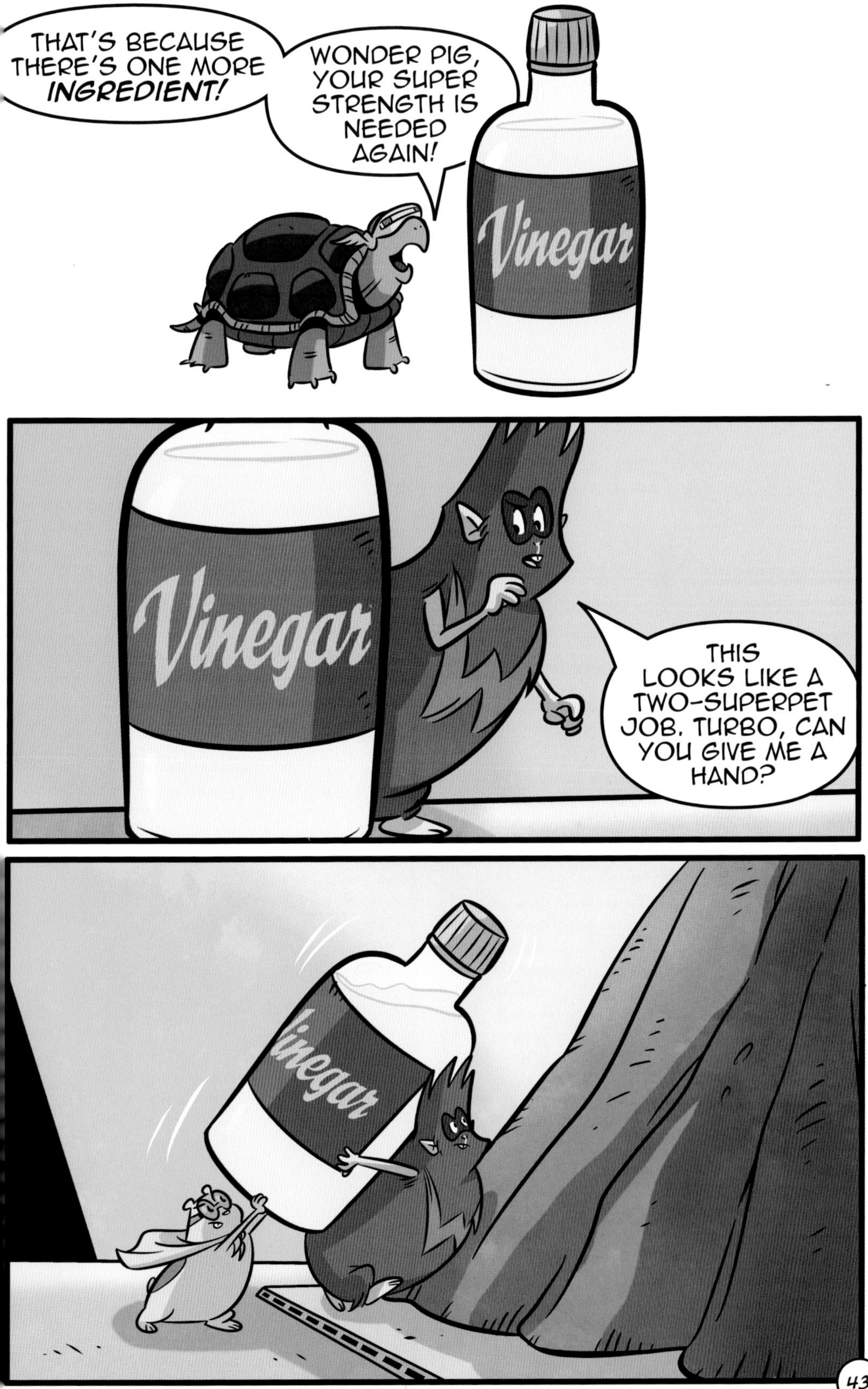
THAT'S BECAUSE THERE'S ONE MORE *INGREDIENT!*
WONDER PIG, YOUR SUPER STRENGTH IS NEEDED AGAIN!
Vinegar
Vinegar
THIS LOOKS LIKE A TWO-SUPERPET JOB. TURBO, CAN YOU GIVE ME A HAND?
inegar

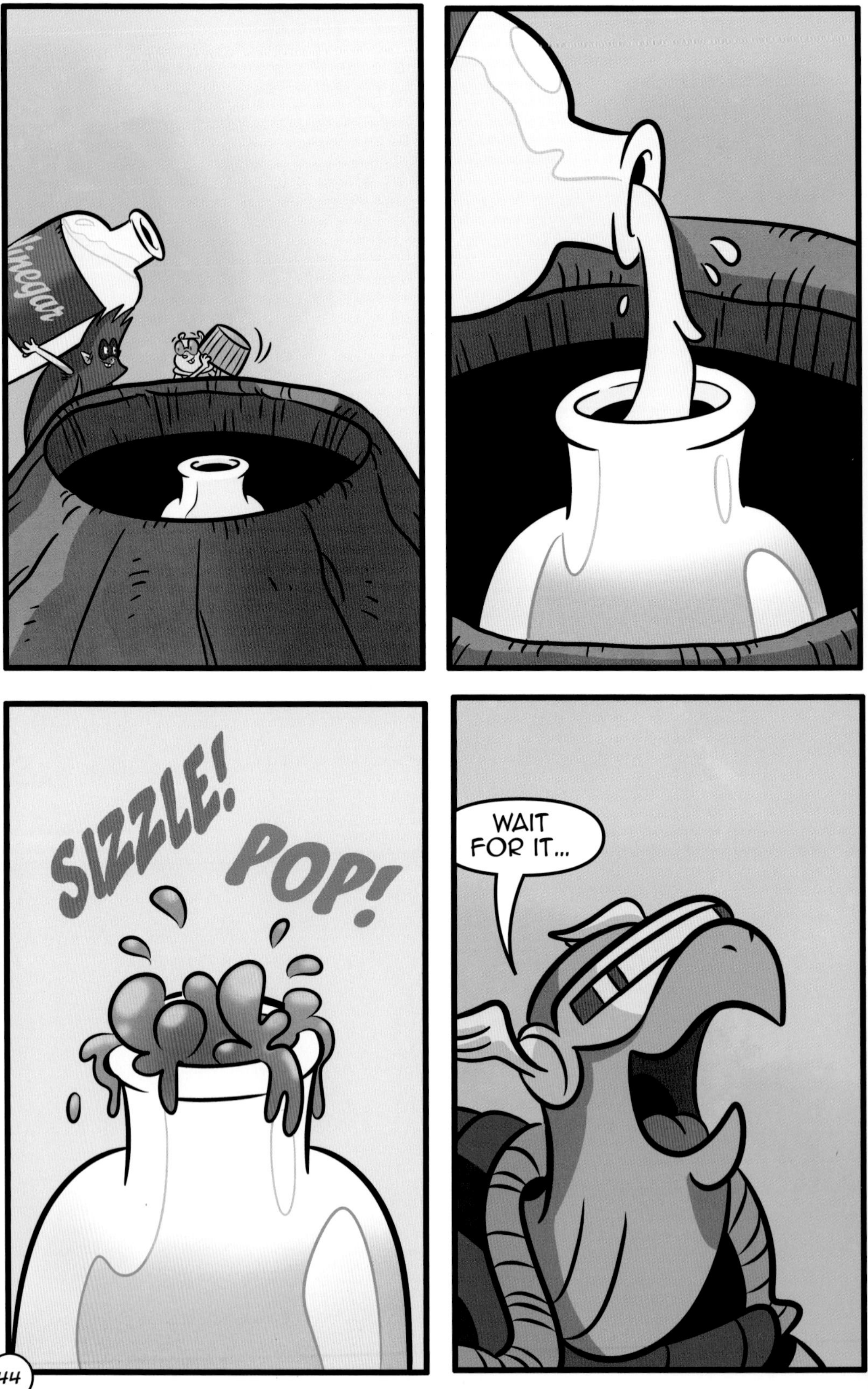
Vinegar
SIZZLE!
POP!
WAIT FOR IT...

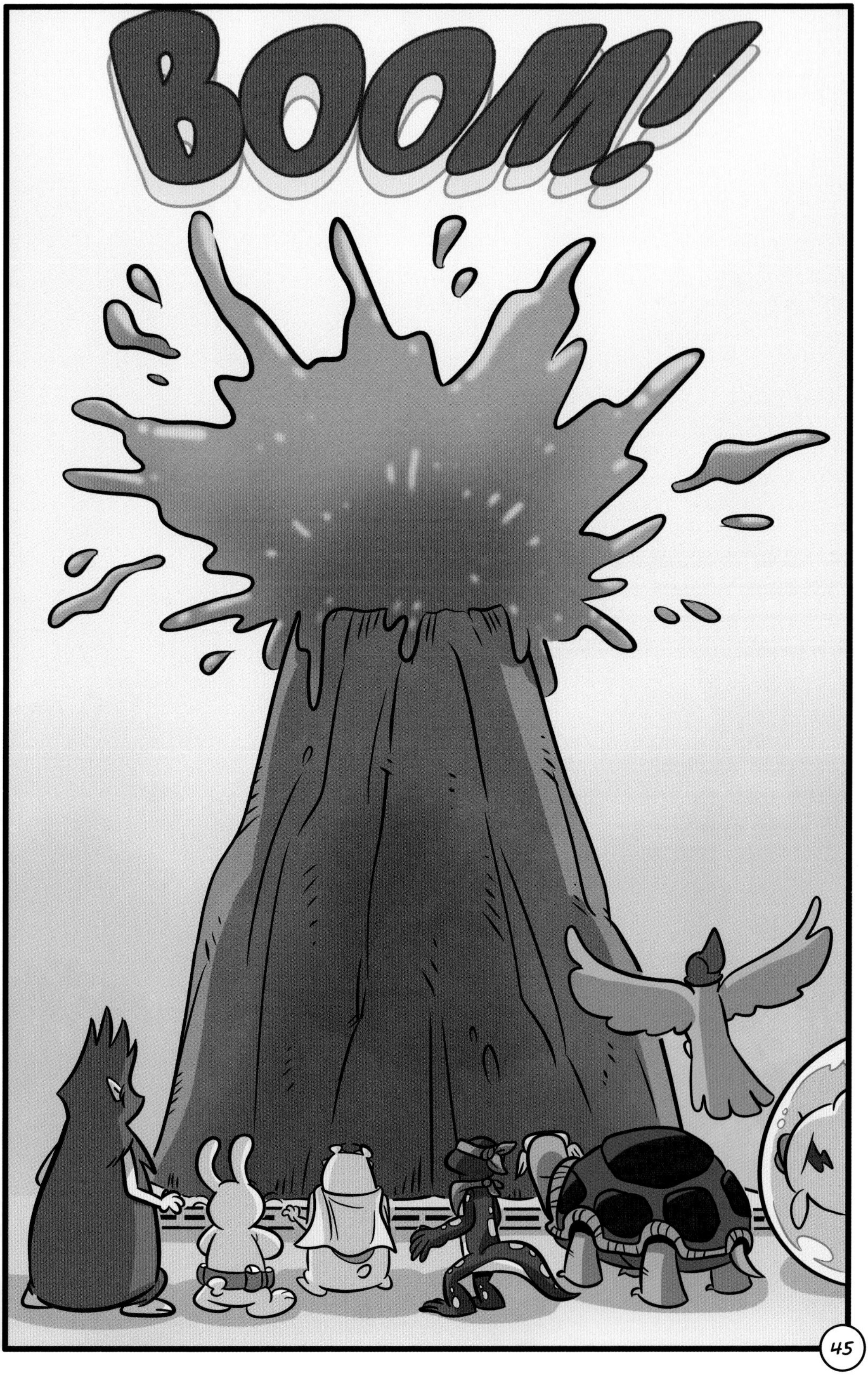
BOOM!

CHAPTER 4

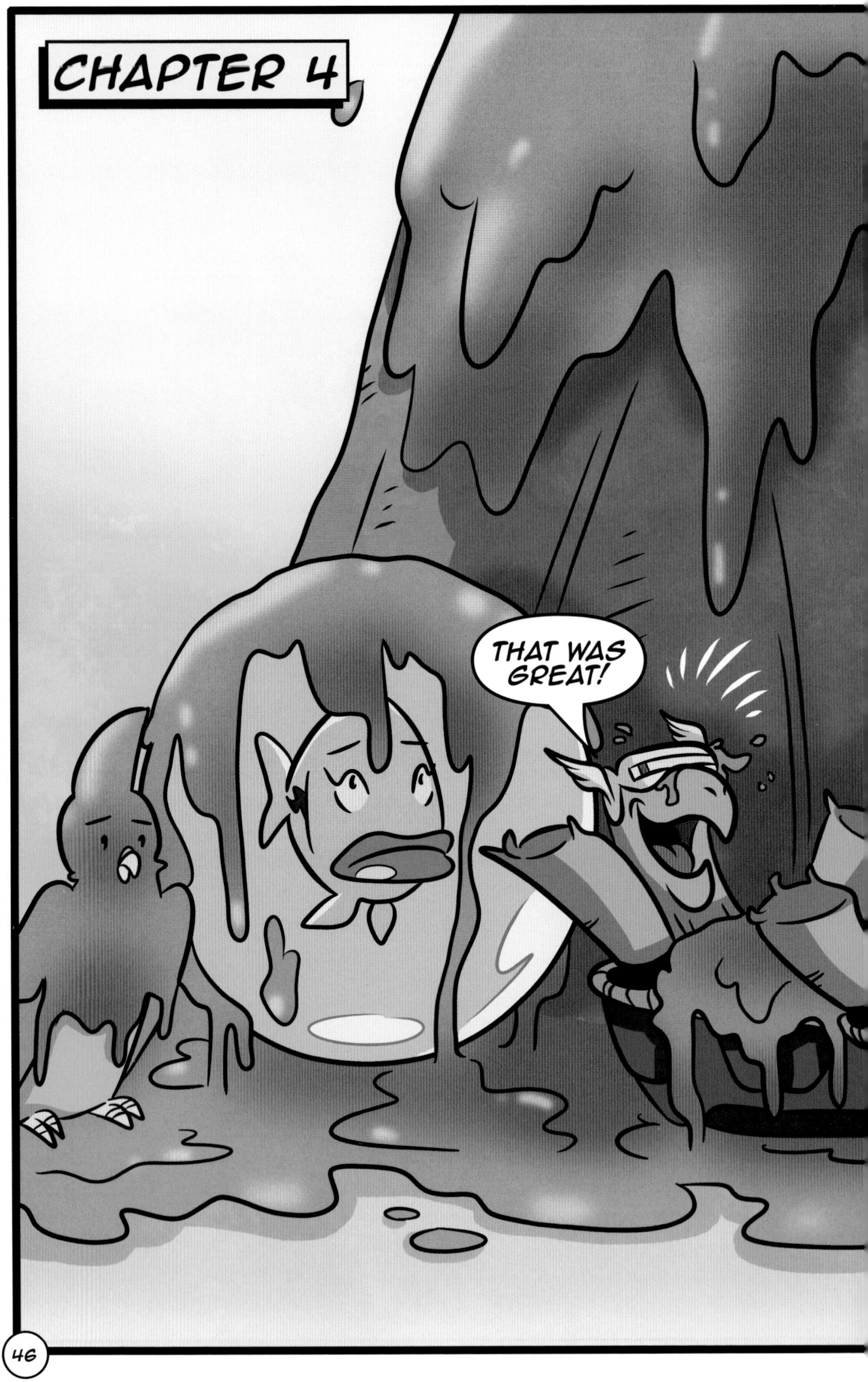

THAT WAS GREAT!

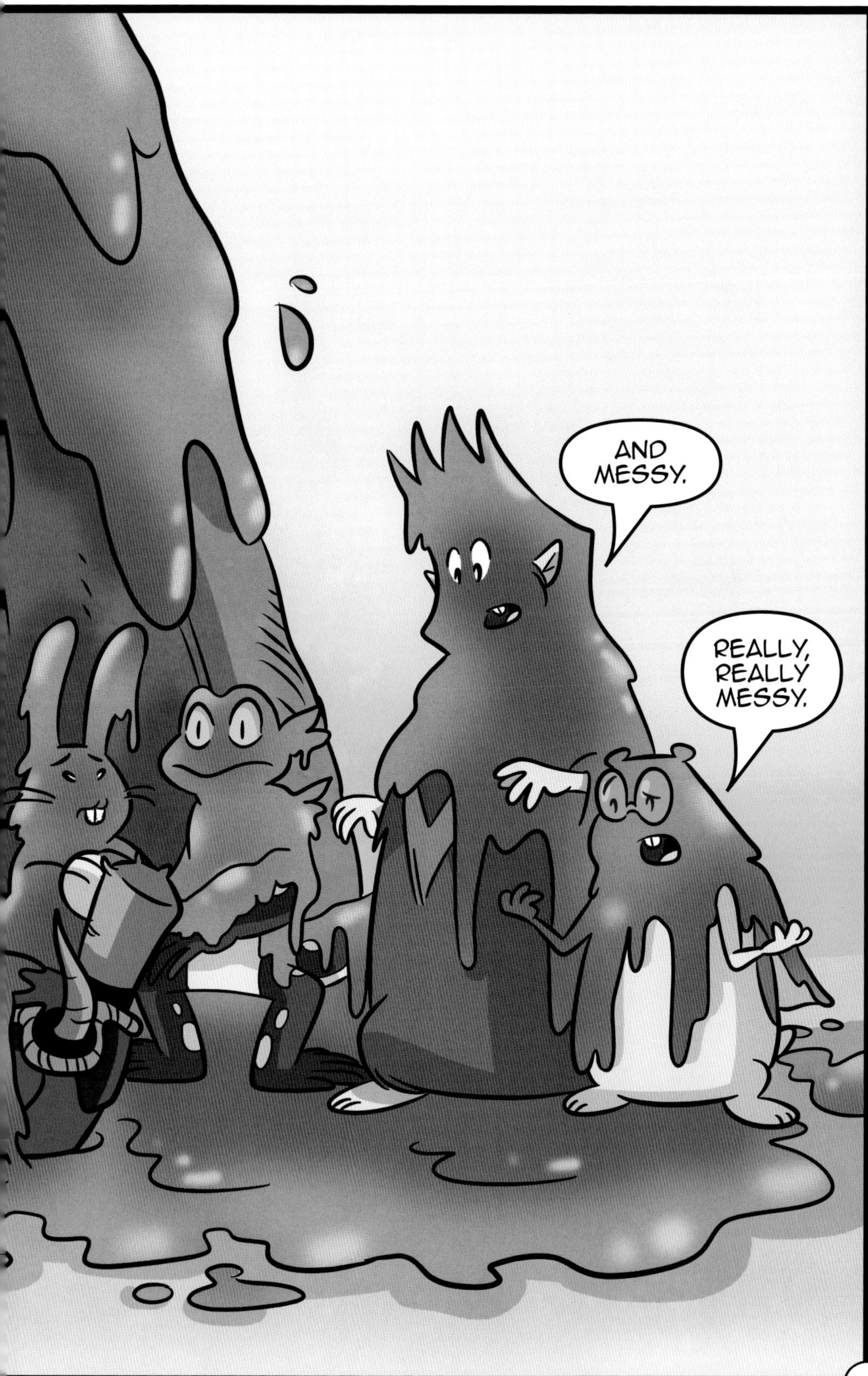
AND MESSY.
REALLY, REALLY MESSY.

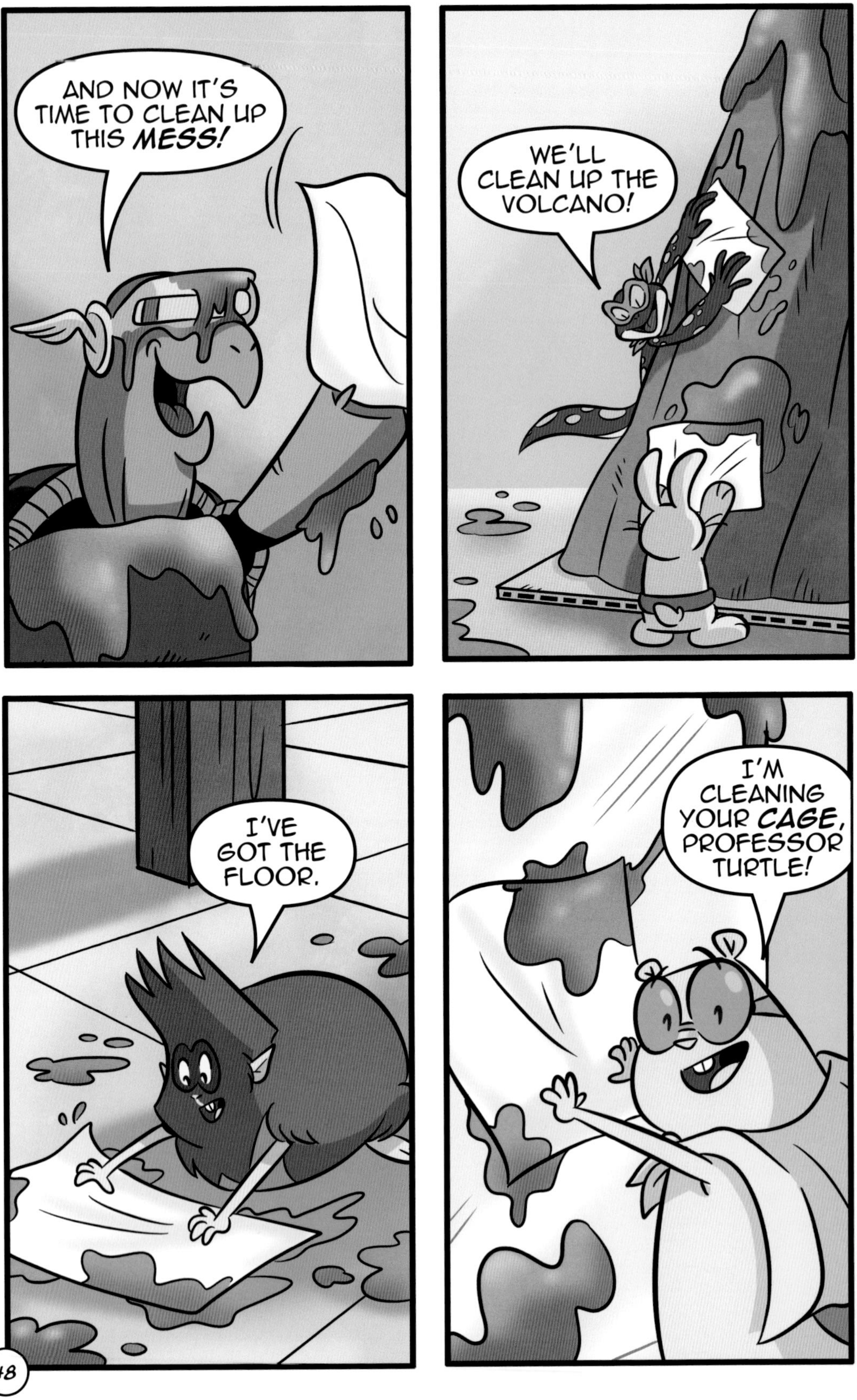
AND NOW IT'S TIME TO CLEAN UP THIS *MESS!*
WE'LL CLEAN UP THE VOLCANO!
I'VE GOT THE FLOOR.
I'M CLEANING YOUR *CAGE*, PROFESSOR TURTLE!

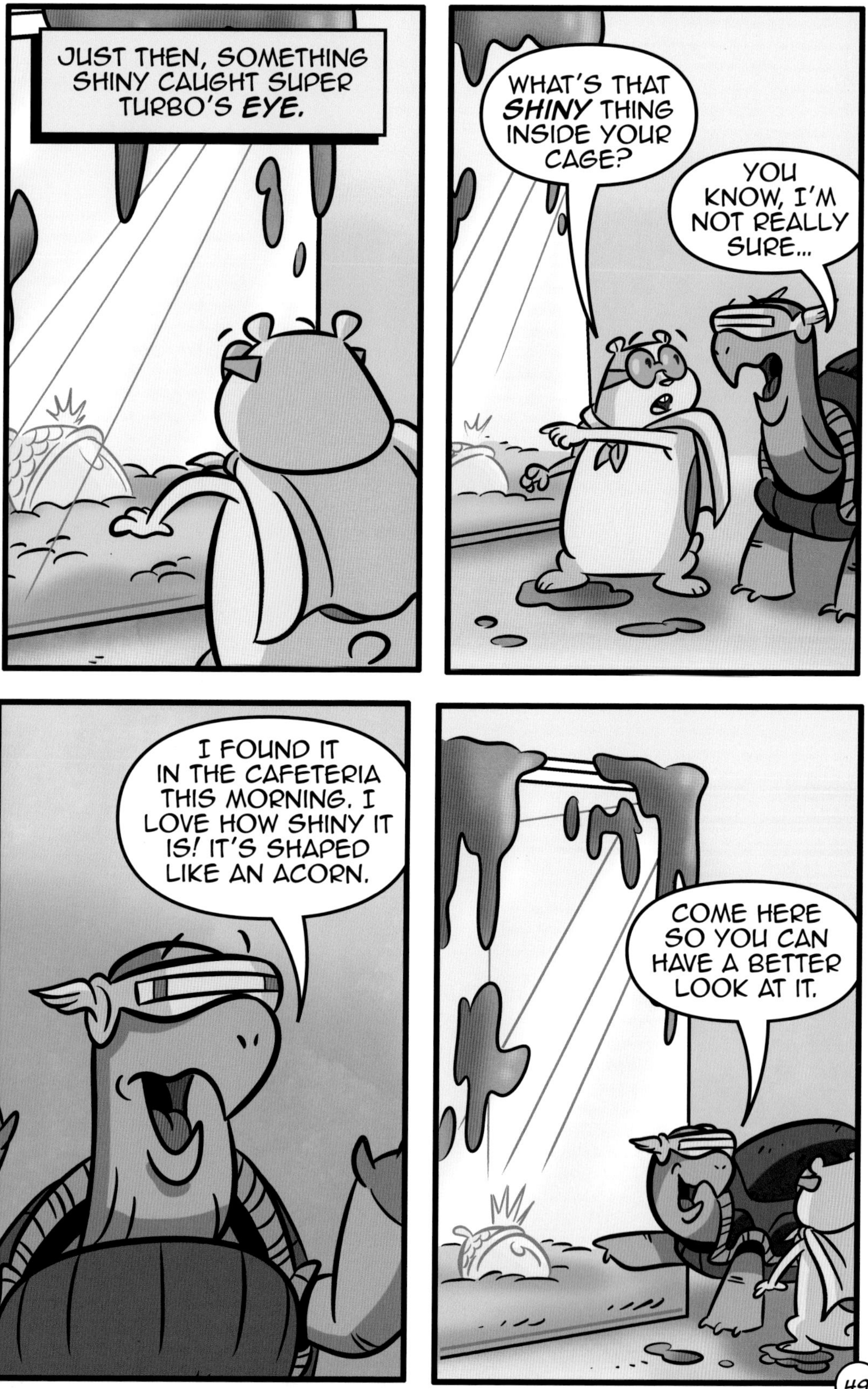
JUST THEN, SOMETHING SHINY CAUGHT SUPER TURBO'S *EYE.*
WHAT'S THAT *SHINY* THING INSIDE YOUR CAGE?
YOU KNOW, I'M NOT REALLY SURE...
I FOUND IT IN THE CAFETERIA THIS MORNING. I LOVE HOW SHINY IT IS! IT'S SHAPED LIKE AN ACORN.
COME HERE SO YOU CAN HAVE A BETTER LOOK AT IT.

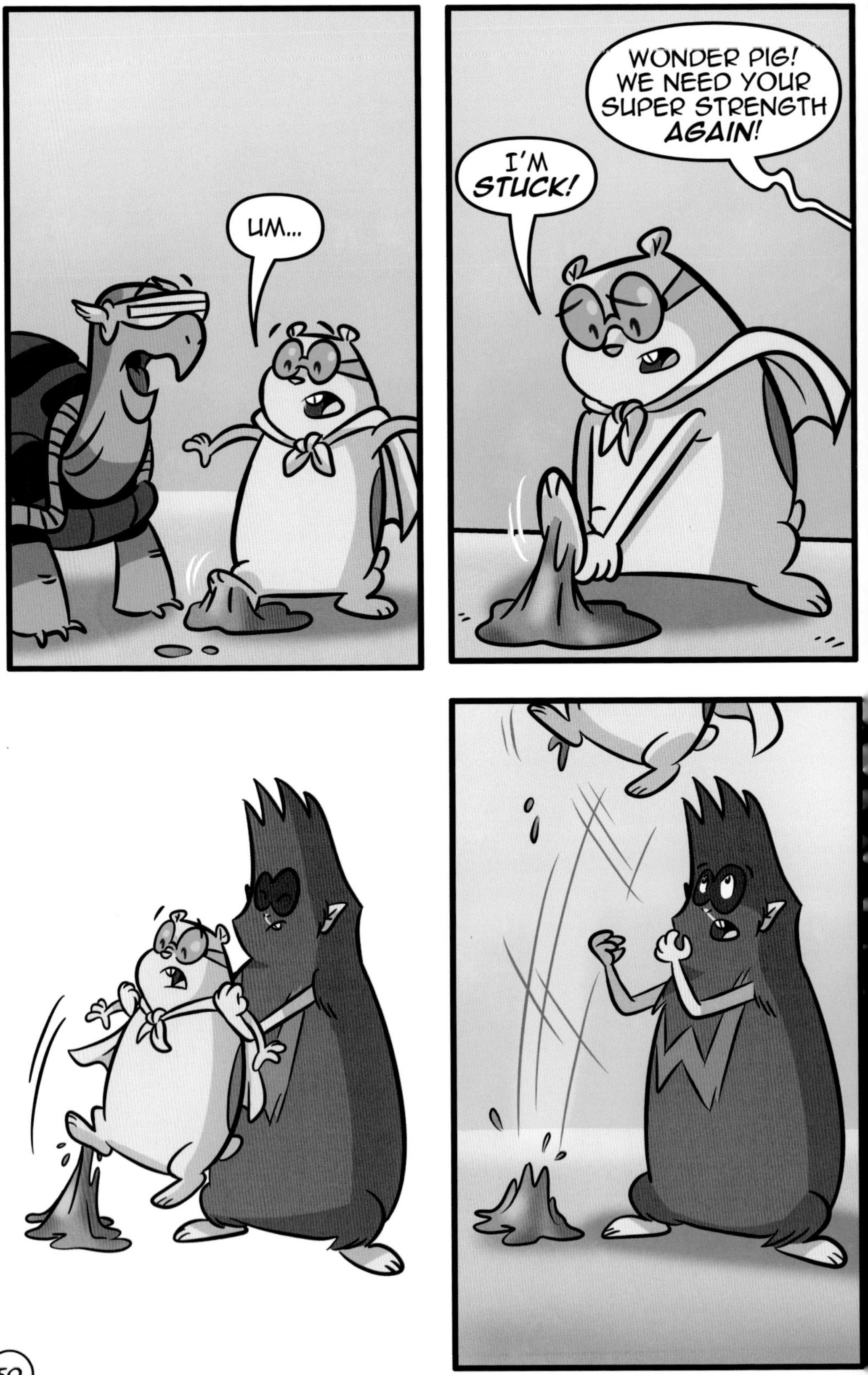
UM...
I'M STUCK!
WONDER PIG! WE NEED YOUR SUPER STRENGTH AGAIN!

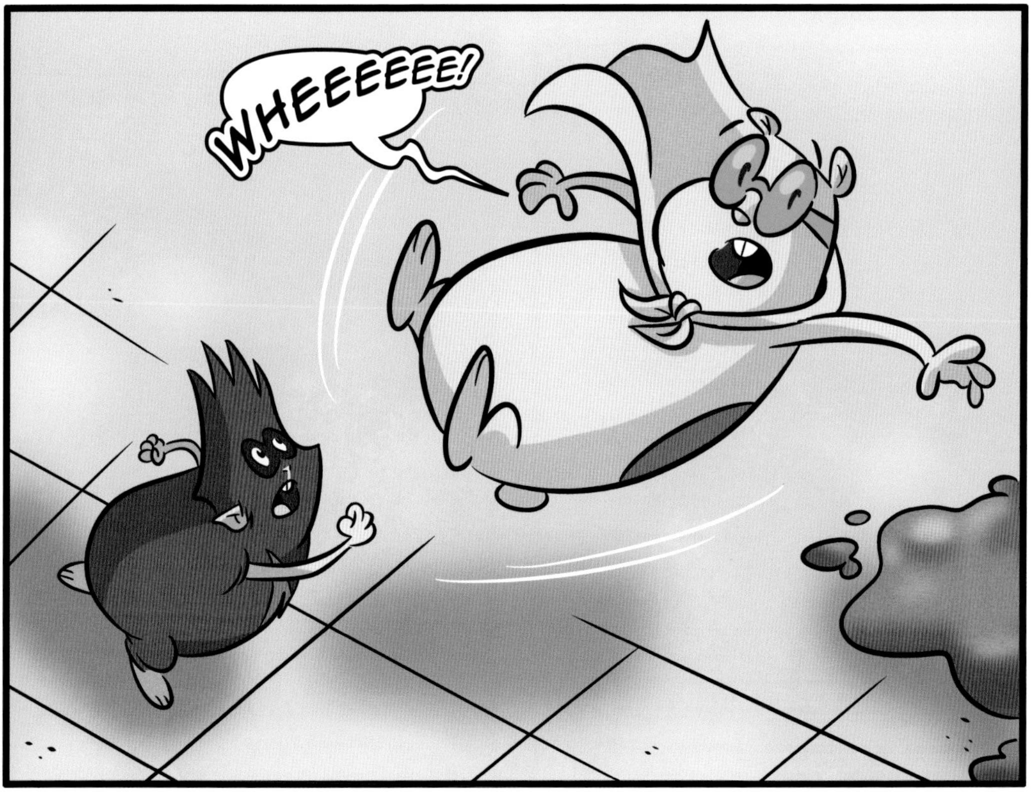
WHEEEEEEE!

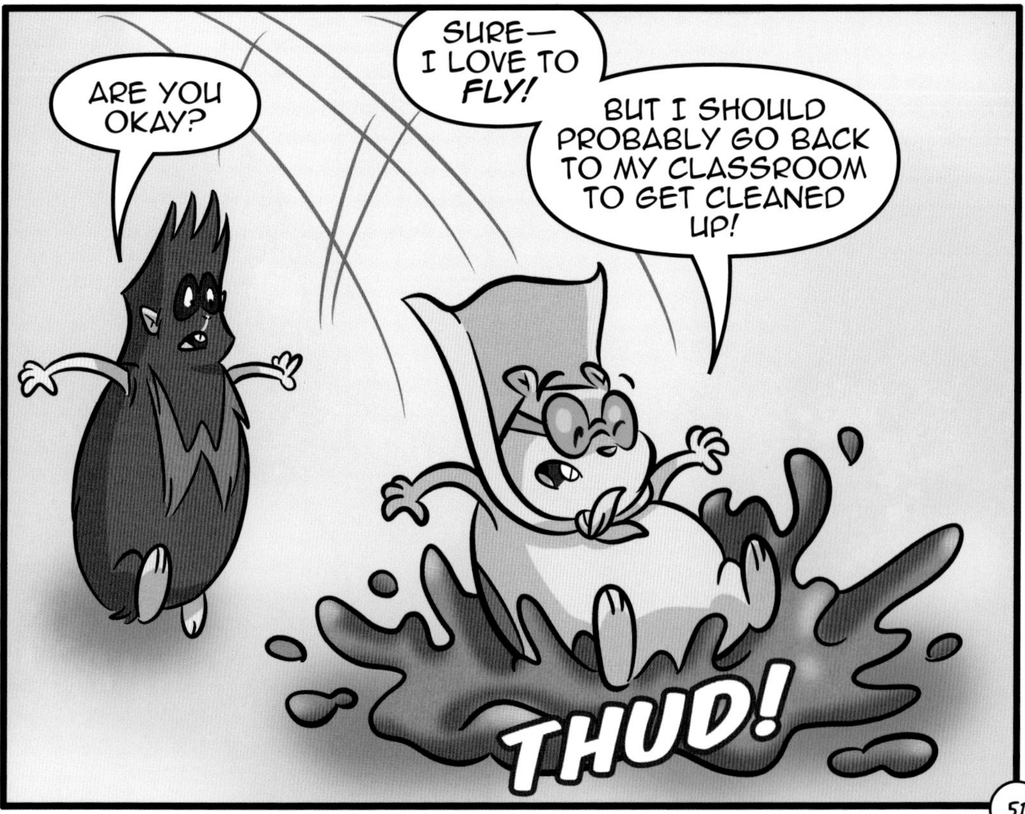
ARE YOU OKAY?
SURE— I LOVE TO *FLY!*
BUT I SHOULD PROBABLY GO BACK TO MY CLASSROOM TO GET CLEANED UP!
THUD!

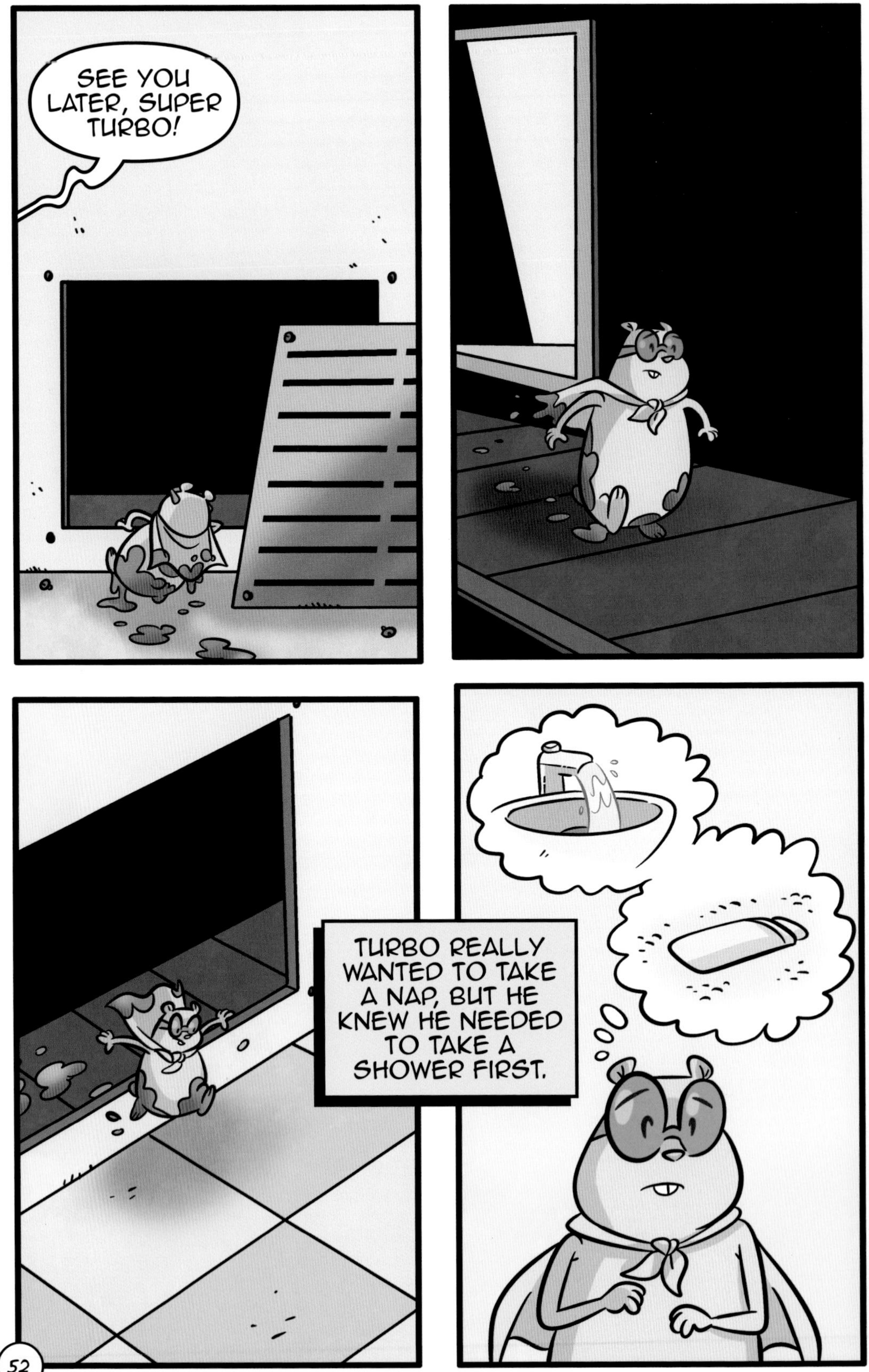
SEE YOU LATER, SUPER TURBO!
TURBO REALLY WANTED TO TAKE A NAP, BUT HE KNEW HE NEEDED TO TAKE A SHOWER FIRST.

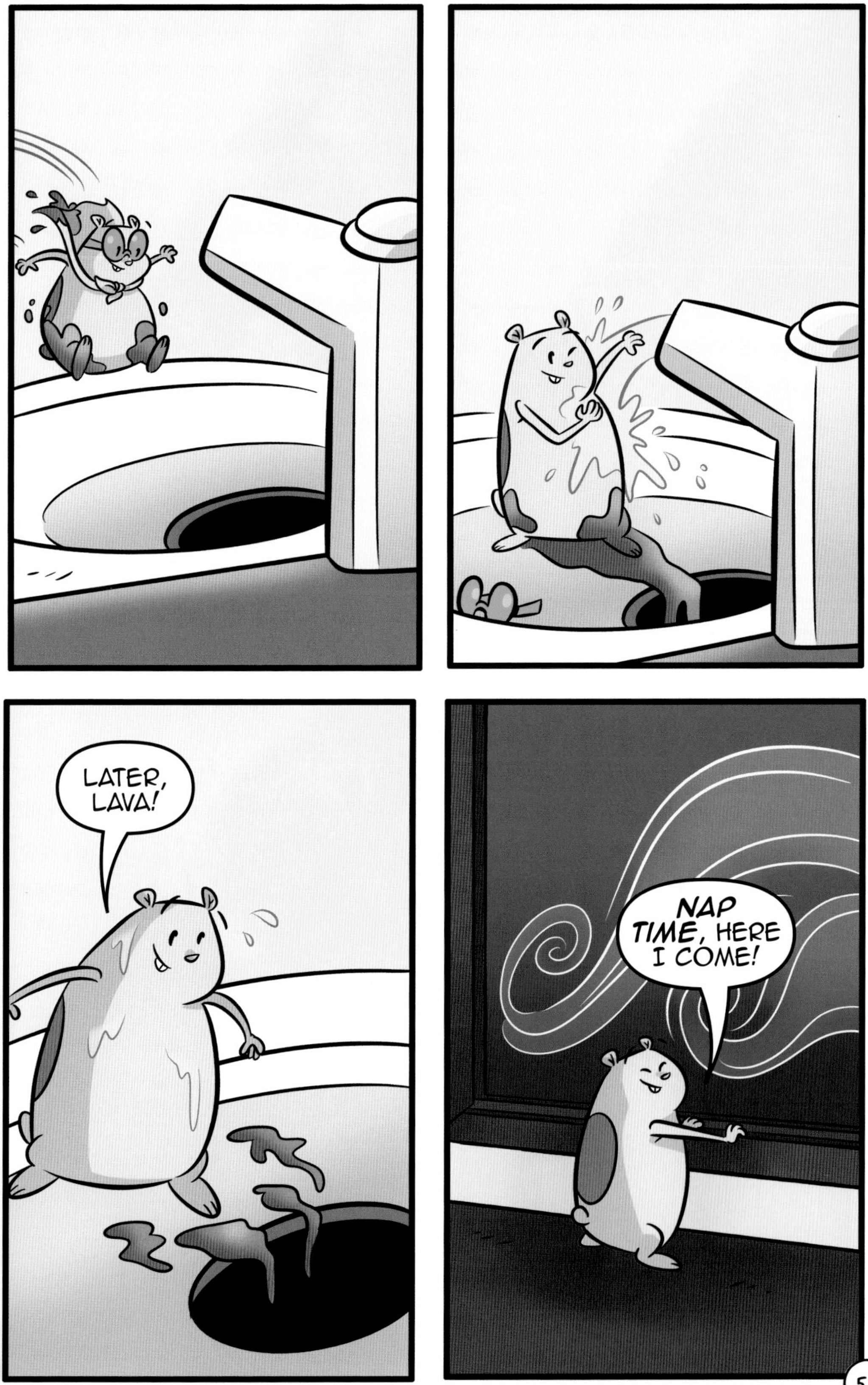
LATER, LAVA!
NAP TIME, HERE I COME!

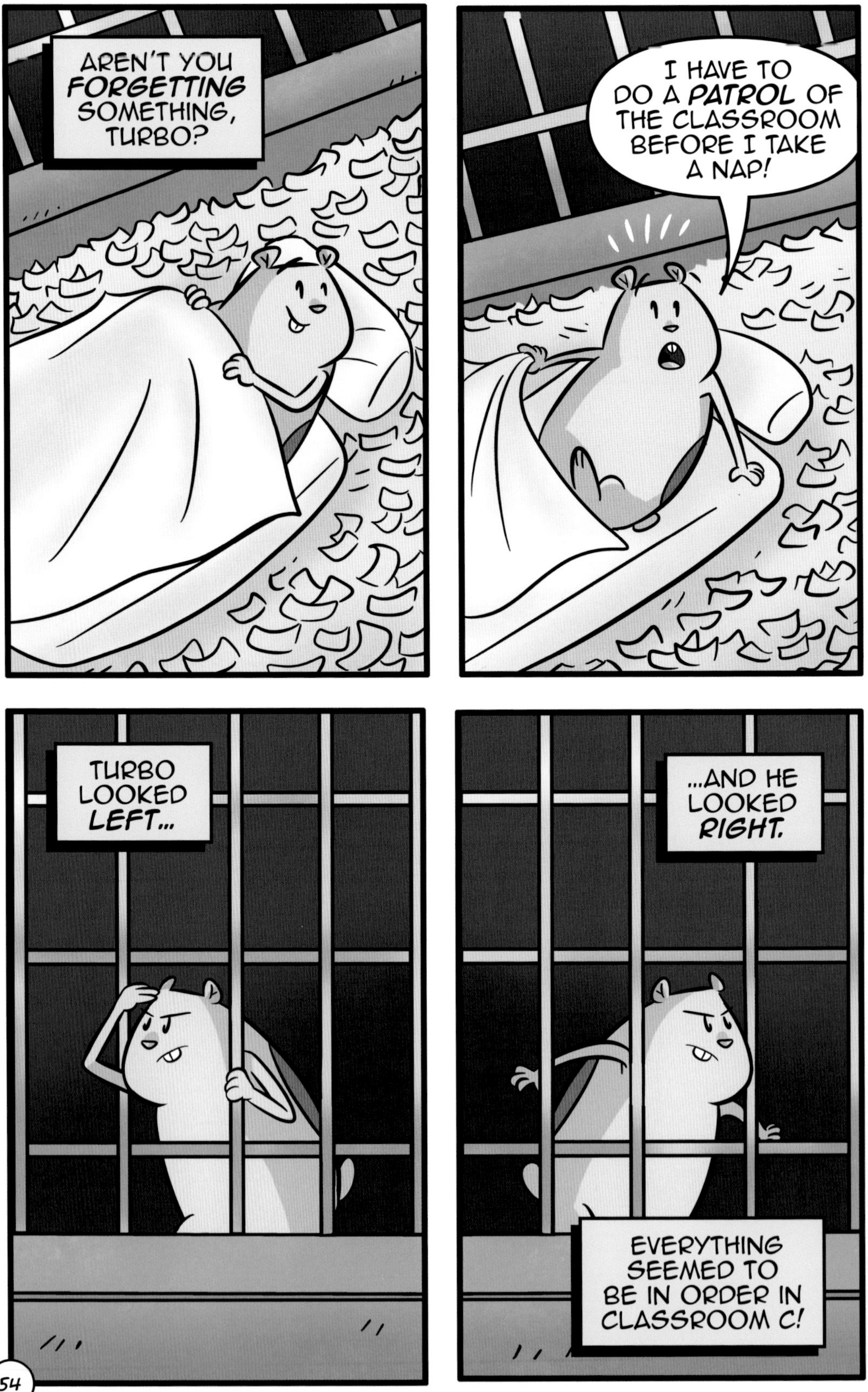
AREN'T YOU FORGETTING SOMETHING, TURBO?
I HAVE TO DO A PATROL OF THE CLASSROOM BEFORE I TAKE A NAP!
TURBO LOOKED LEFT...
...AND HE LOOKED RIGHT.
EVERYTHING SEEMED TO BE IN ORDER IN CLASSROOM C!

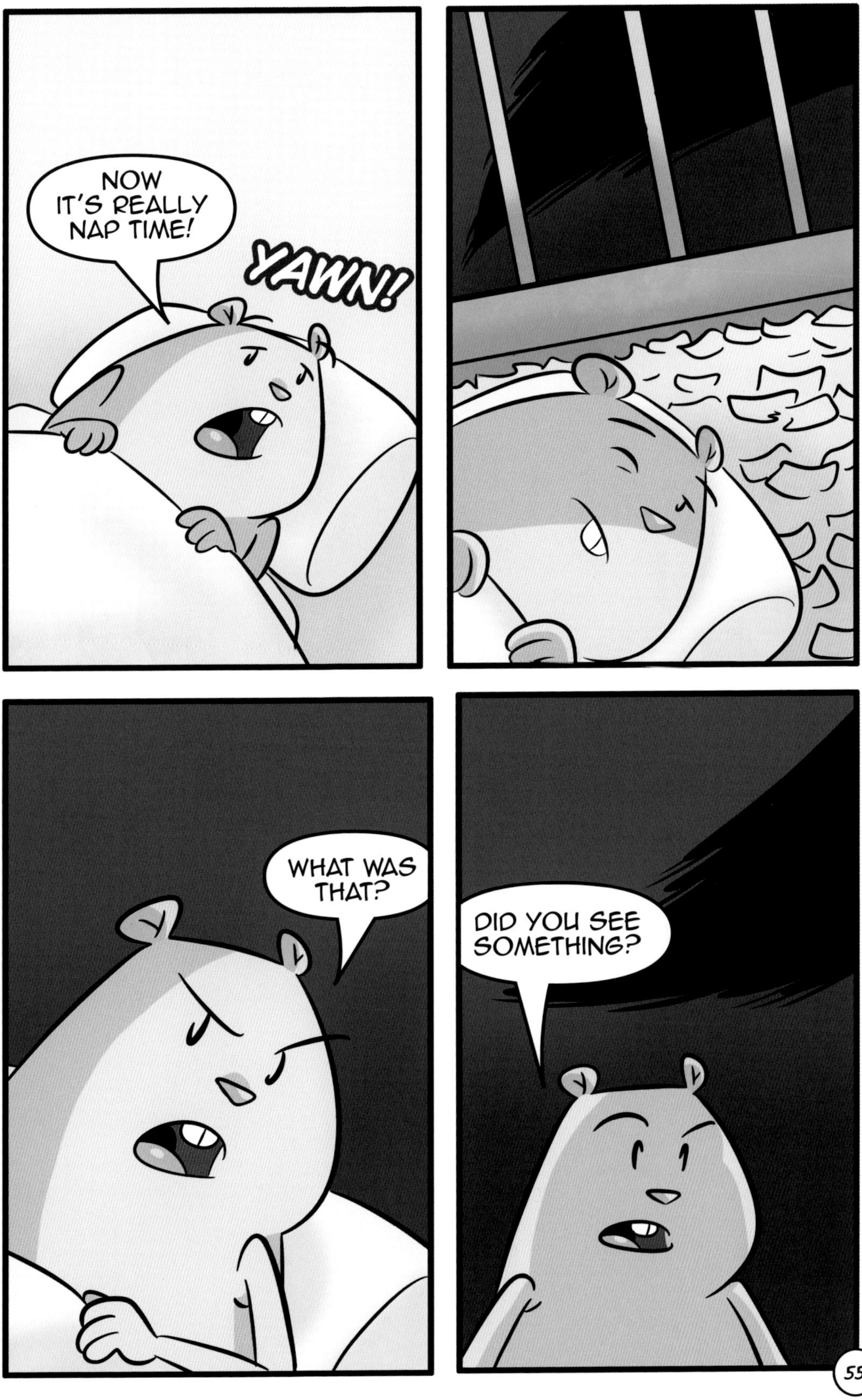
NOW IT'S REALLY NAP TIME!
YAWN!
WHAT WAS THAT?
DID YOU SEE SOMETHING?

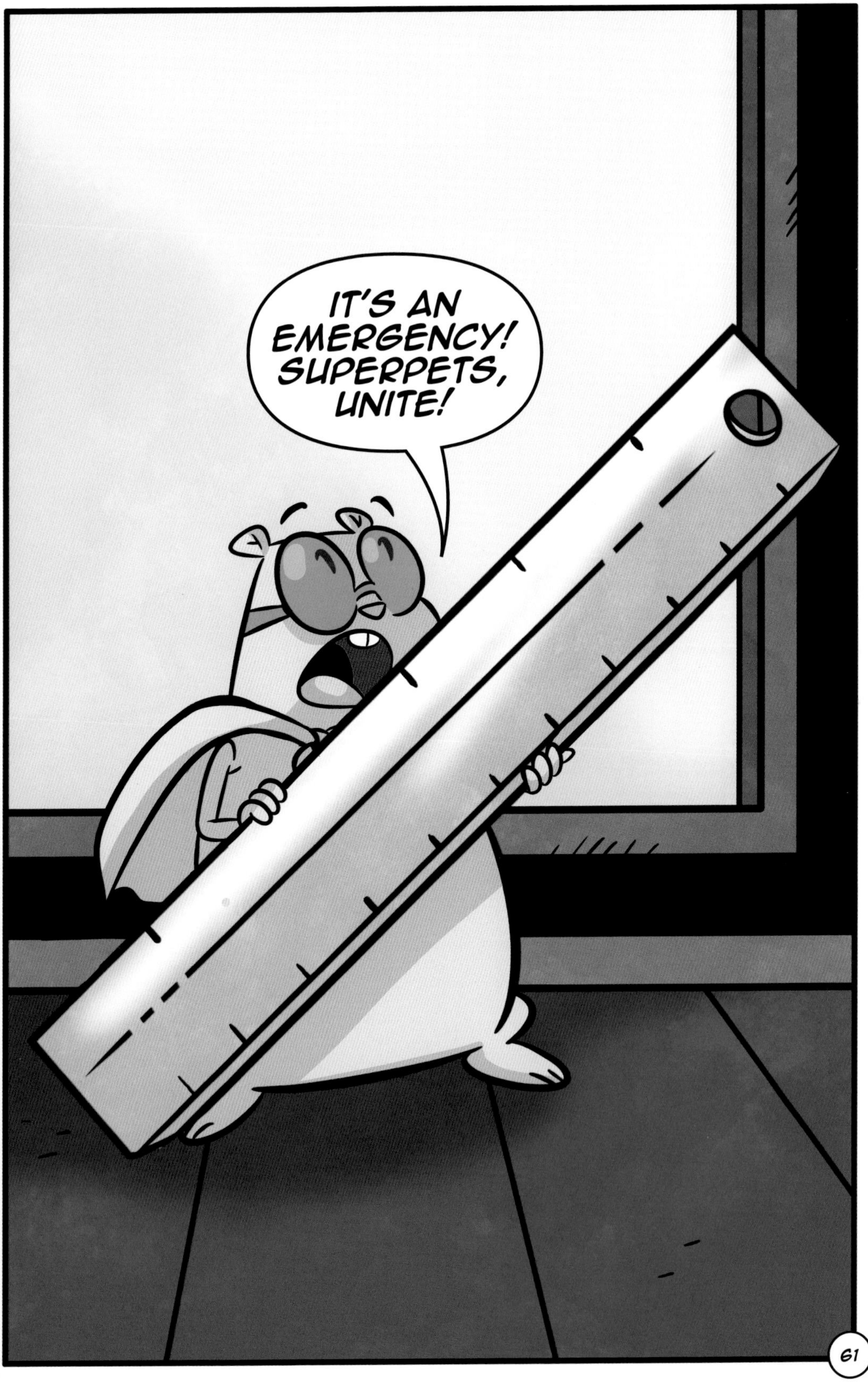
IT'S AN EMERGENCY! SUPERPETS, UNITE!

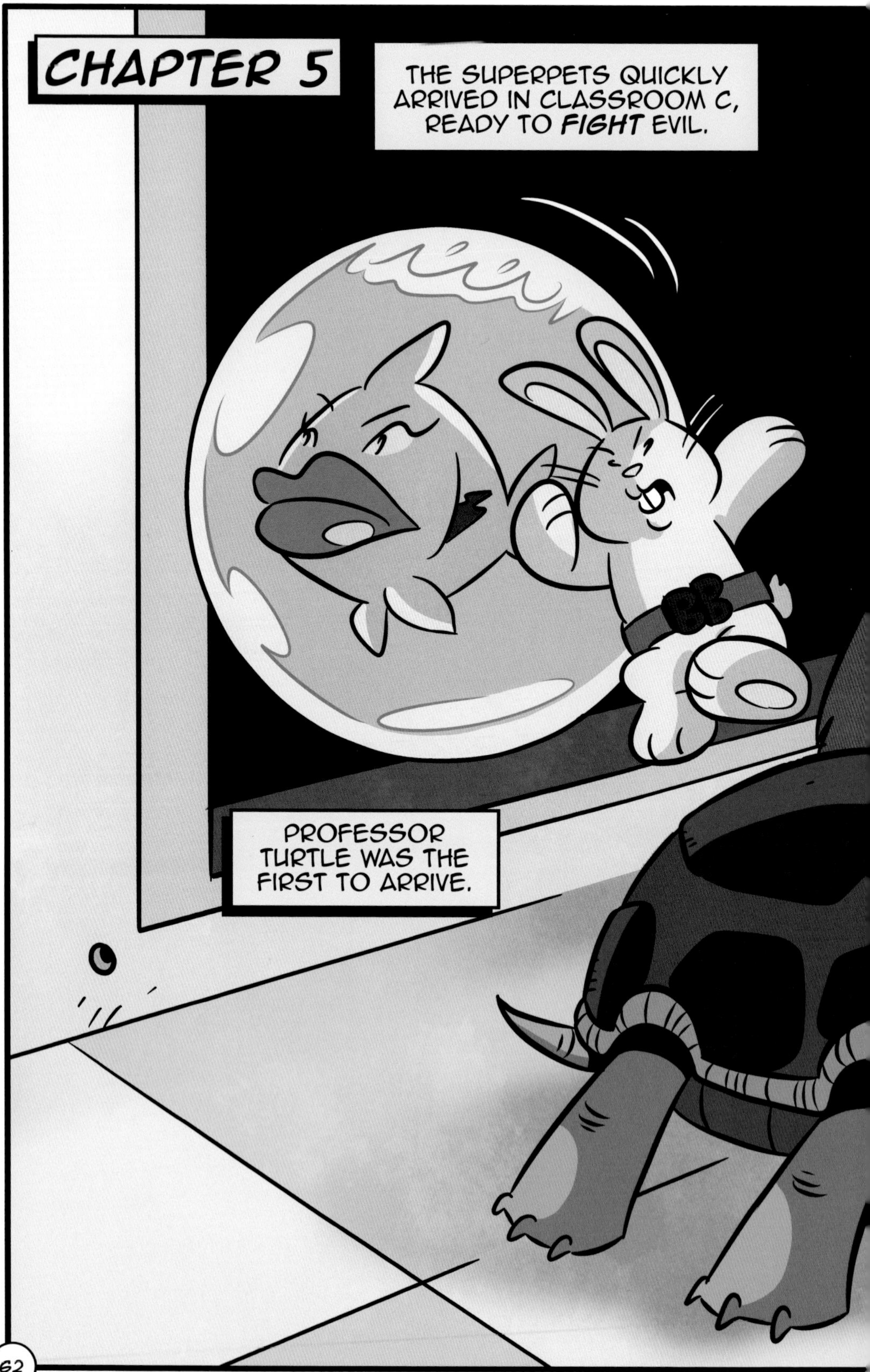
CHAPTER 5
THE SUPERPETS QUICKLY ARRIVED IN CLASSROOM C, READY TO FIGHT EVIL.
PROFESSOR TURTLE WAS THE FIRST TO ARRIVE.

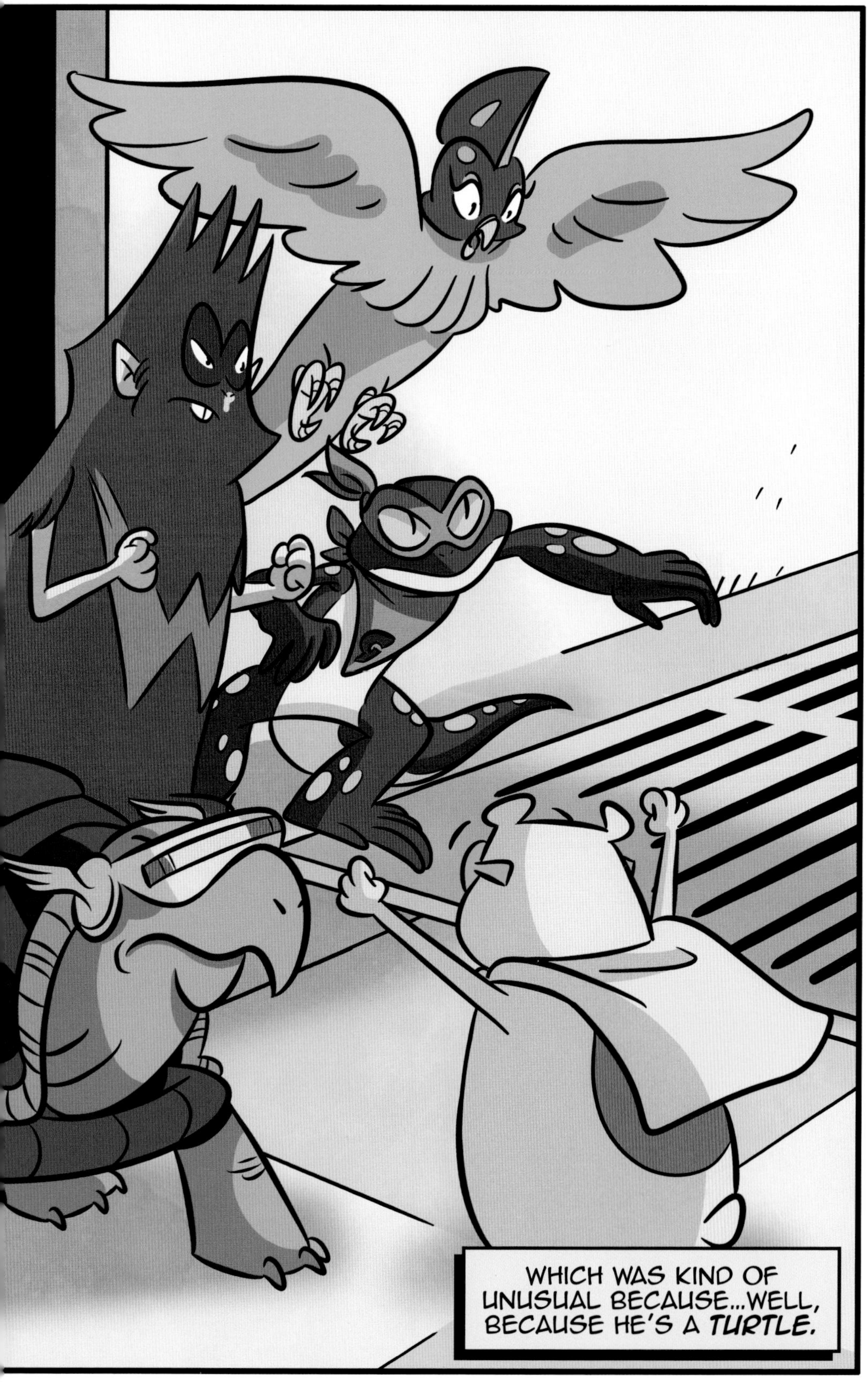
WHICH WAS KIND OF UNUSUAL BECAUSE...WELL, BECAUSE HE'S A *TURTLE.*

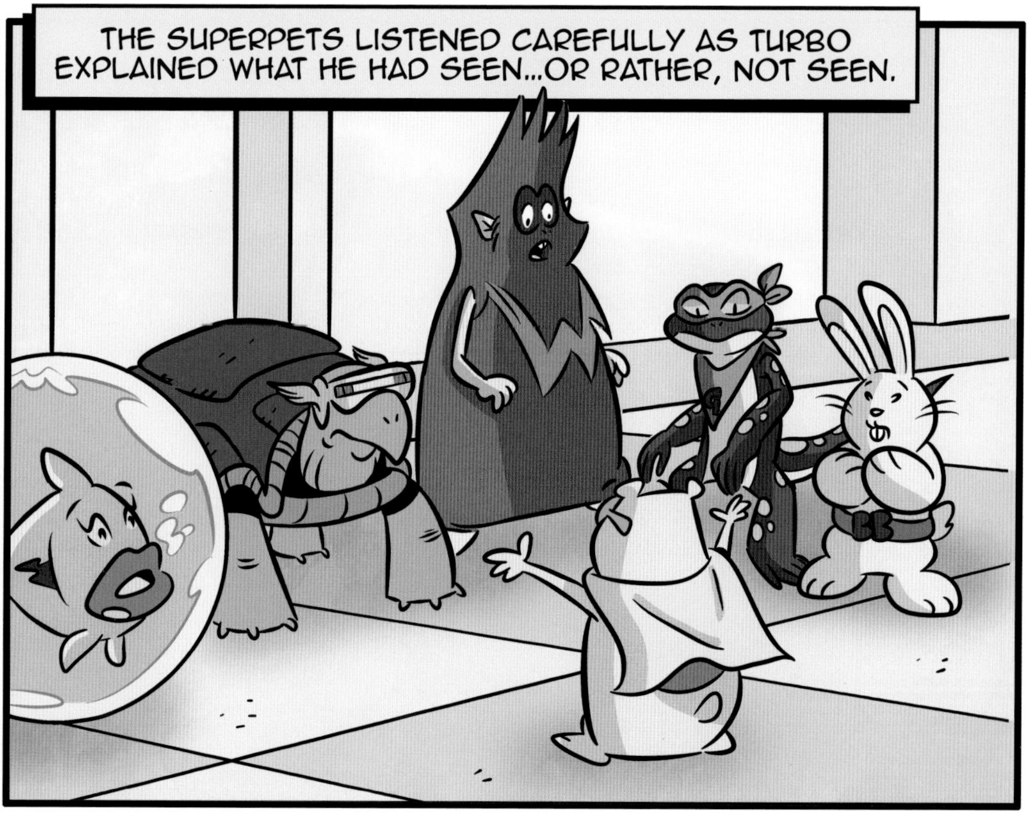
THE SUPERPETS LISTENED CAREFULLY AS TURBO EXPLAINED WHAT HE HAD SEEN...OR RATHER, NOT SEEN.

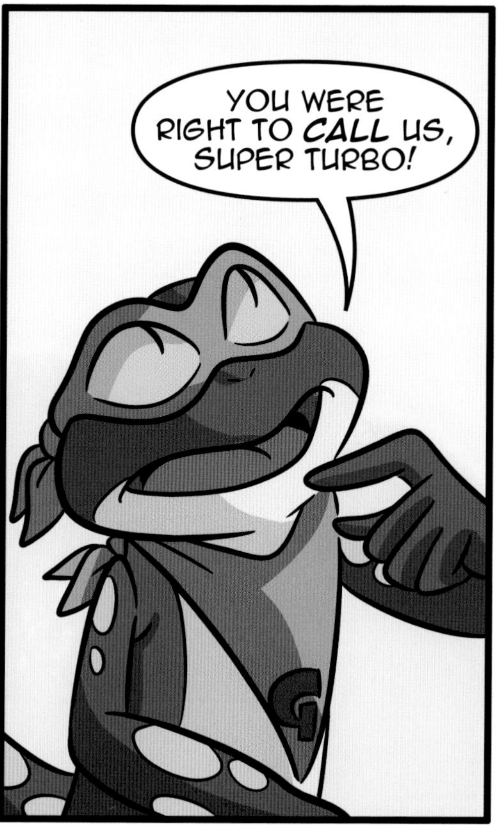
YOU WERE RIGHT TO *CALL* US, SUPER TURBO!

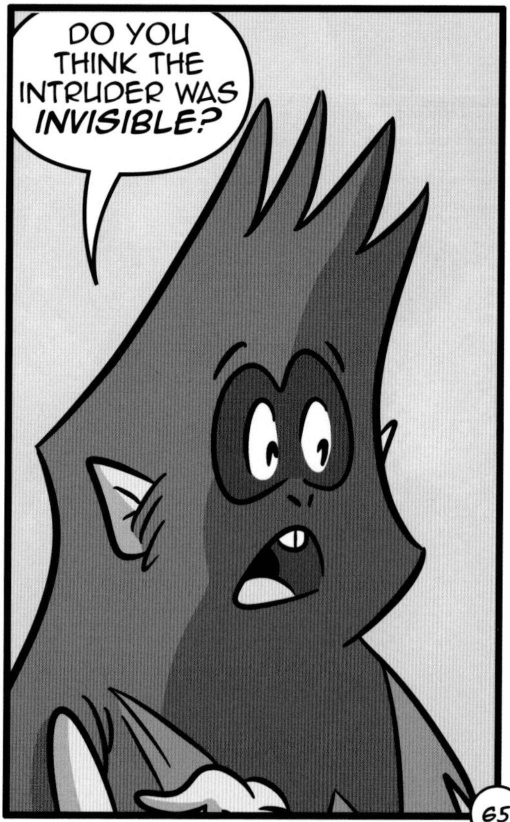
DO YOU THINK THE INTRUDER WAS *INVISIBLE?*

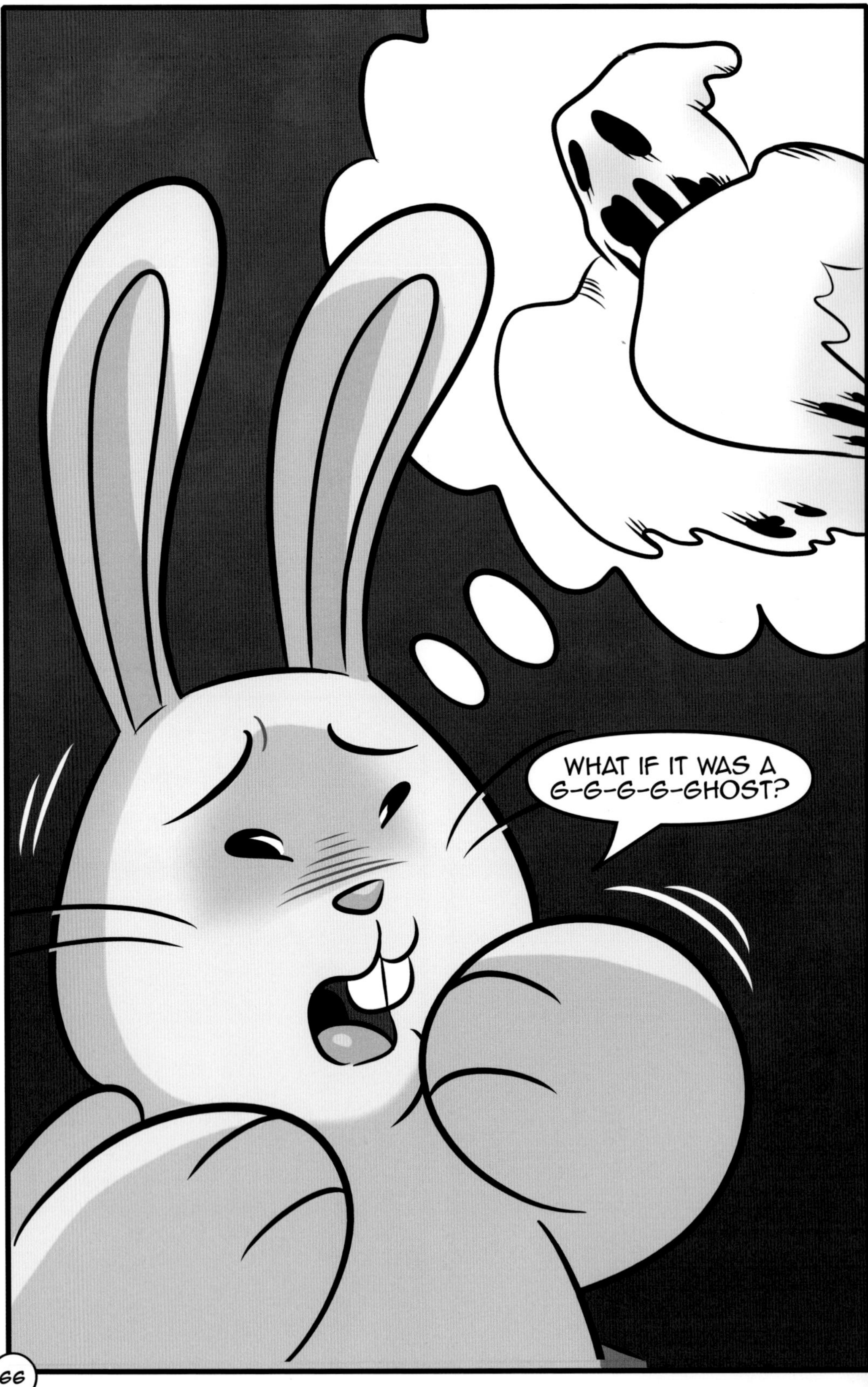
WHAT IF IT WAS A G-G-G-G-GHOST?

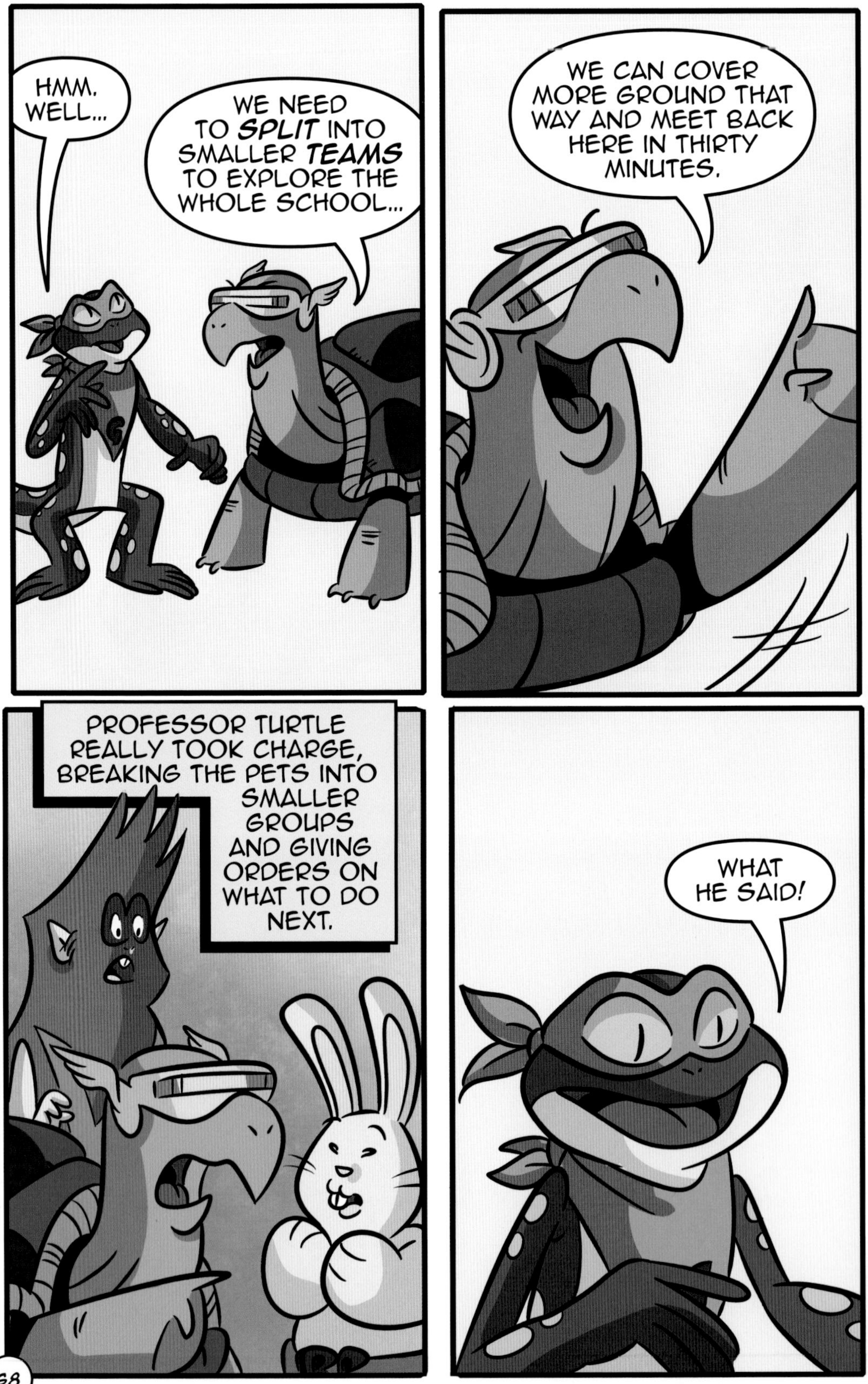
HMM. WELL...
WE NEED TO SPLIT INTO SMALLER TEAMS TO EXPLORE THE WHOLE SCHOOL...
WE CAN COVER MORE GROUND THAT WAY AND MEET BACK HERE IN THIRTY MINUTES.
PROFESSOR TURTLE REALLY TOOK CHARGE, BREAKING THE PETS INTO SMALLER GROUPS AND GIVING ORDERS ON WHAT TO DO NEXT.
WHAT HE SAID!

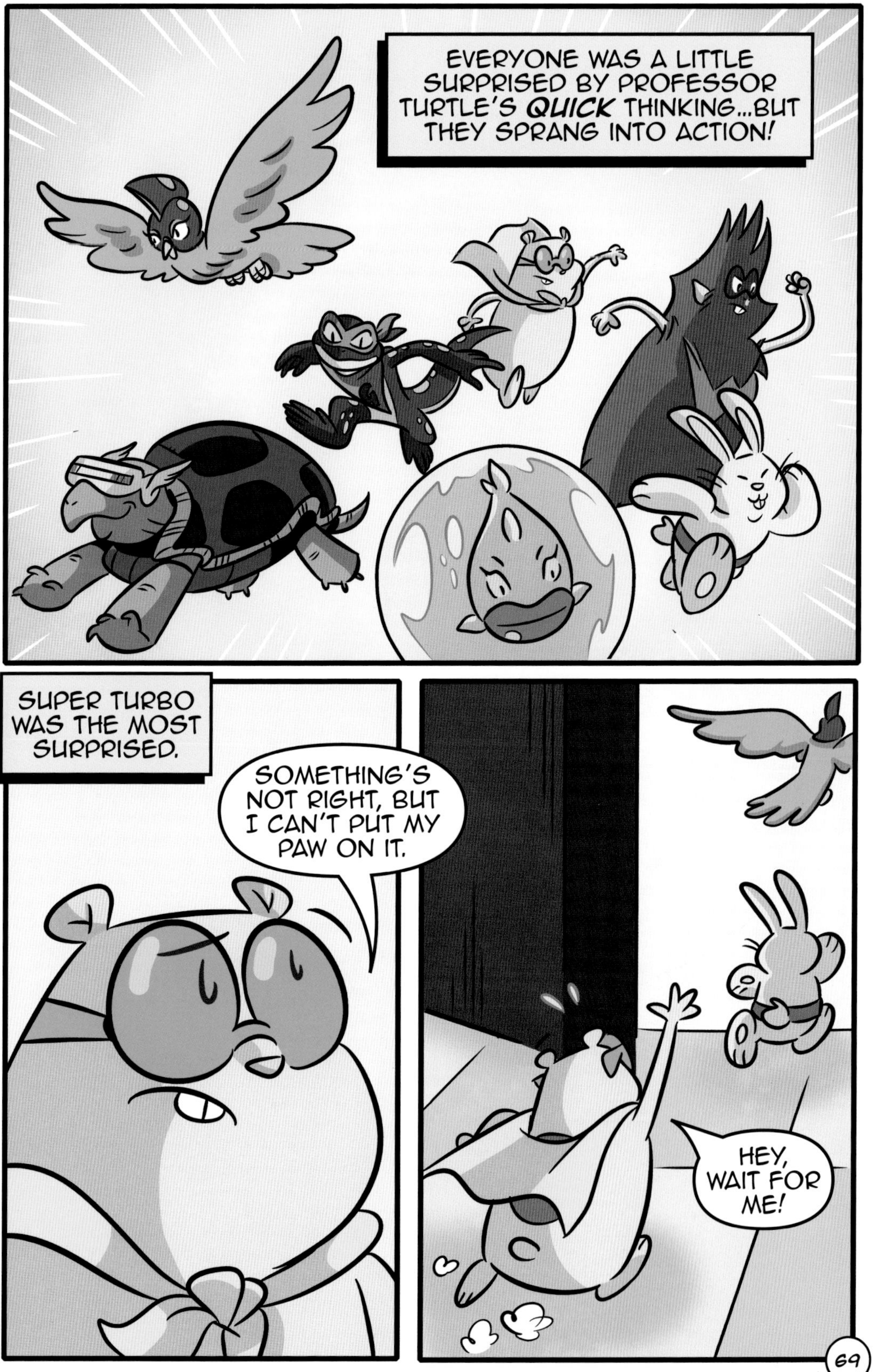
EVERYONE WAS A LITTLE SURPRISED BY PROFESSOR TURTLE'S *QUICK* THINKING...BUT THEY SPRANG INTO ACTION!
SUPER TURBO WAS THE MOST SURPRISED.
SOMETHING'S NOT RIGHT, BUT I CAN'T PUT MY PAW ON IT.
HEY, WAIT FOR ME!

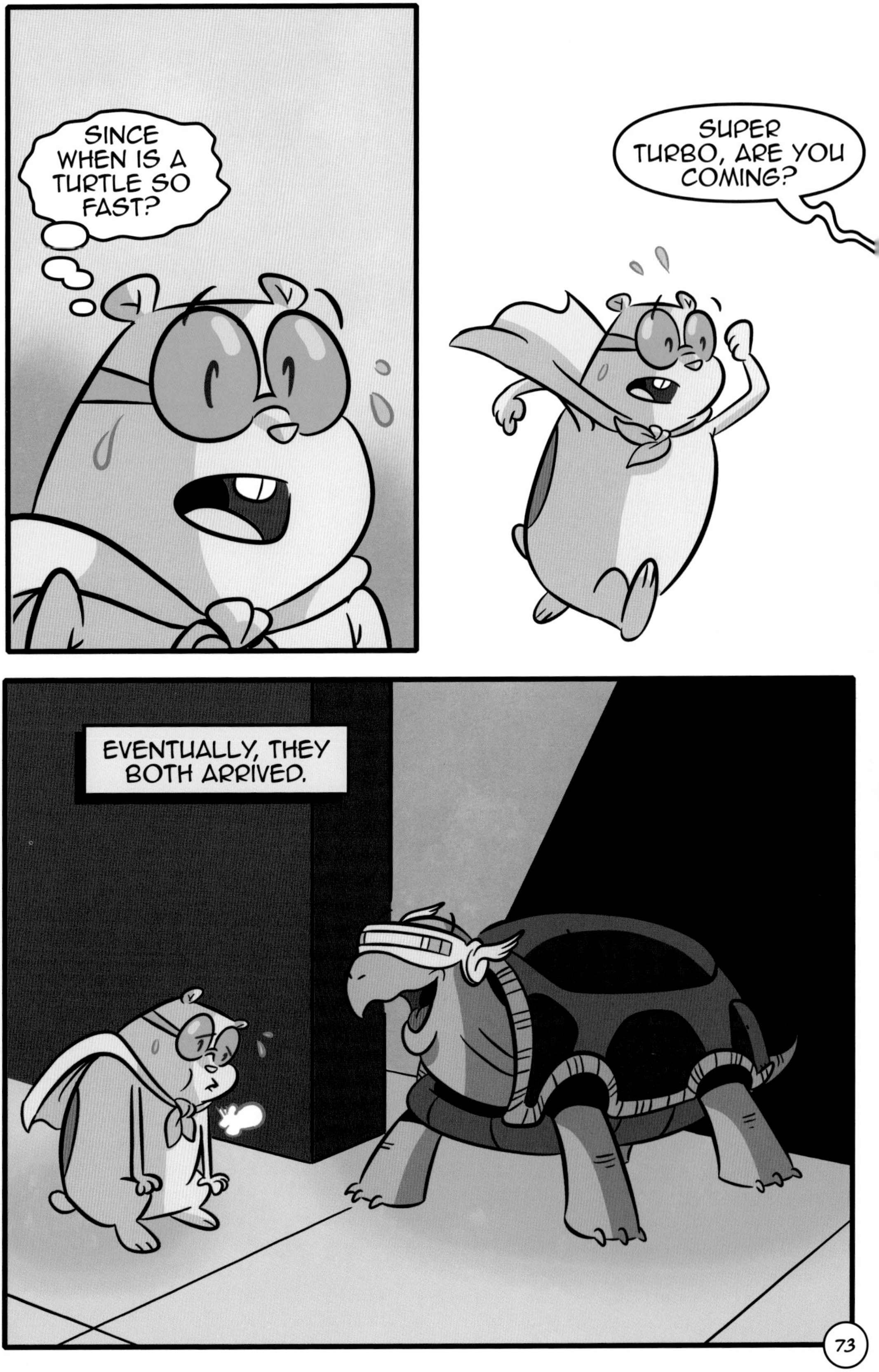
SINCE WHEN IS A TURTLE SO FAST?
SUPER TURBO, ARE YOU COMING?
EVENTUALLY, THEY BOTH ARRIVED.

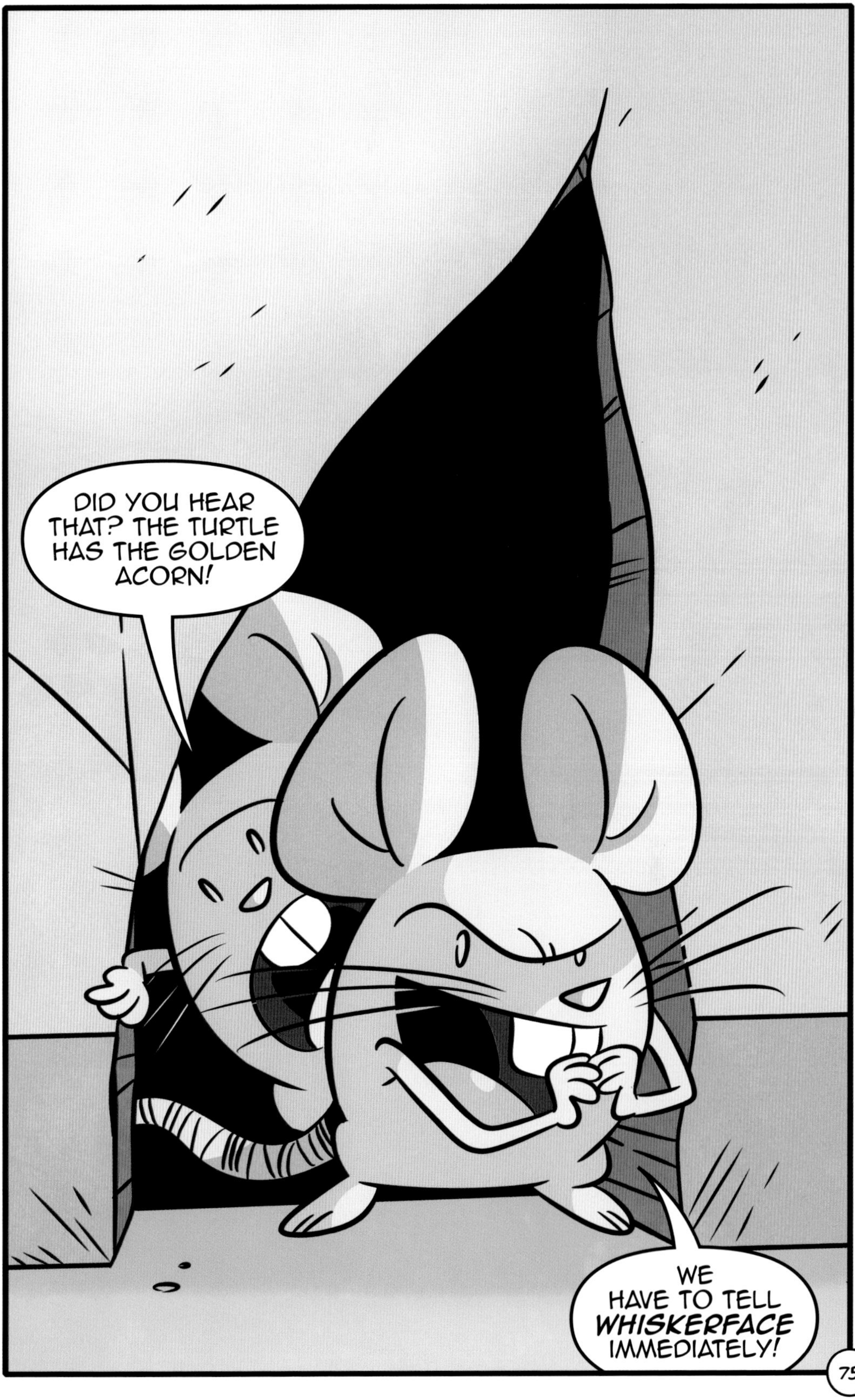

DID YOU HEAR THAT? THE TURTLE HAS THE GOLDEN ACORN!
WE HAVE TO TELL WHISKERFACE IMMEDIATELY!

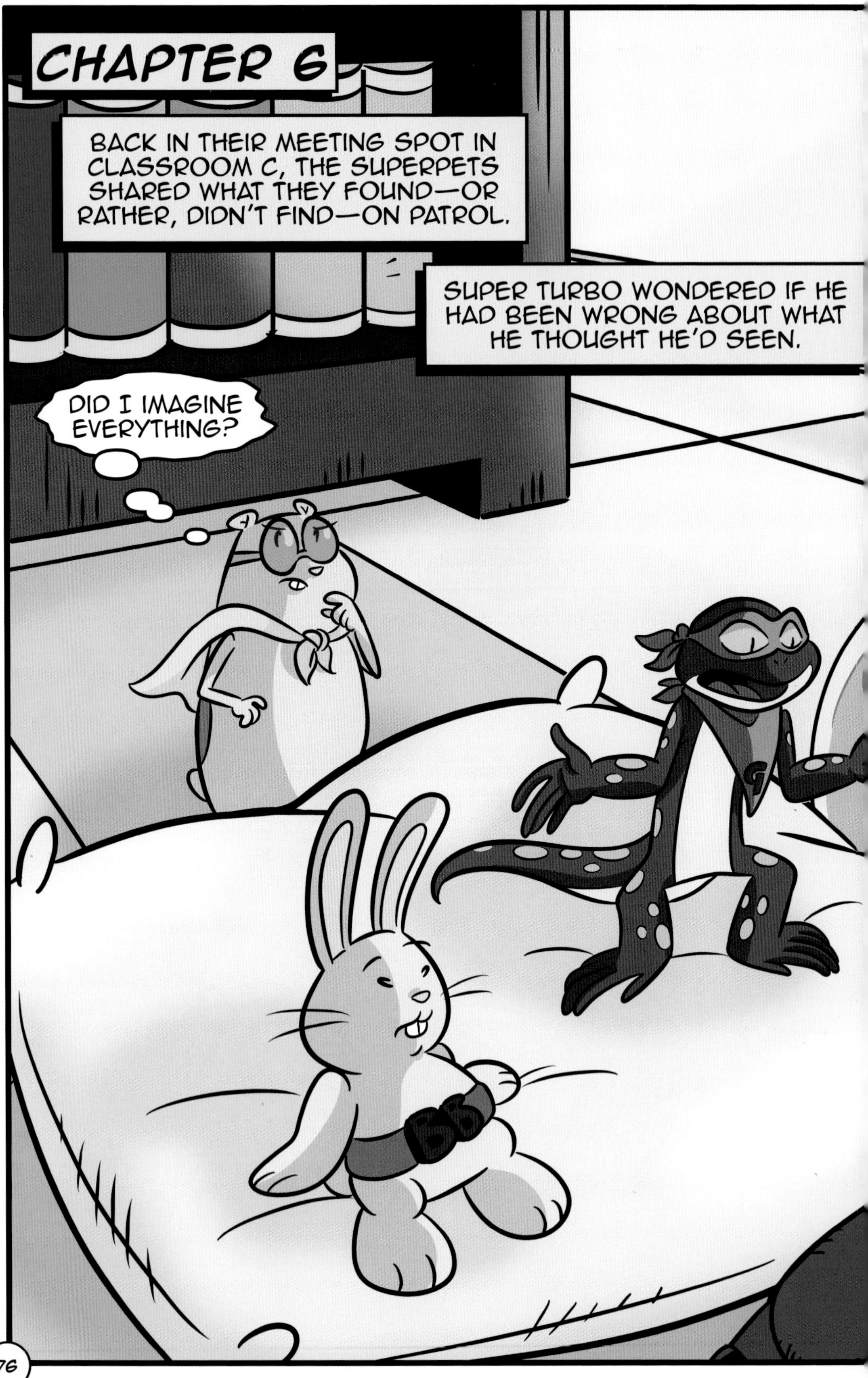
CHAPTER 6
BACK IN THEIR MEETING SPOT IN CLASSROOM C, THE SUPERPETS SHARED WHAT THEY FOUND—OR RATHER, DIDN'T FIND—ON PATROL.
SUPER TURBO WONDERED IF HE HAD BEEN WRONG ABOUT WHAT HE THOUGHT HE'D SEEN.
DID I IMAGINE EVERYTHING?

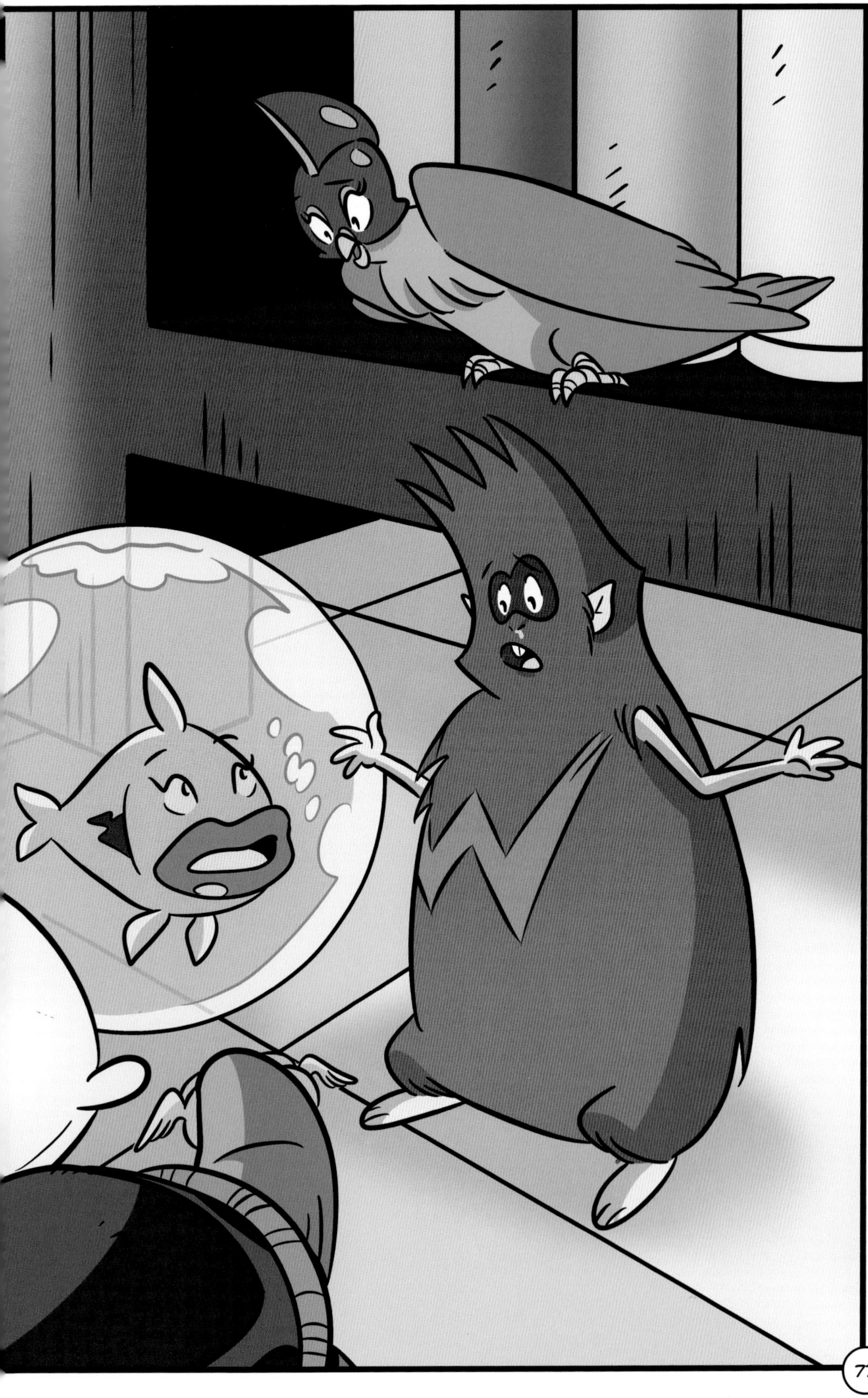

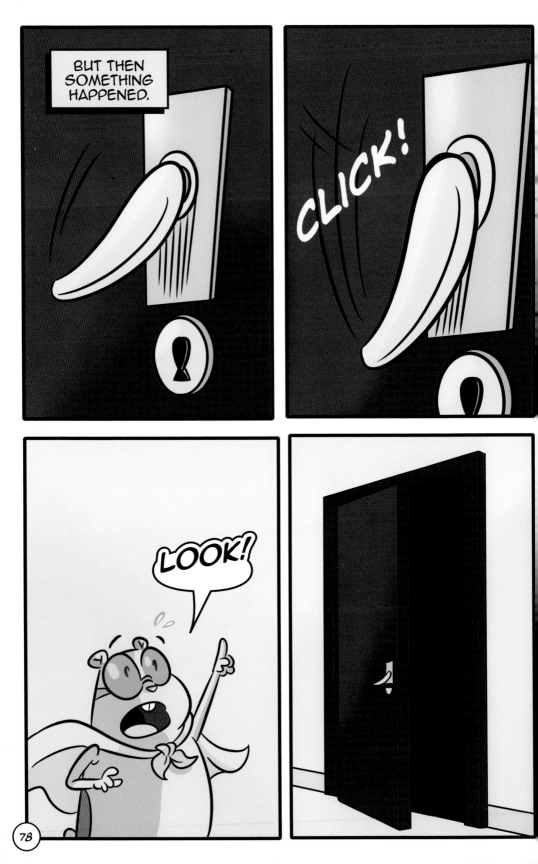

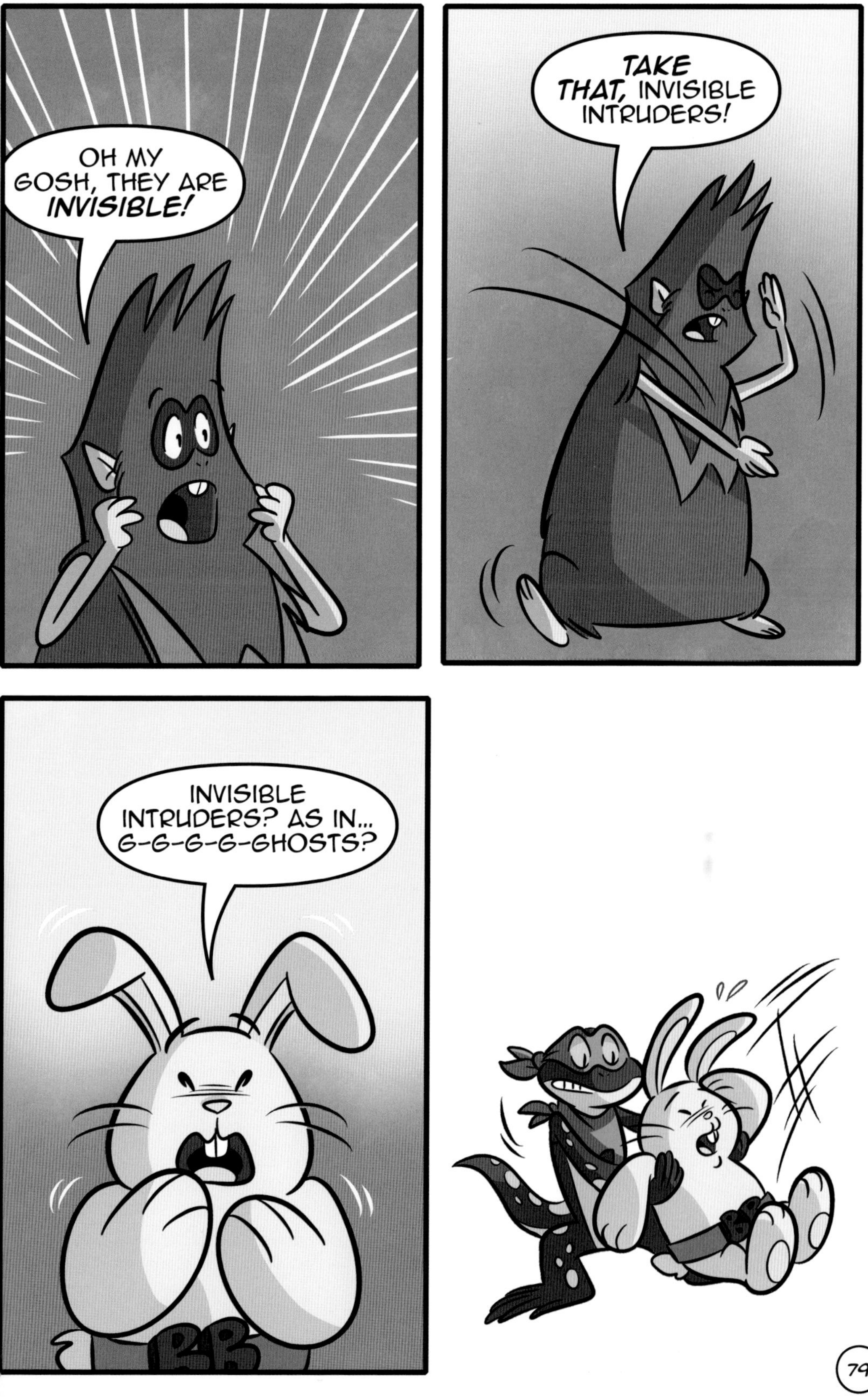
OH MY GOSH, THEY ARE *INVISIBLE!*
TAKE THAT, INVISIBLE INTRUDERS!
INVISIBLE INTRUDERS? AS IN... G-G-G-G-GHOSTS?

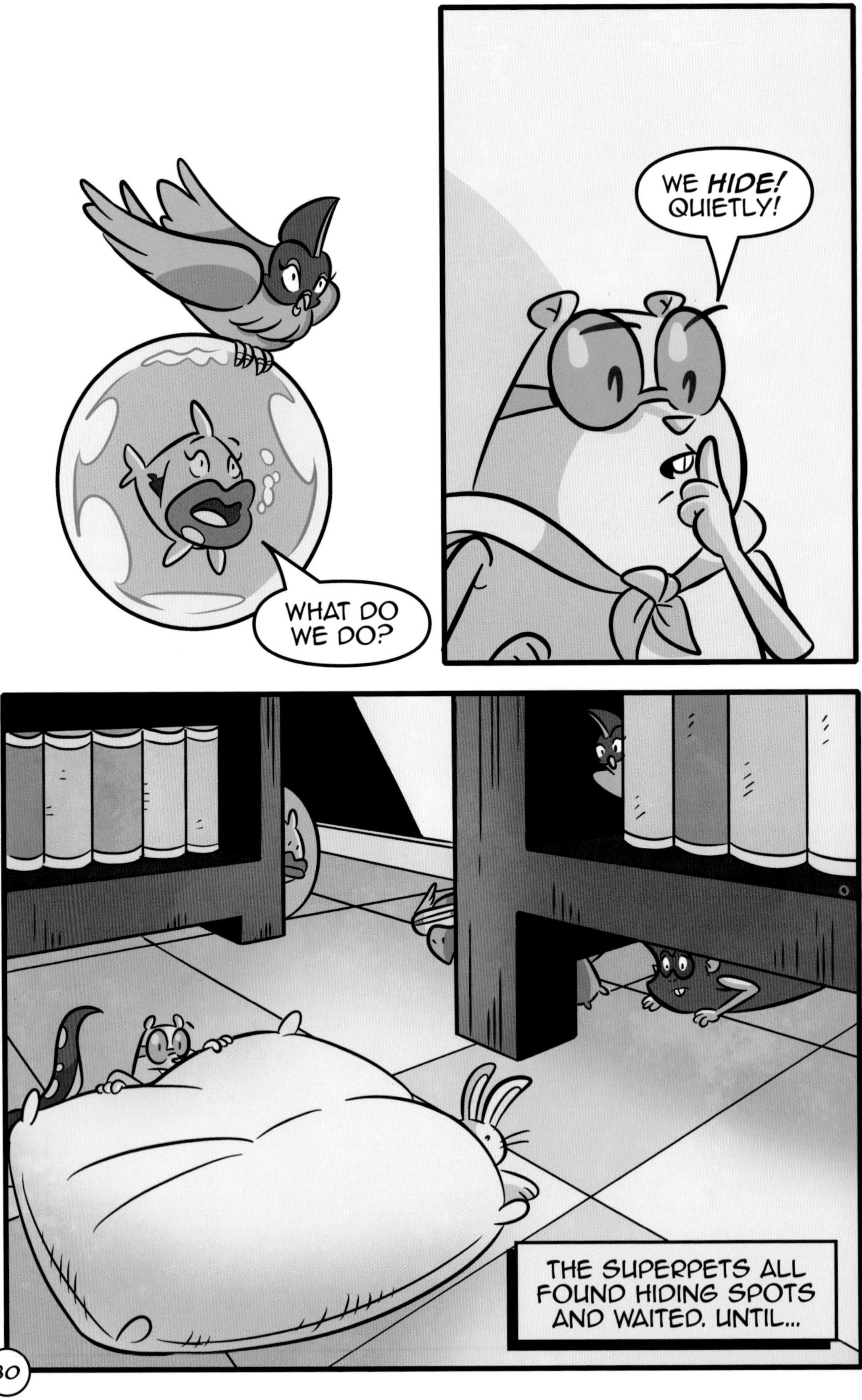
WHAT DO WE DO?
WE HIDE! QUIETLY!
THE SUPERPETS ALL FOUND HIDING SPOTS AND WAITED. UNTIL...

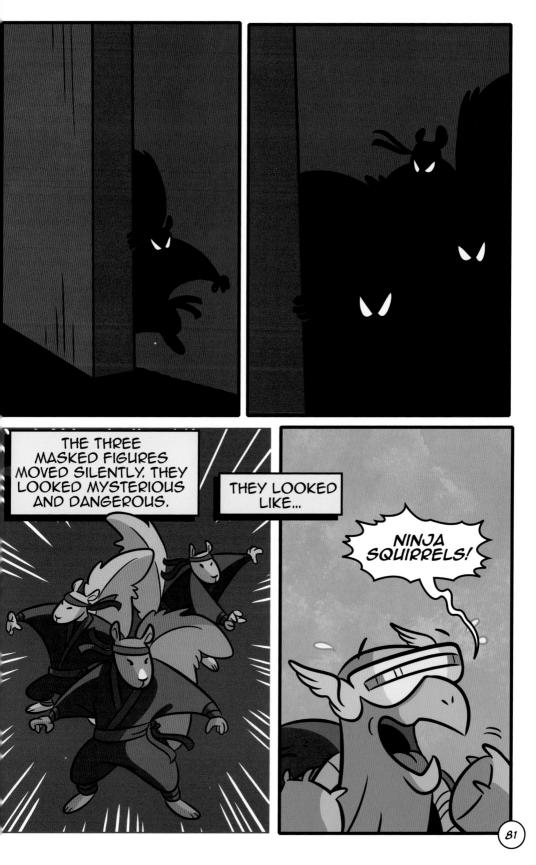

THE THREE MASKED FIGURES MOVED SILENTLY. THEY LOOKED MYSTERIOUS AND DANGEROUS.

THEY LOOKED LIKE...

NINJA SQUIRRELS!

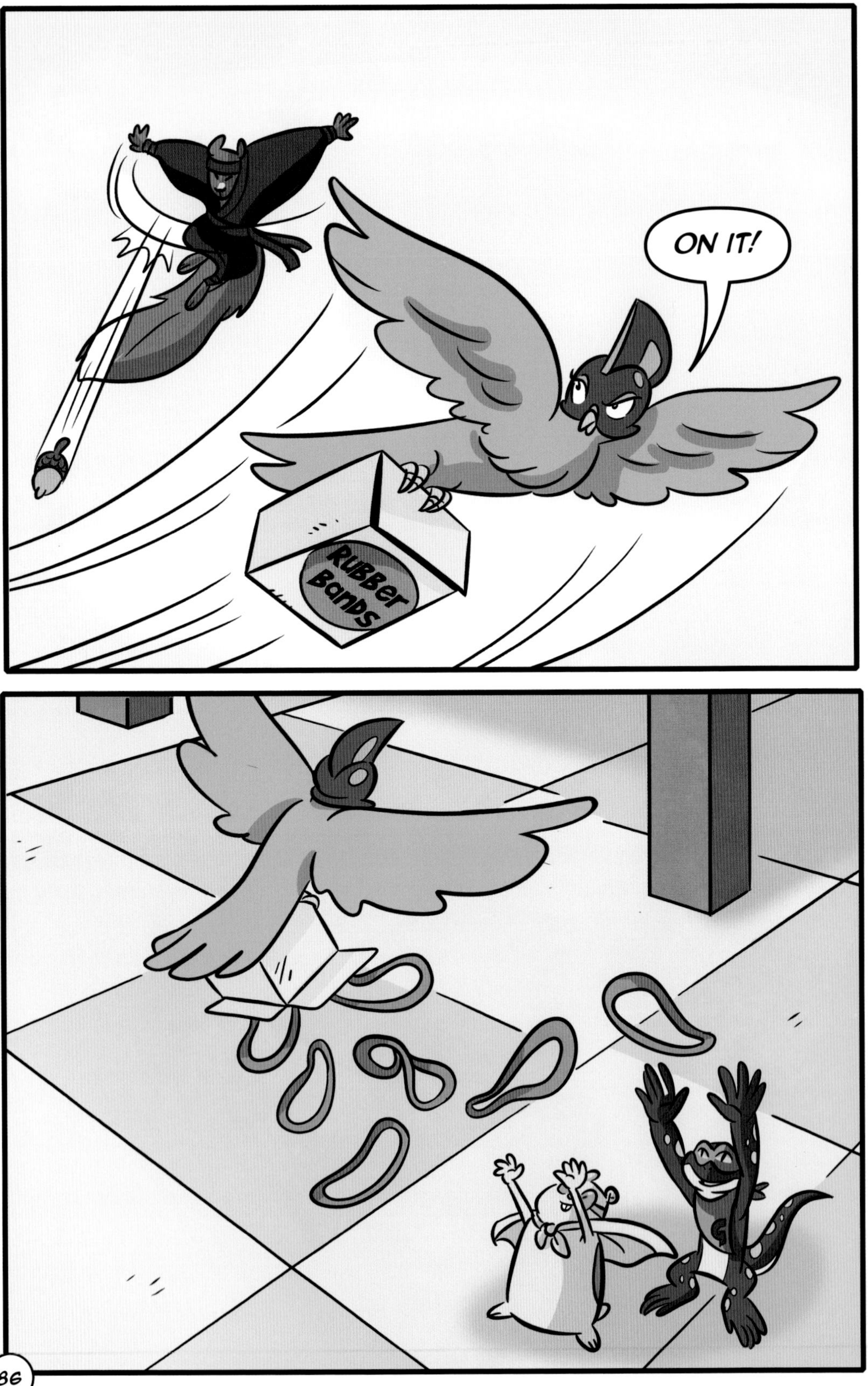
ON IT!
RUBBER BANDS

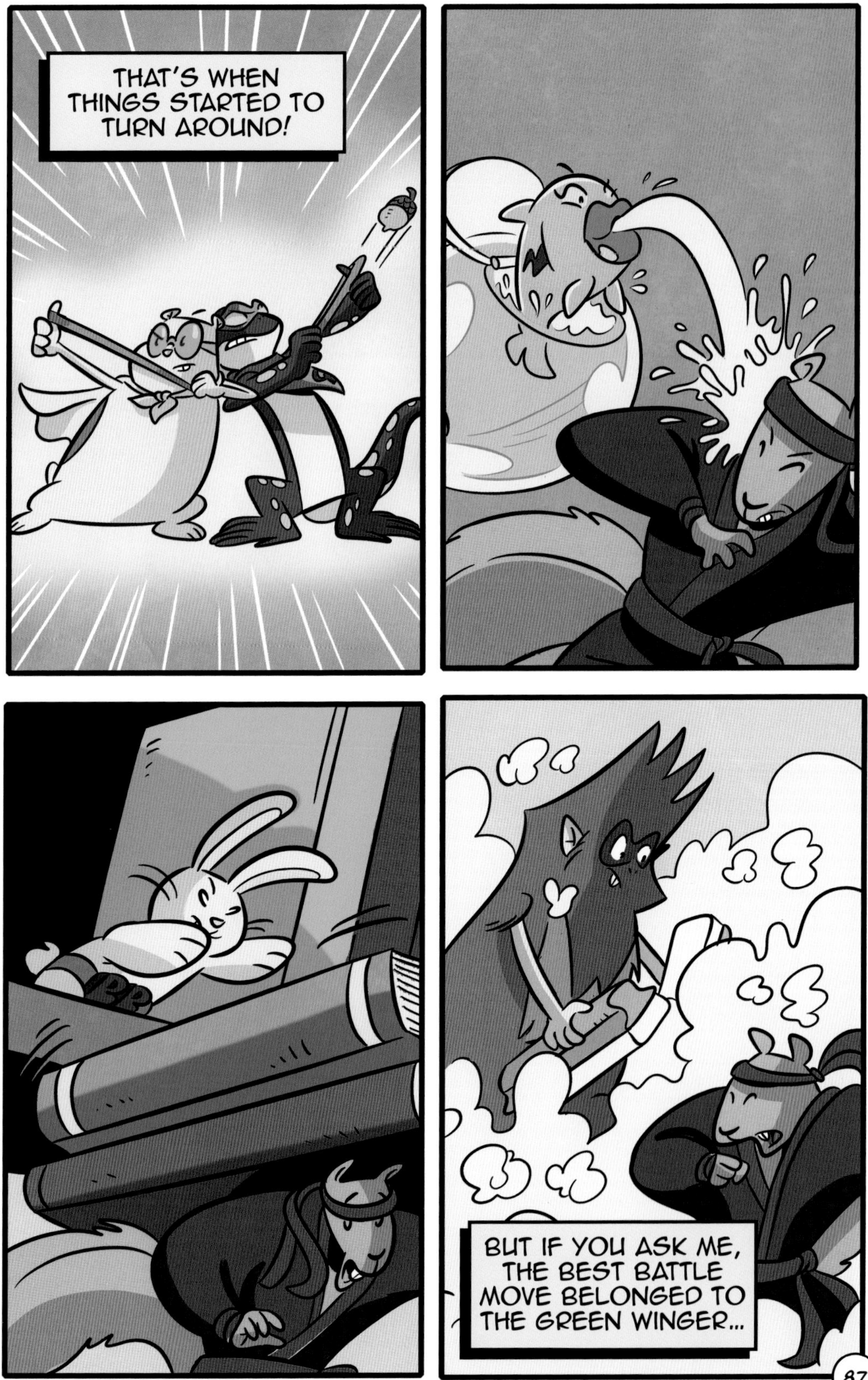
THAT'S WHEN THINGS STARTED TO TURN AROUND!
BUT IF YOU ASK ME, THE BEST BATTLE MOVE BELONGED TO THE GREEN WINGER...

AS THE BATTLE RAGED ON, SUPER TURBO REALIZED SOMETHING...

WHAT SORT OF OFFICIAL CLASSROOM PET ALLOWED THIS TO HAPPEN?

THEY WERE MAKING A HUGE MESS. IN *HIS* CLASSROOM!

NOT ON MY WATCH!

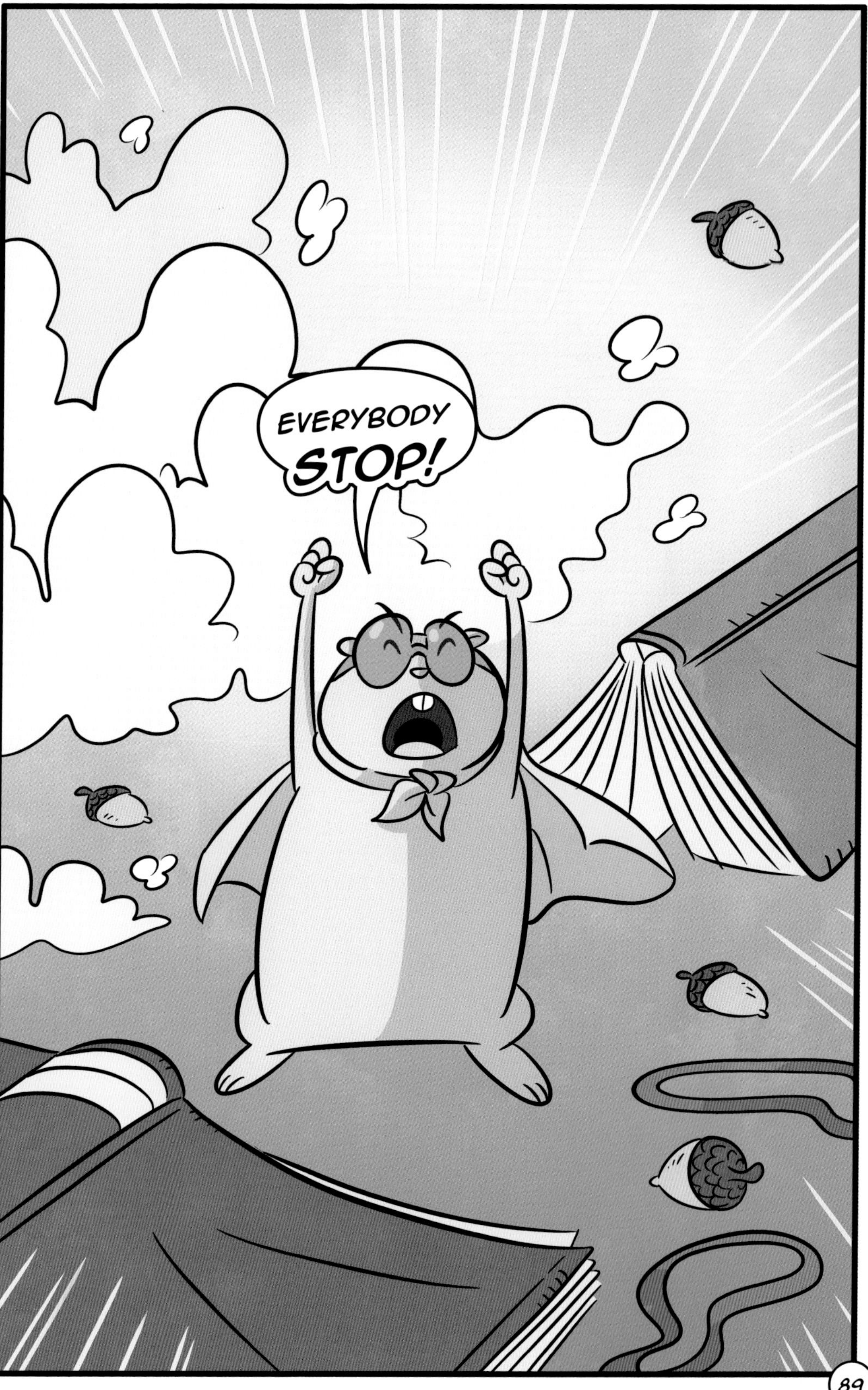
EVERYBODY STOP!

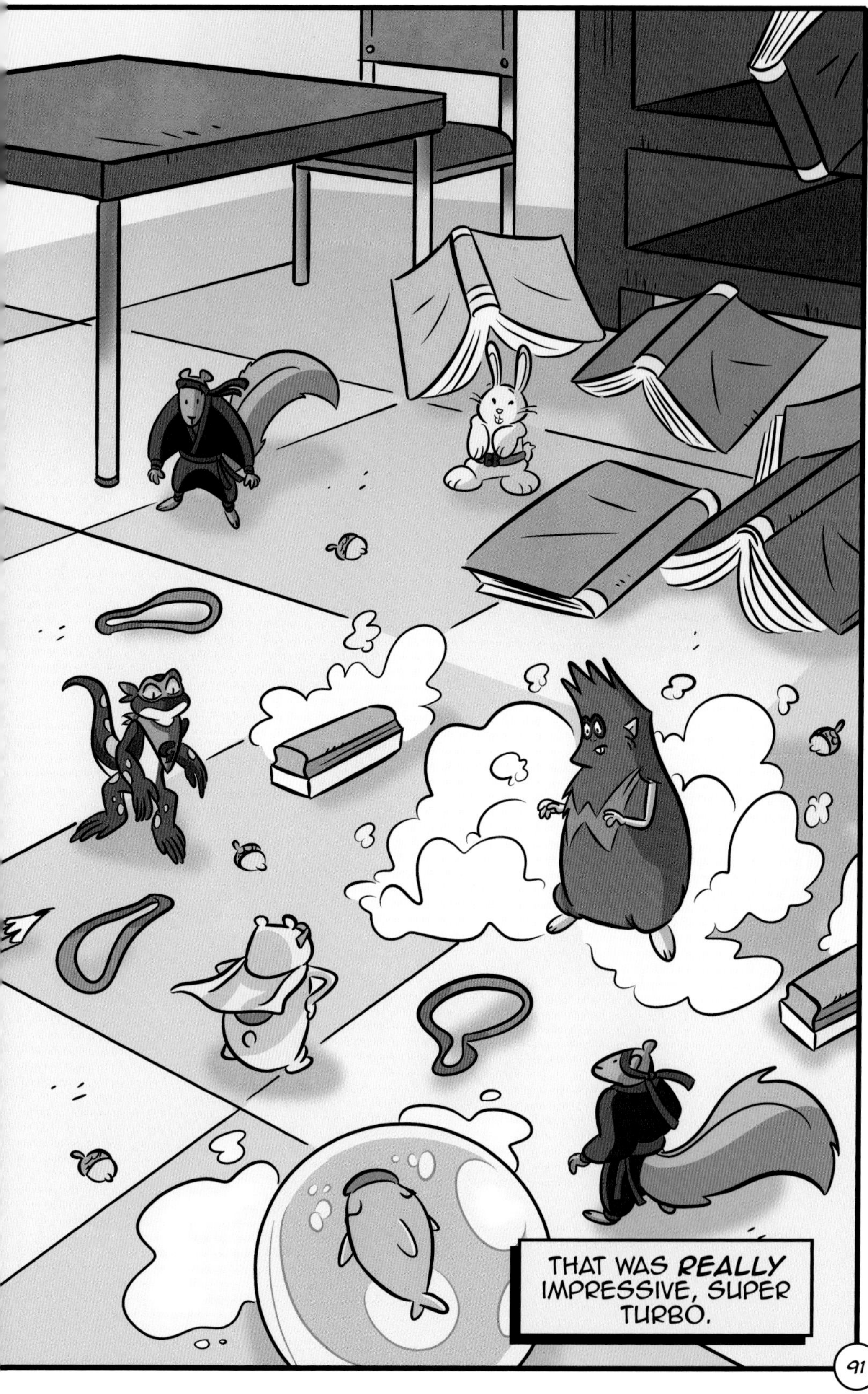
THAT WAS *REALLY* IMPRESSIVE, SUPER TURBO.

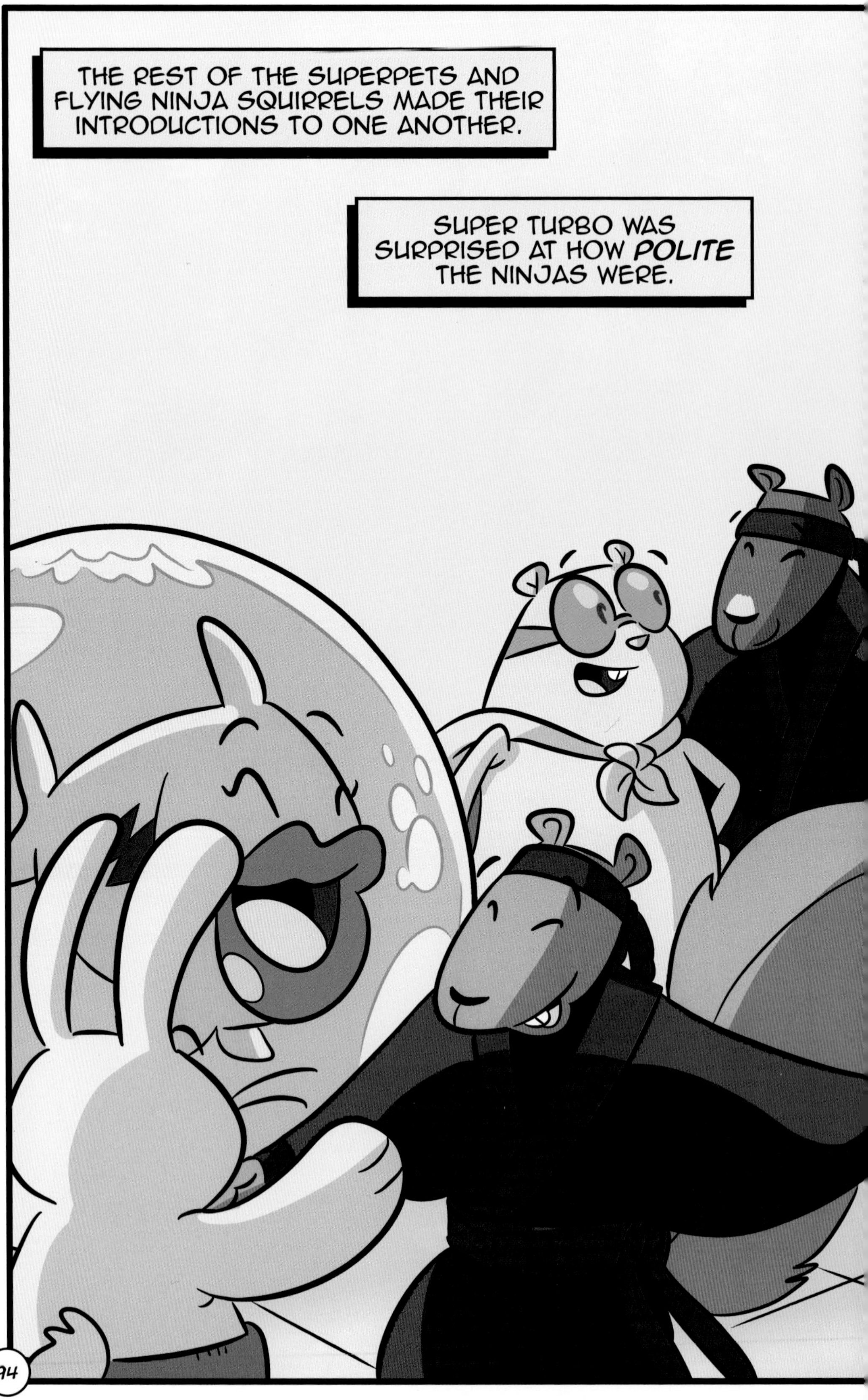
THE REST OF THE SUPERPETS AND FLYING NINJA SQUIRRELS MADE THEIR INTRODUCTIONS TO ONE ANOTHER.
SUPER TURBO WAS SURPRISED AT HOW *POLITE* THE NINJAS WERE.

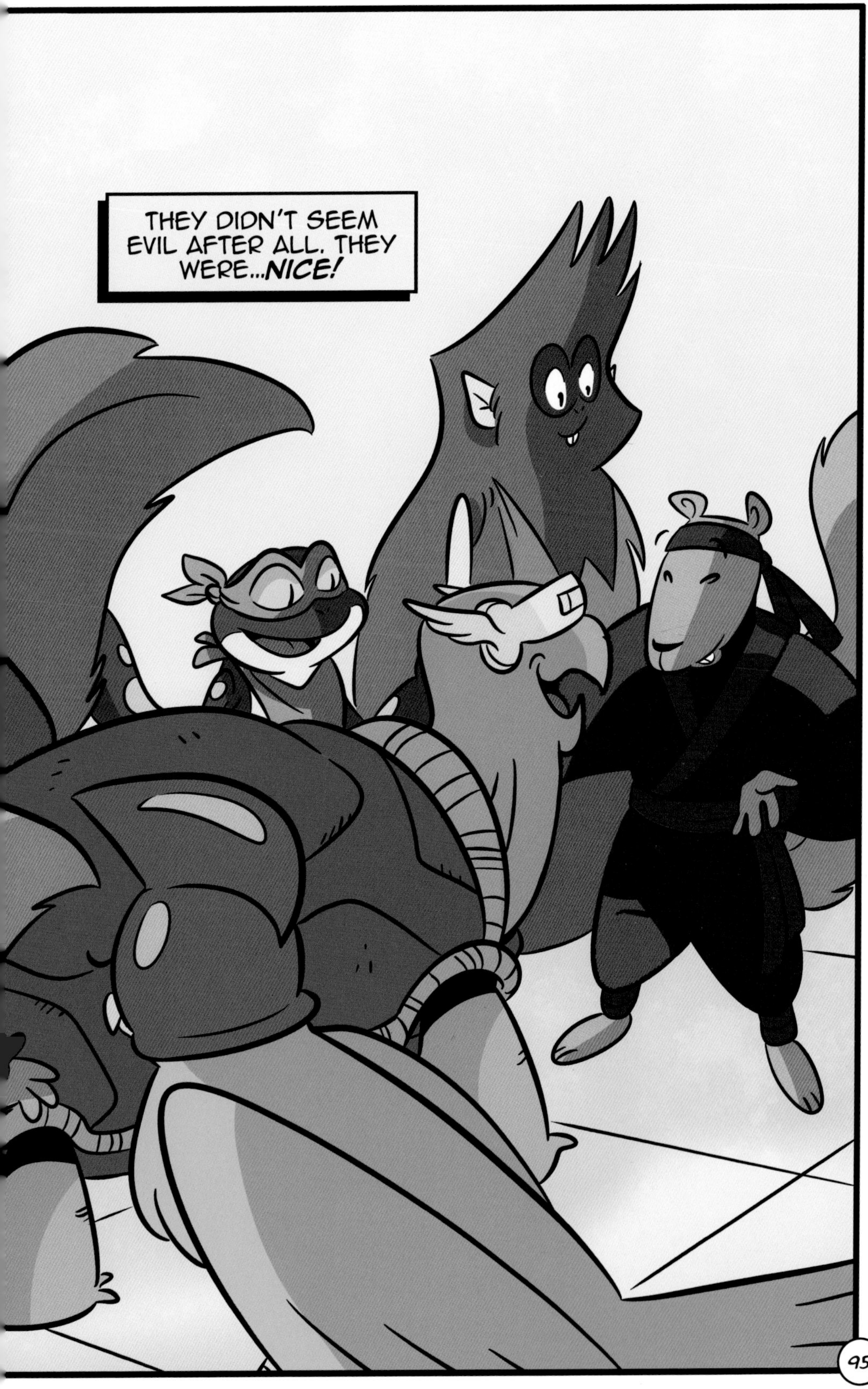
THEY DIDN'T SEEM EVIL AFTER ALL. THEY WERE...NICE!

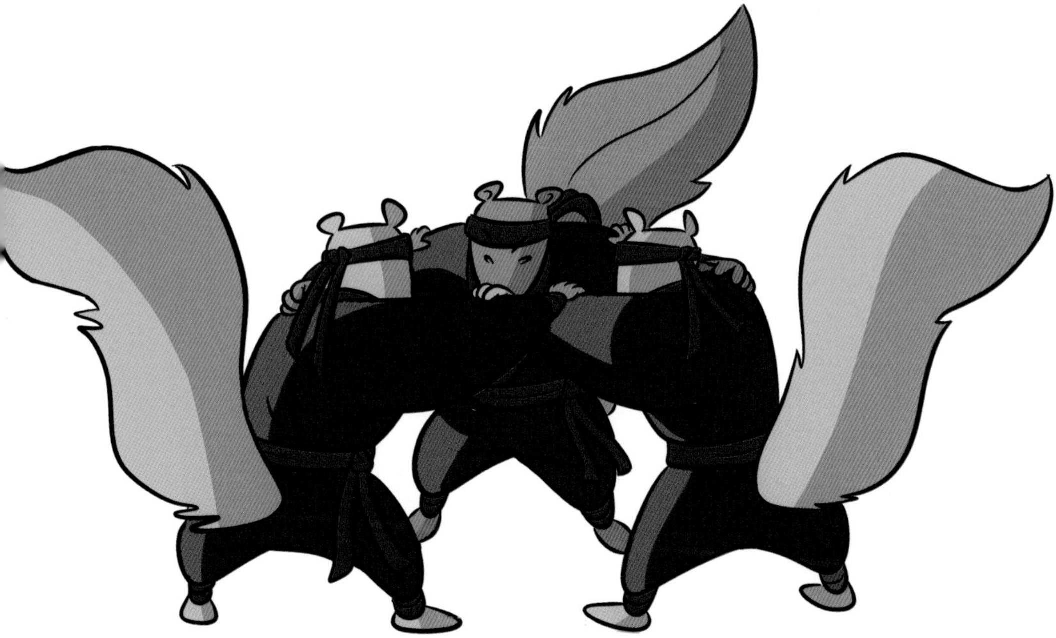

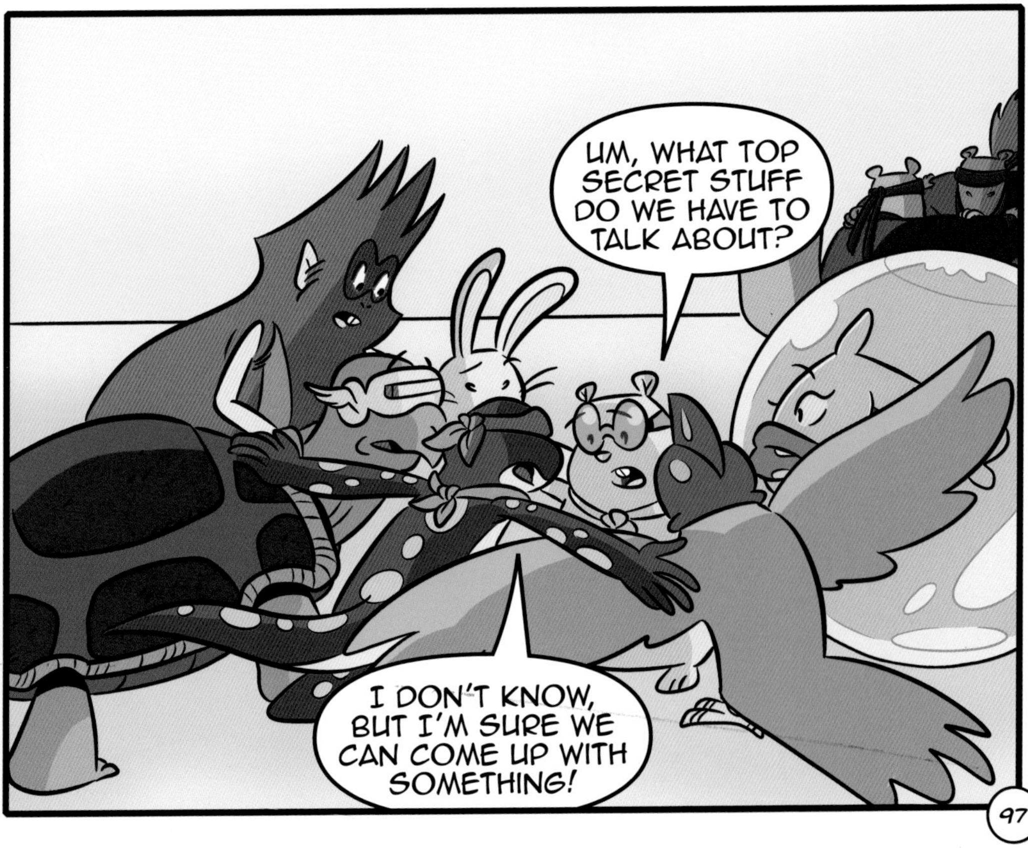
UM, WHAT TOP SECRET STUFF DO WE HAVE TO TALK ABOUT?
I DON'T KNOW, BUT I'M SURE WE CAN COME UP WITH SOMETHING!

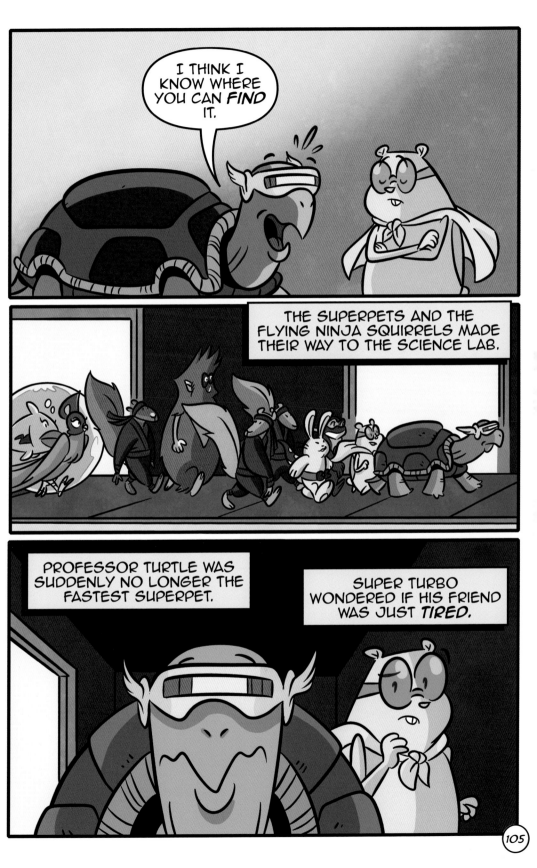

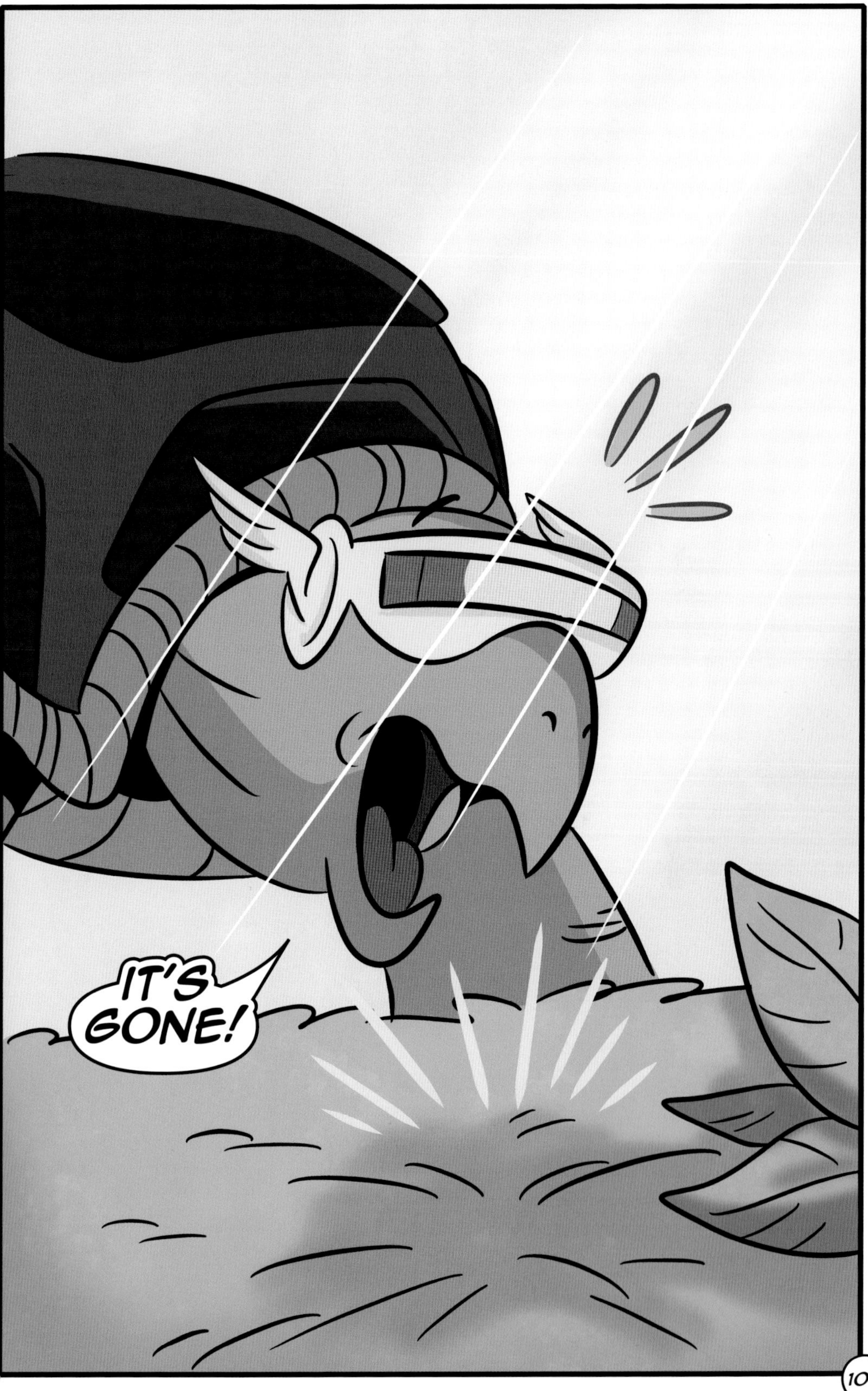
IT'S GONE!

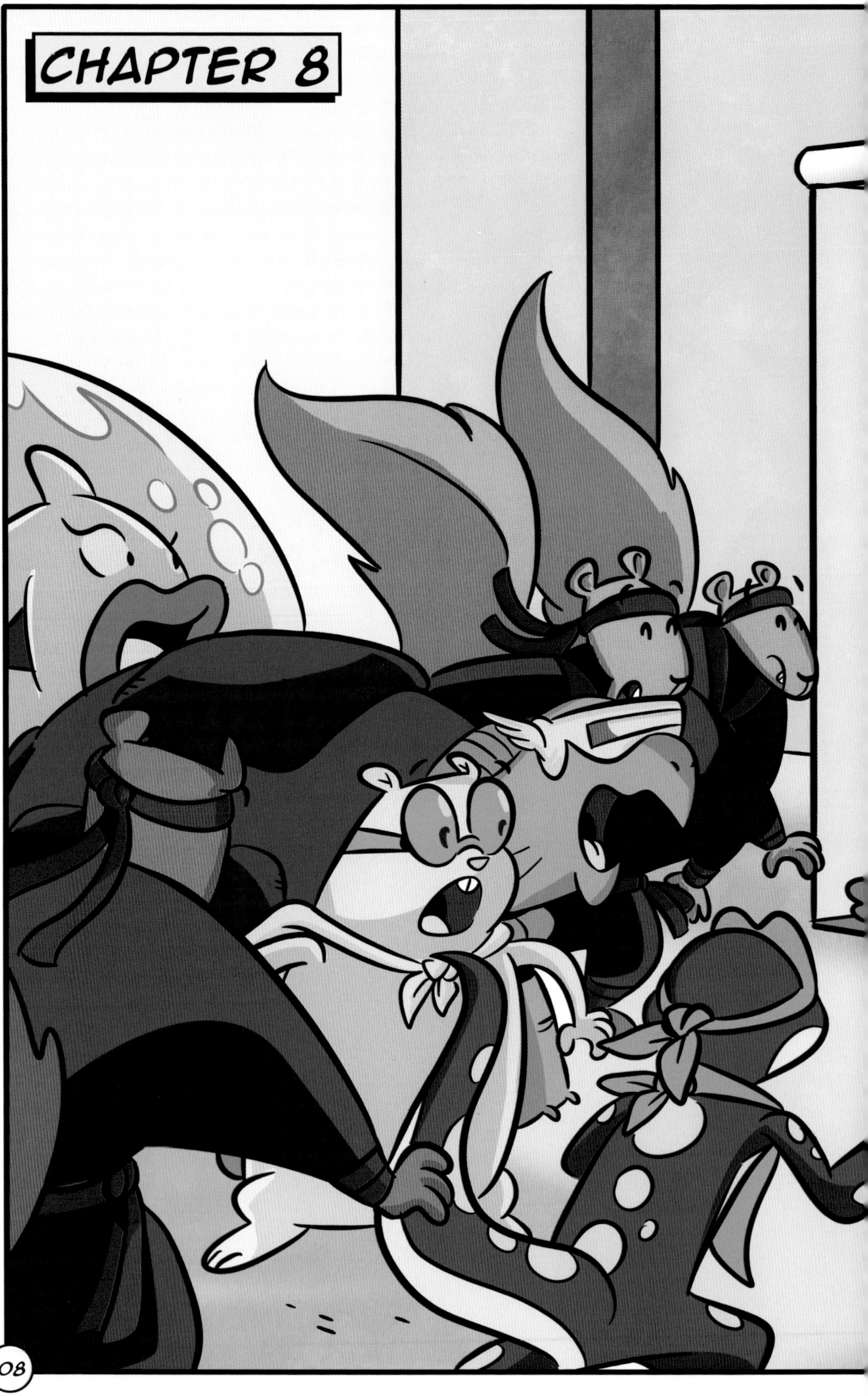
CHAPTER 8

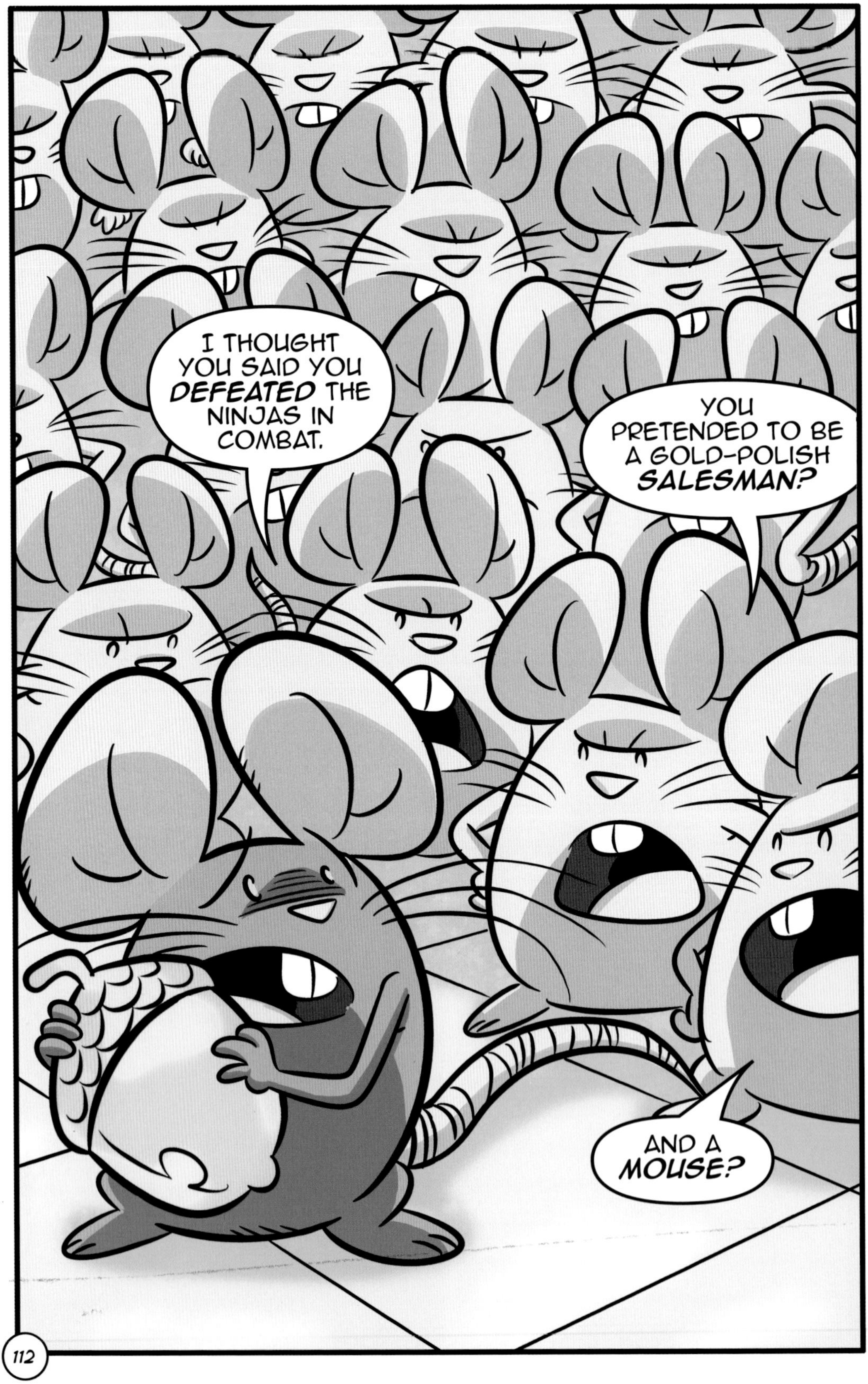
I THOUGHT YOU SAID YOU *DEFEATED* THE NINJAS IN COMBAT.
YOU PRETENDED TO BE A GOLD-POLISH *SALESMAN?*
AND A *MOUSE?*

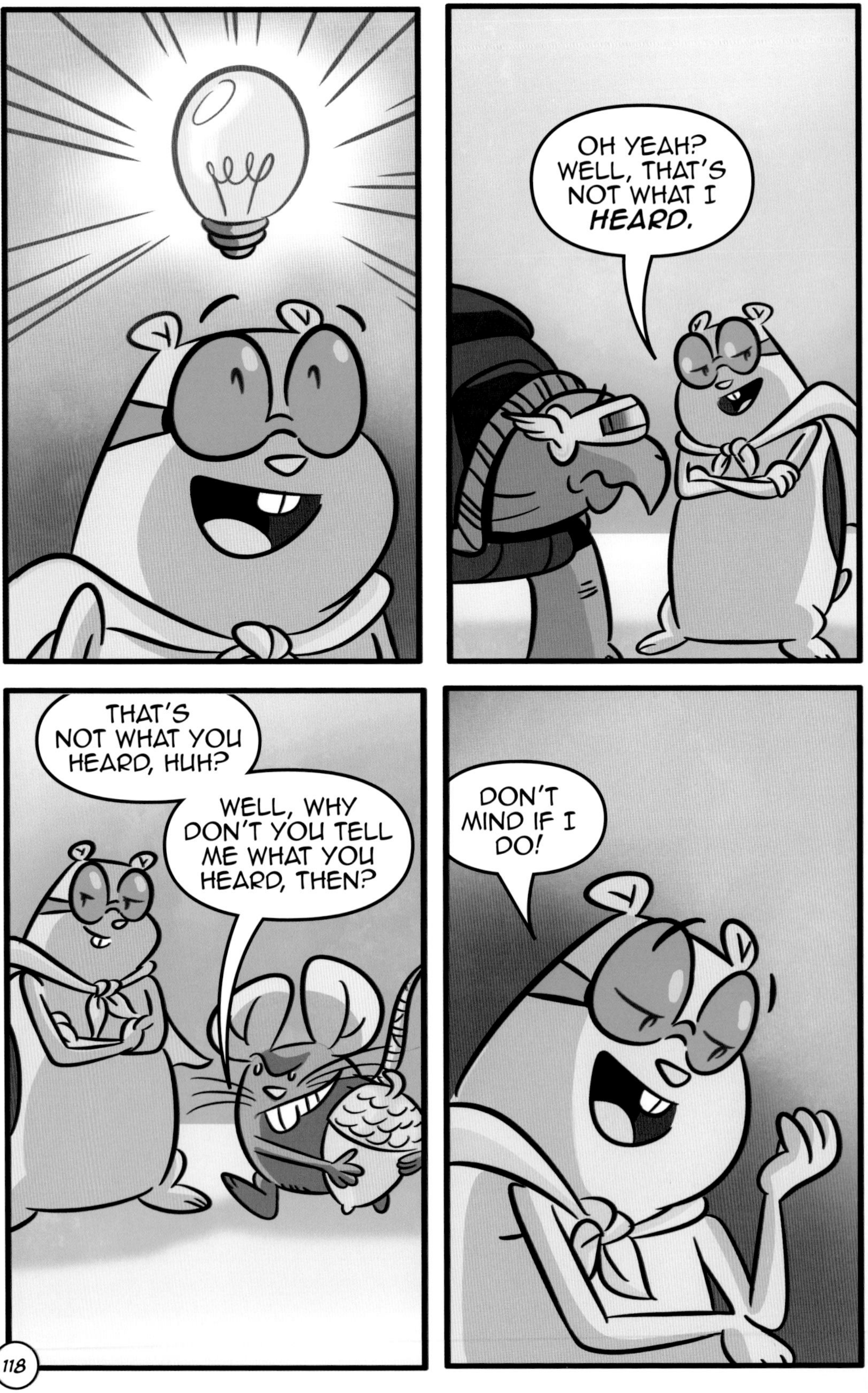
OH YEAH? WELL, THAT'S NOT WHAT I *HEARD.*
THAT'S NOT WHAT YOU HEARD, HUH?
WELL, WHY DON'T YOU TELL ME WHAT YOU HEARD, THEN?
DON'T MIND IF I DO!

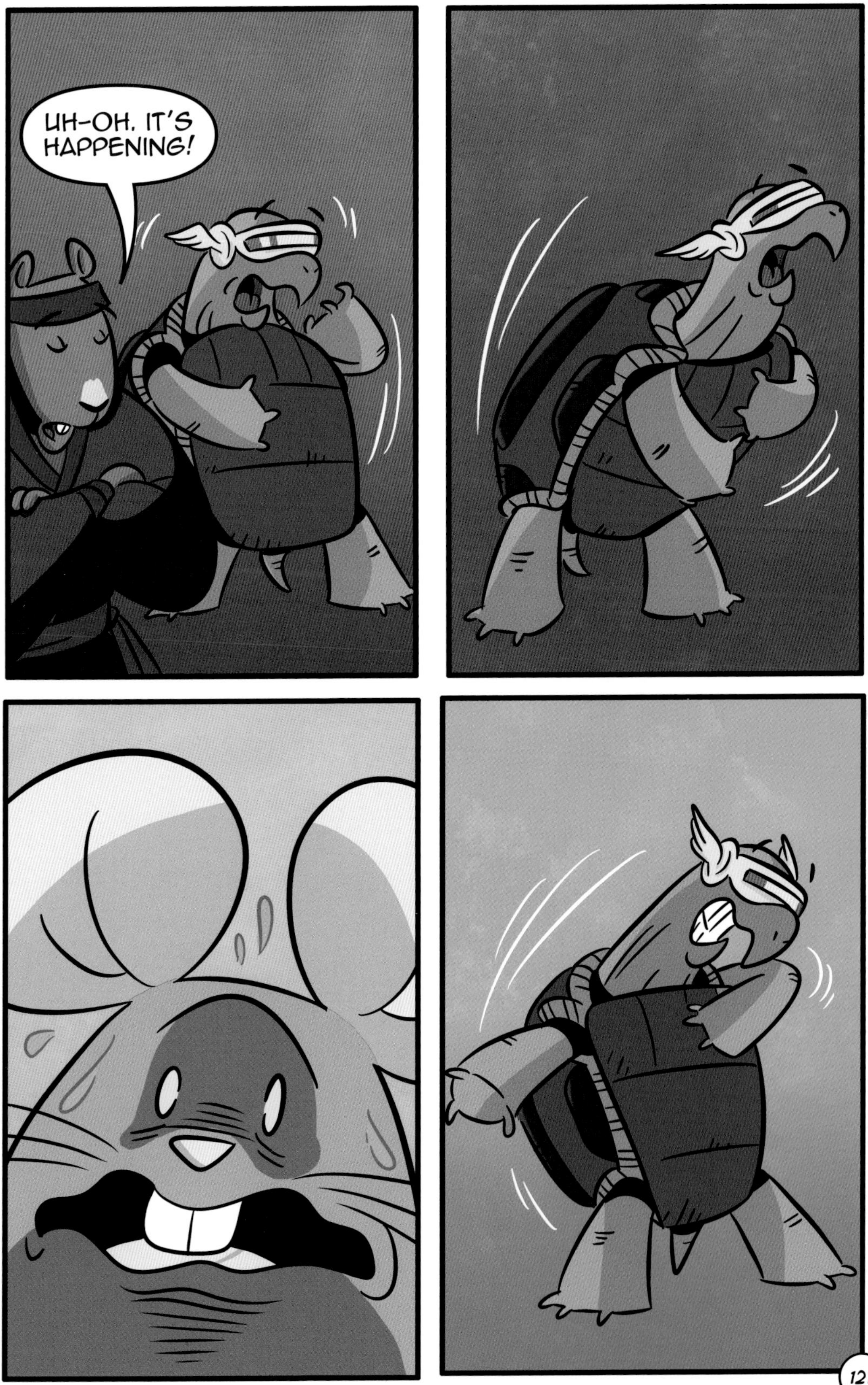
UH-OH. IT'S HAPPENING!

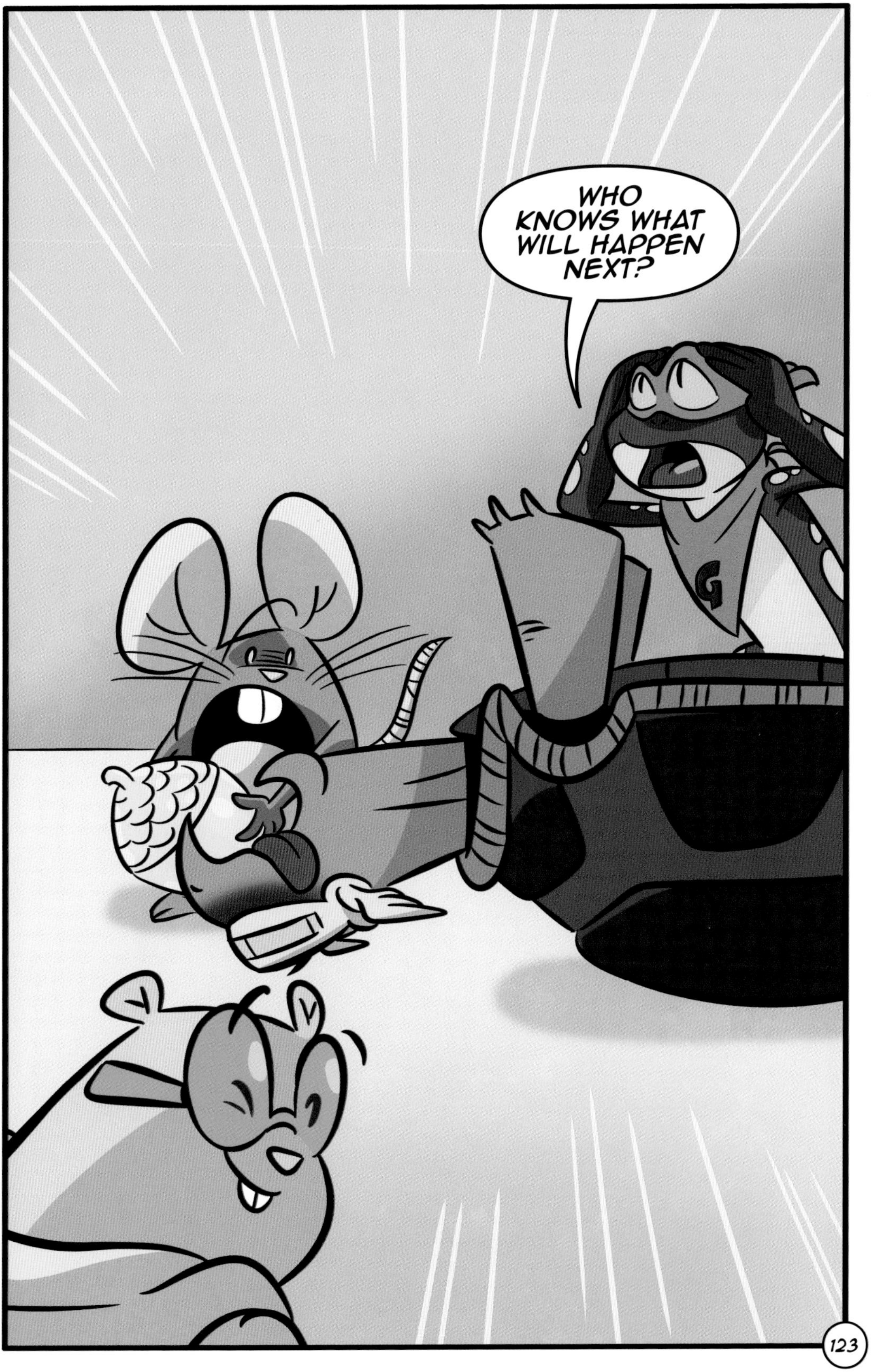
WHO KNOWS WHAT WILL HAPPEN NEXT?

CHAPTER 9

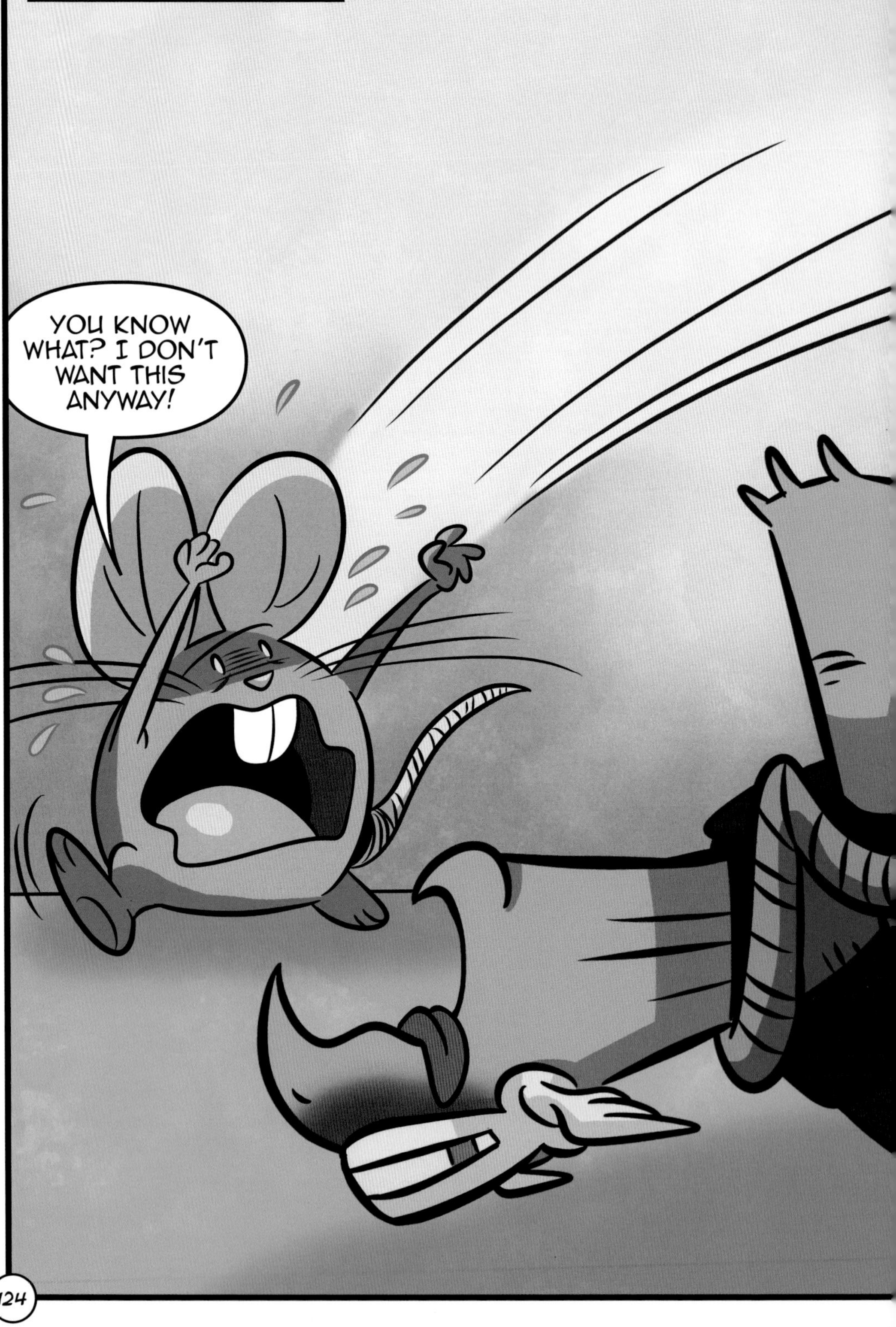
YOU KNOW WHAT? I DON'T WANT THIS ANYWAY!

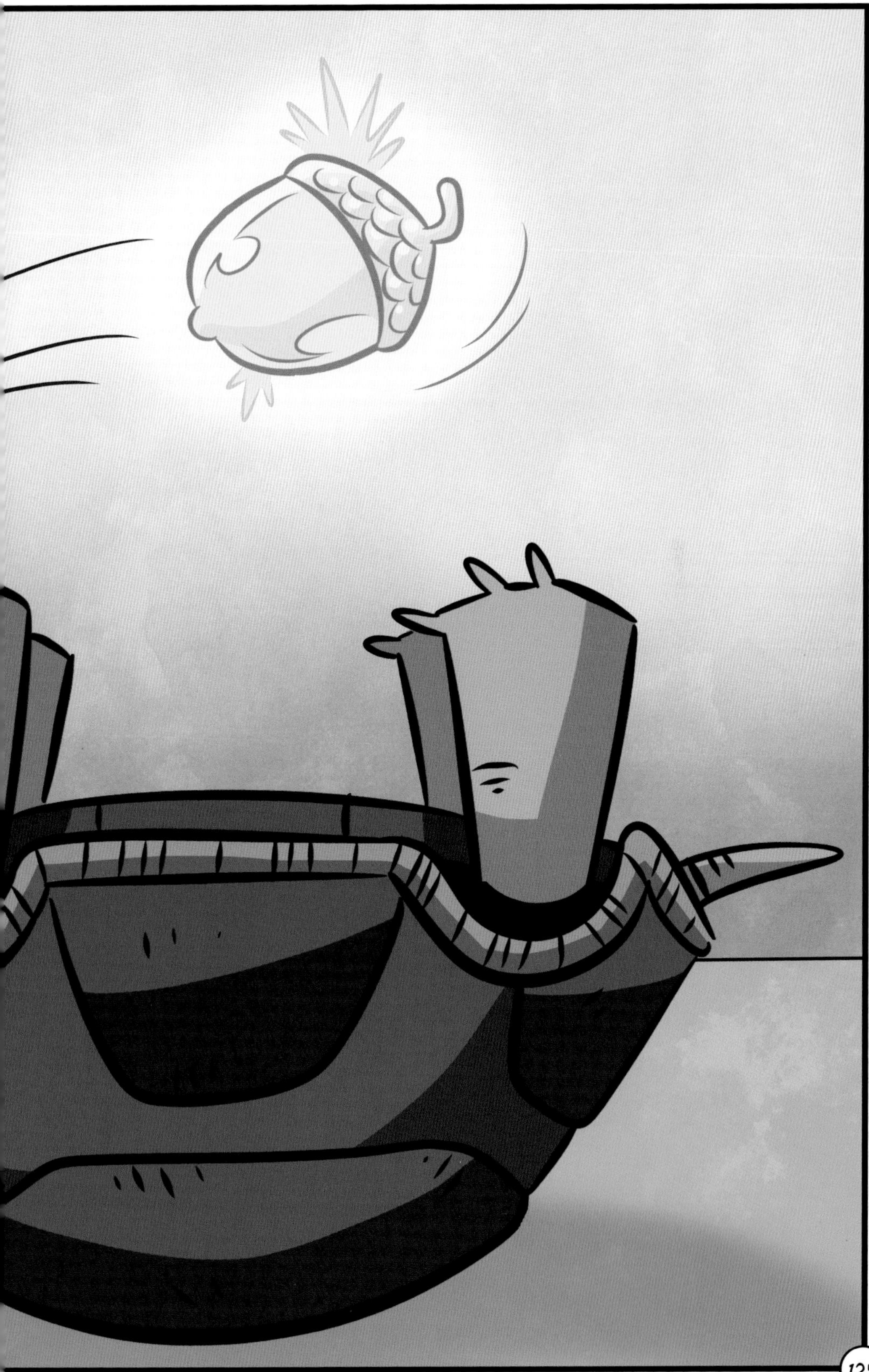

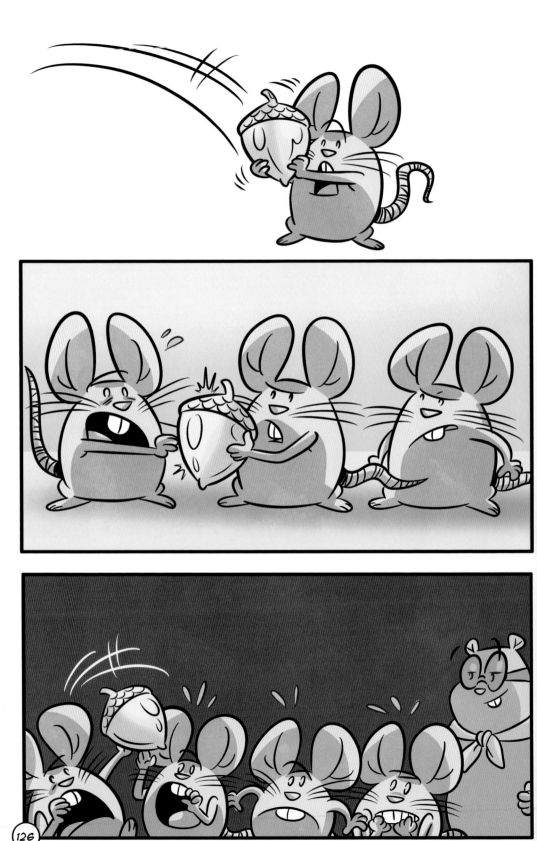

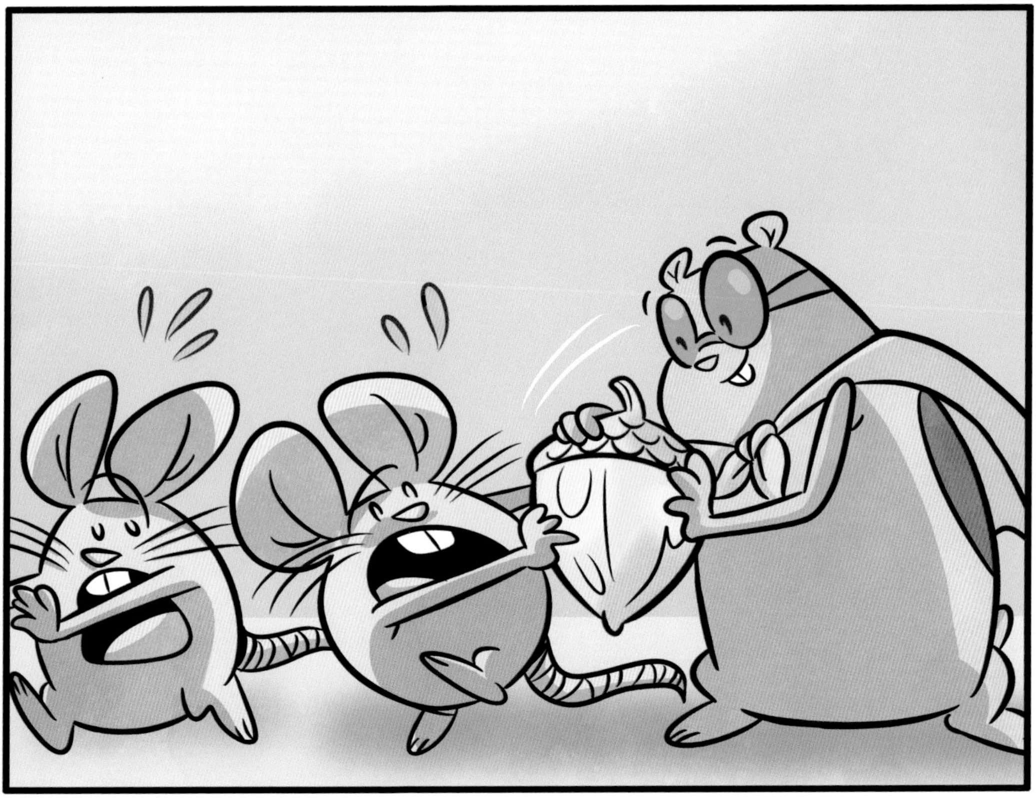

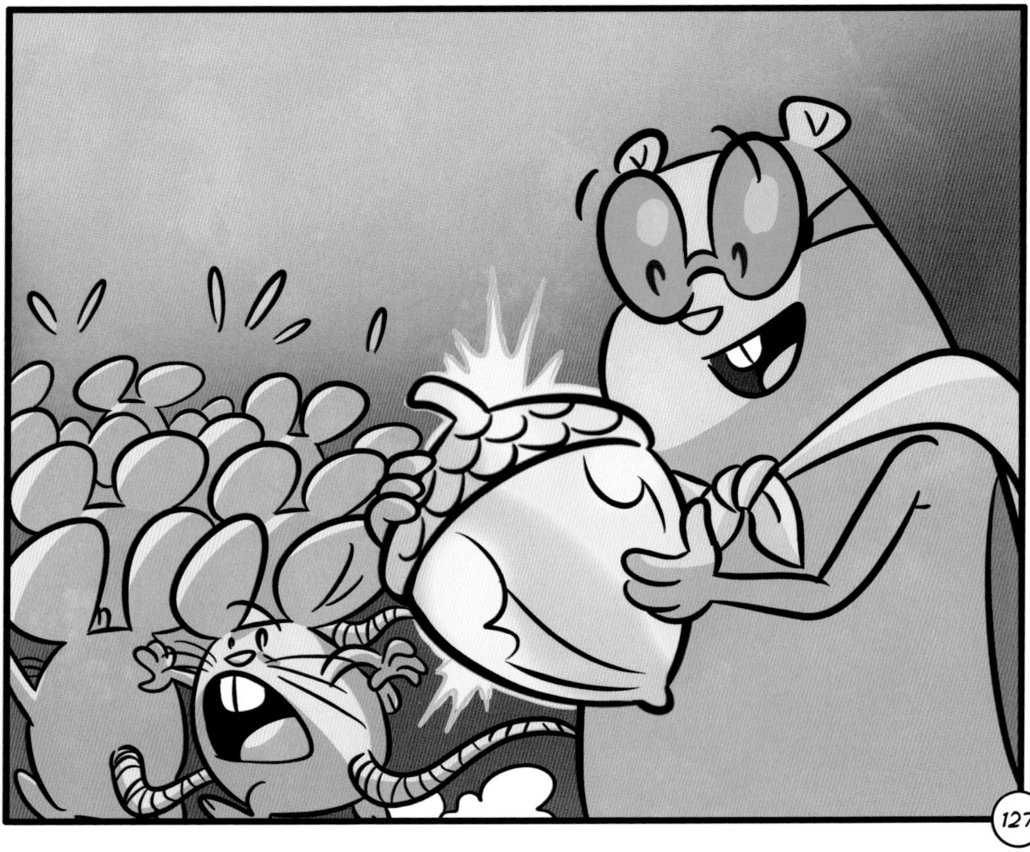

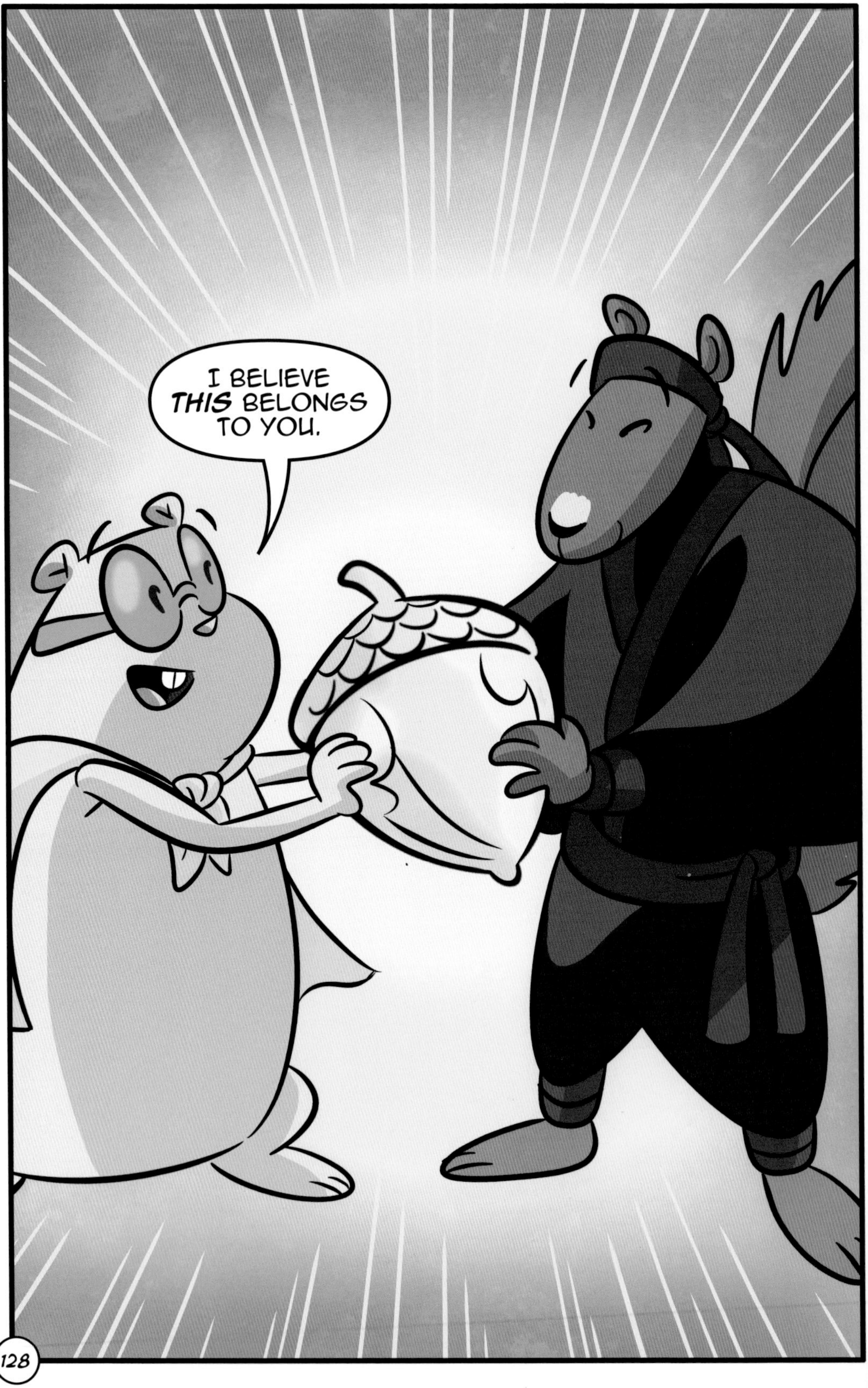
I BELIEVE THIS BELONGS TO YOU.

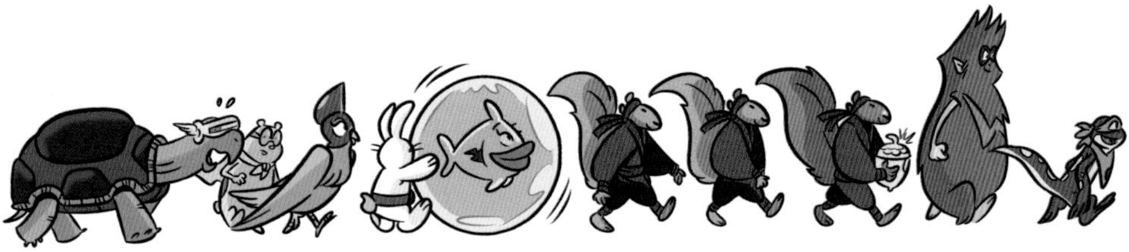

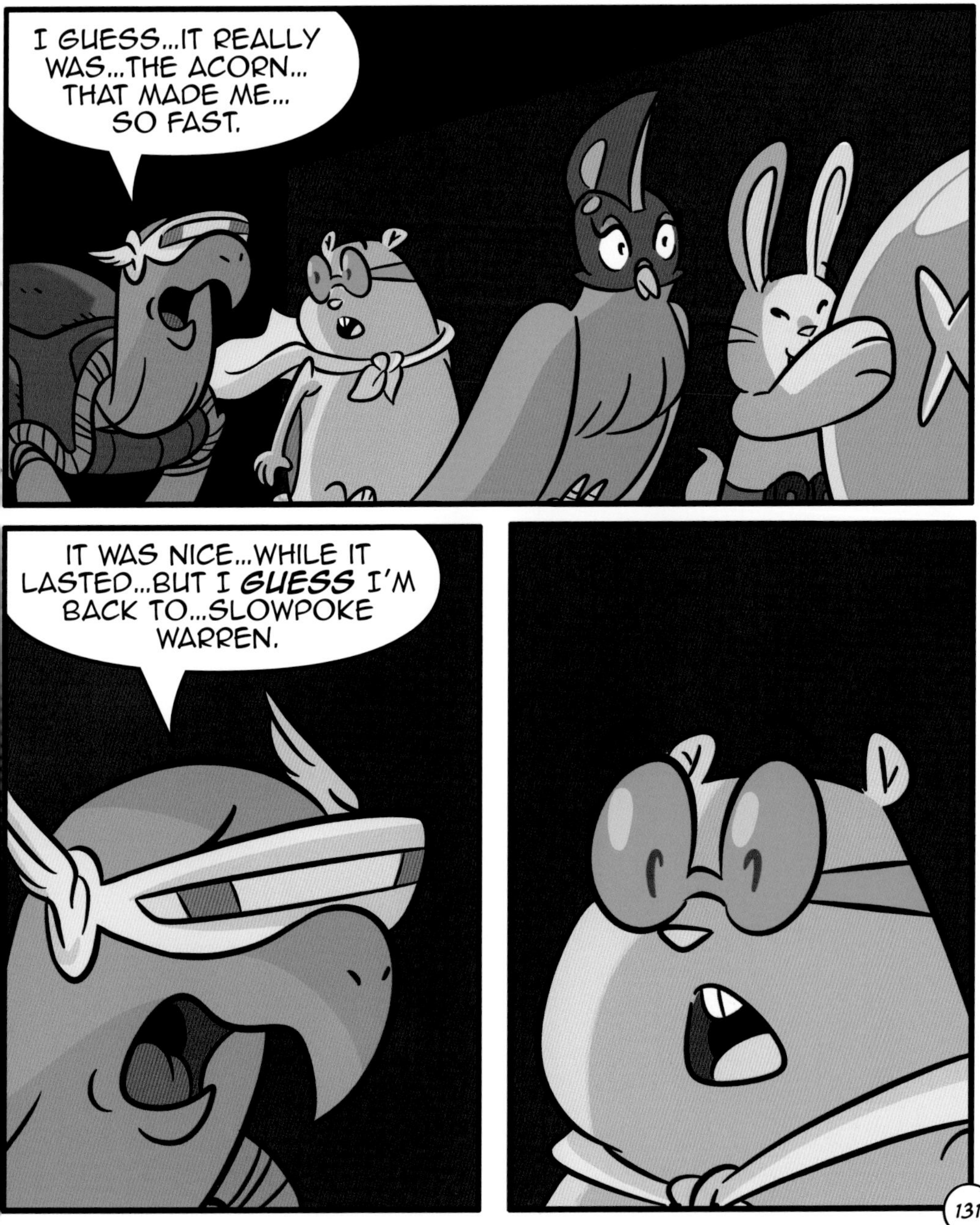
I GUESS...IT REALLY WAS...THE ACORN... THAT MADE ME... SO FAST.
IT WAS NICE...WHILE IT LASTED...BUT I *GUESS* I'M BACK TO...SLOWPOKE WARREN.

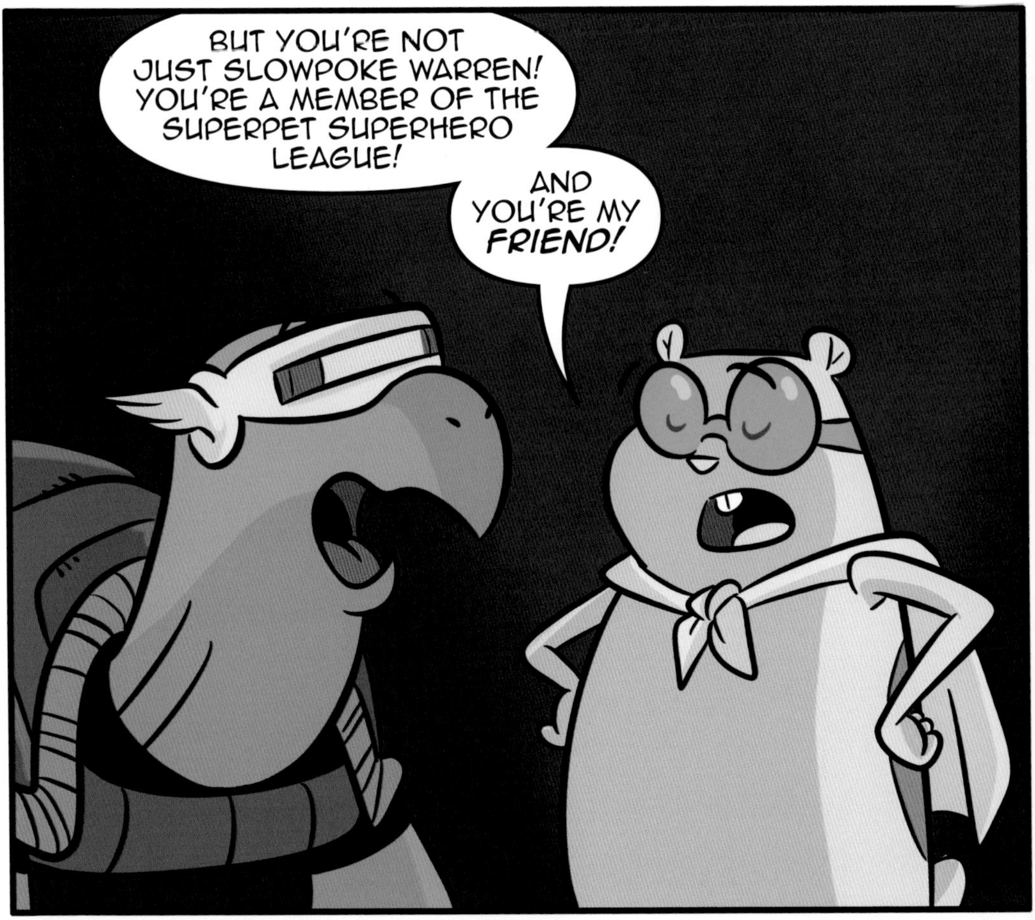
BUT YOU'RE NOT JUST SLOWPOKE WARREN! YOU'RE A MEMBER OF THE SUPERPET SUPERHERO LEAGUE!
AND YOU'RE MY *FRIEND!*

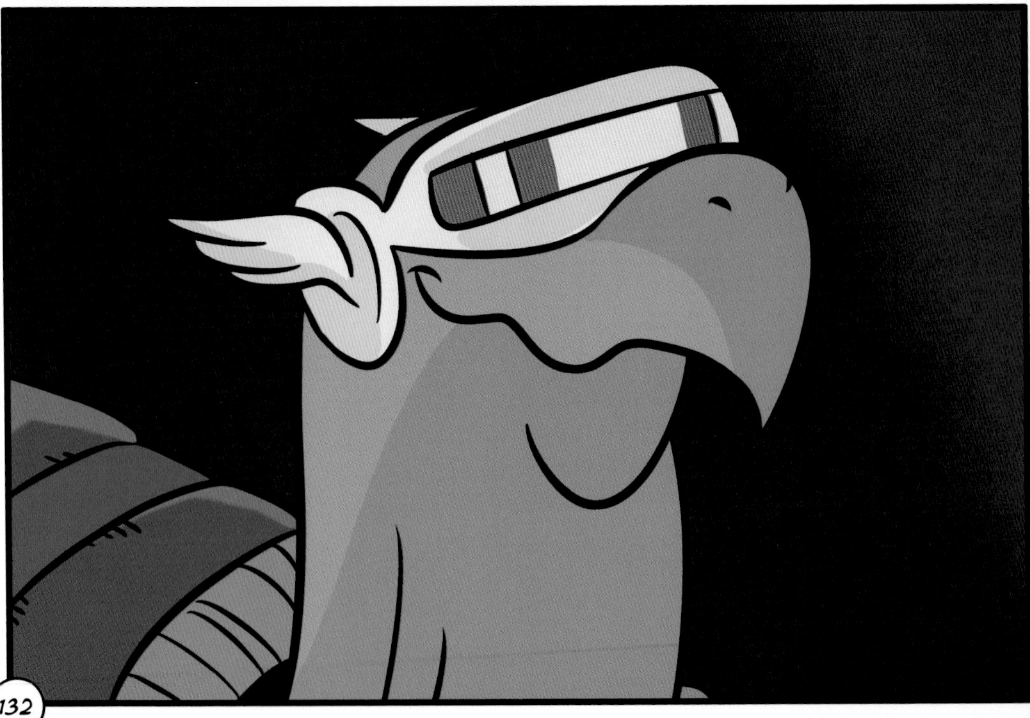

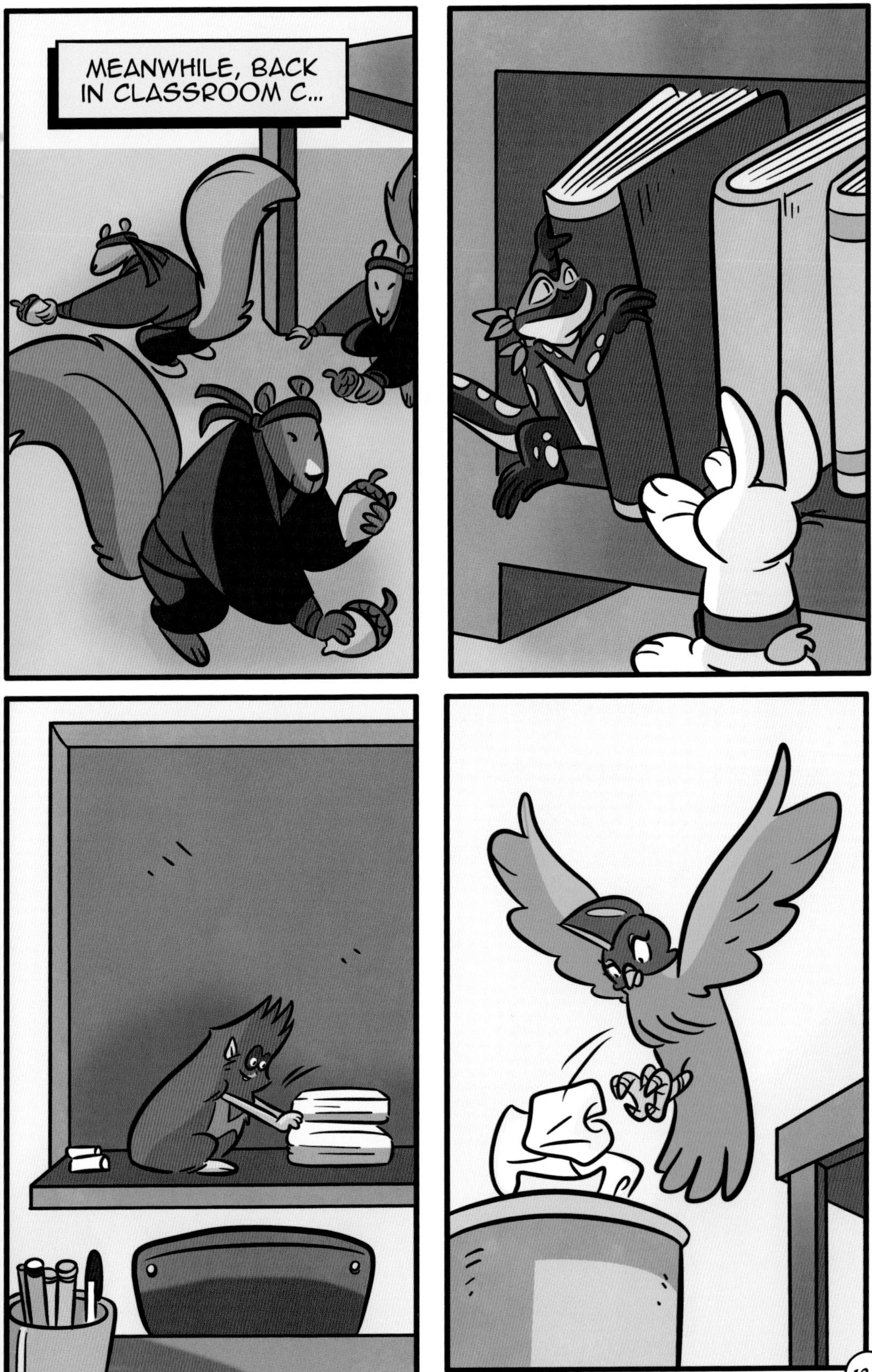
MEANWHILE, BACK IN CLASSROOM C...

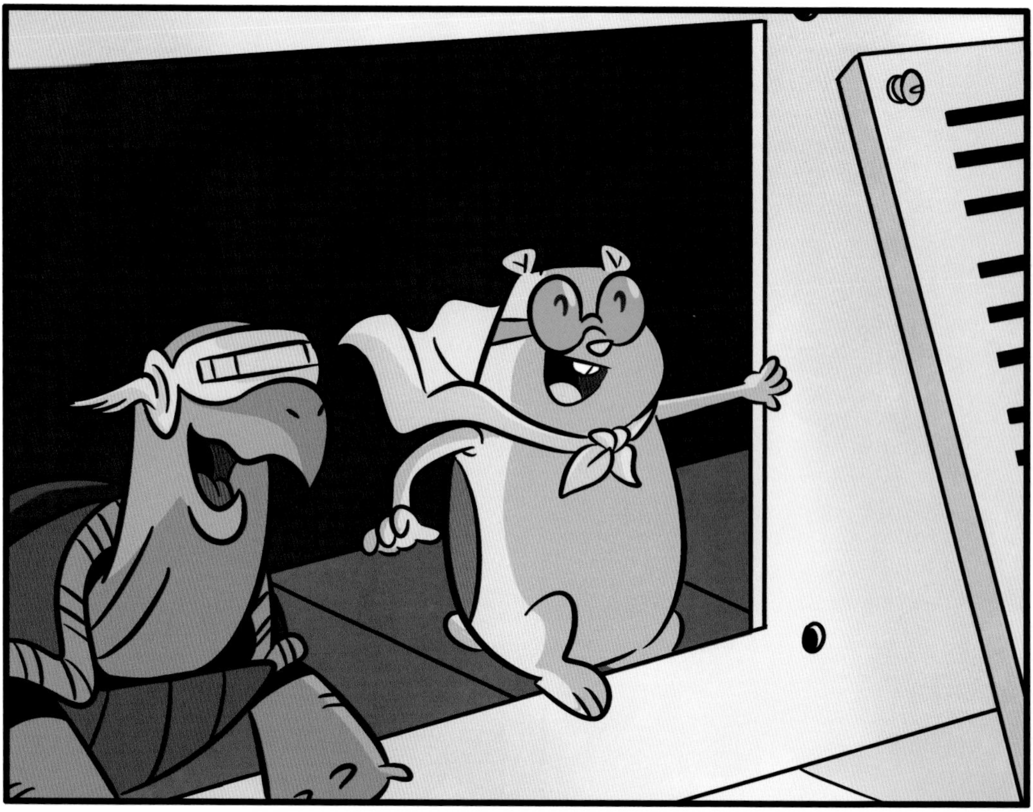

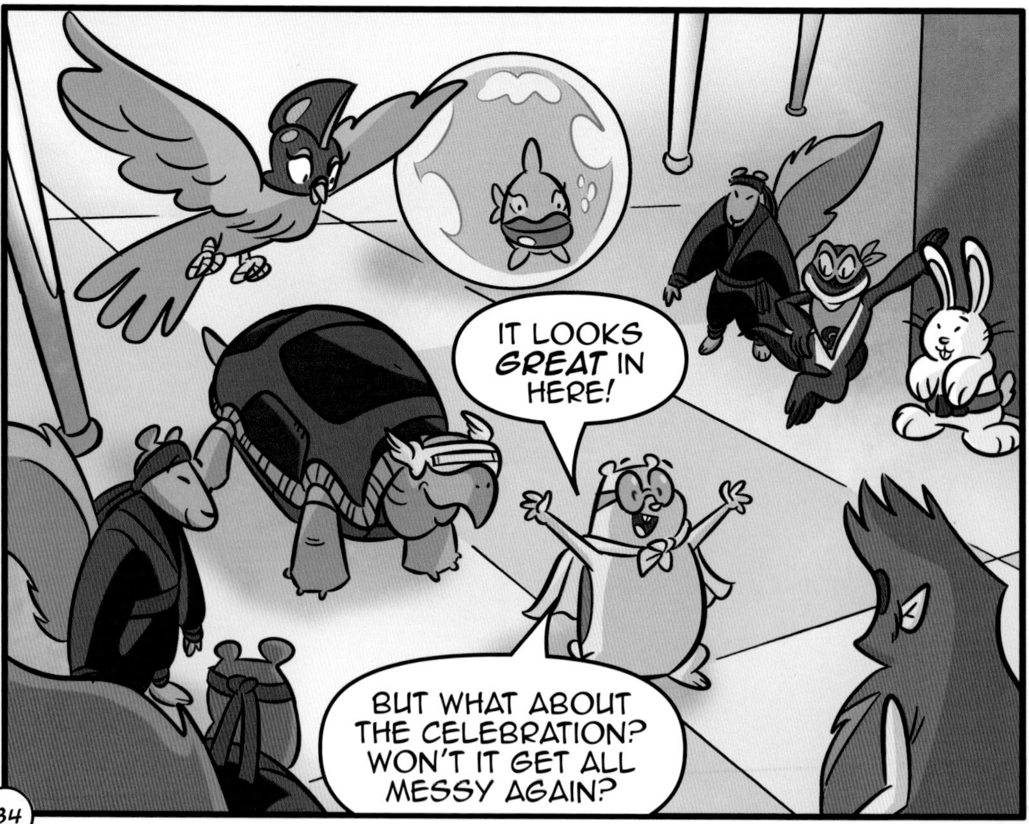
IT LOOKS GREAT IN HERE!
BUT WHAT ABOUT THE CELEBRATION? WON'T IT GET ALL MESSY AGAIN?

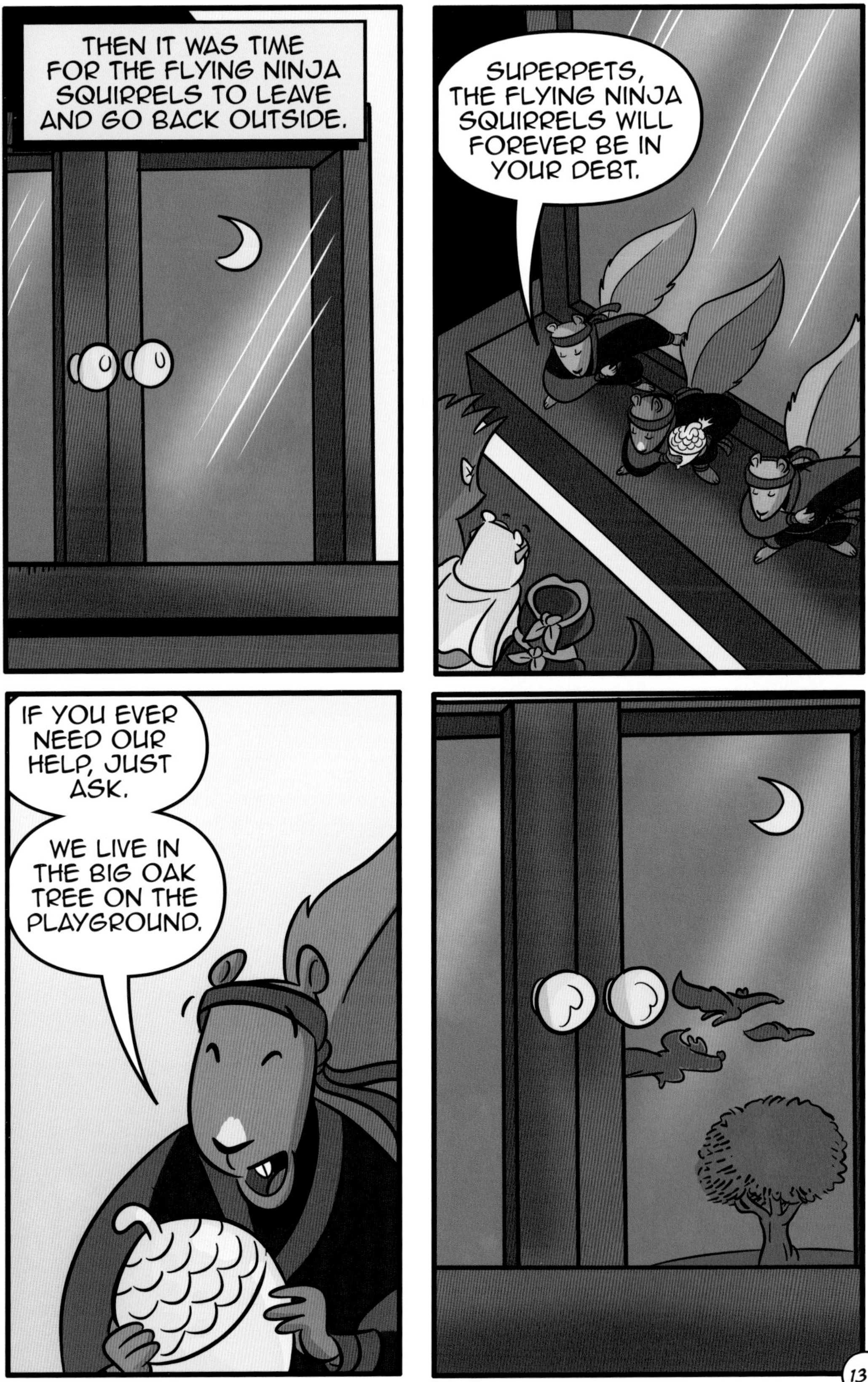
THEN IT WAS TIME FOR THE FLYING NINJA SQUIRRELS TO LEAVE AND GO BACK OUTSIDE.
SUPERPETS, THE FLYING NINJA SQUIRRELS WILL FOREVER BE IN YOUR DEBT.
IF YOU EVER NEED OUR HELP, JUST ASK.
WE LIVE IN THE BIG OAK TREE ON THE PLAYGROUND.

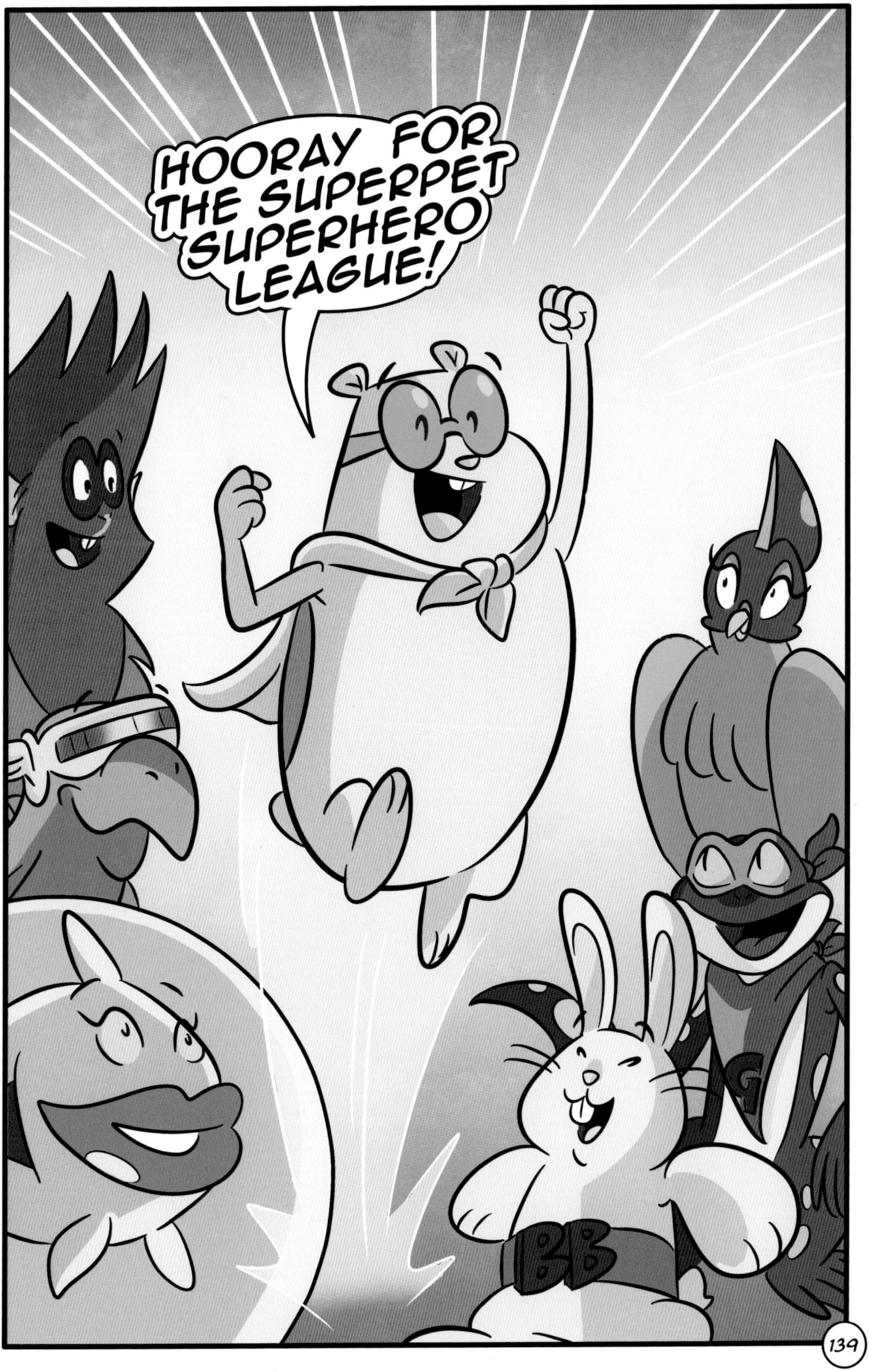
HOORAY FOR THE SUPERPET SUPERHERO LEAGUE!
BB
G

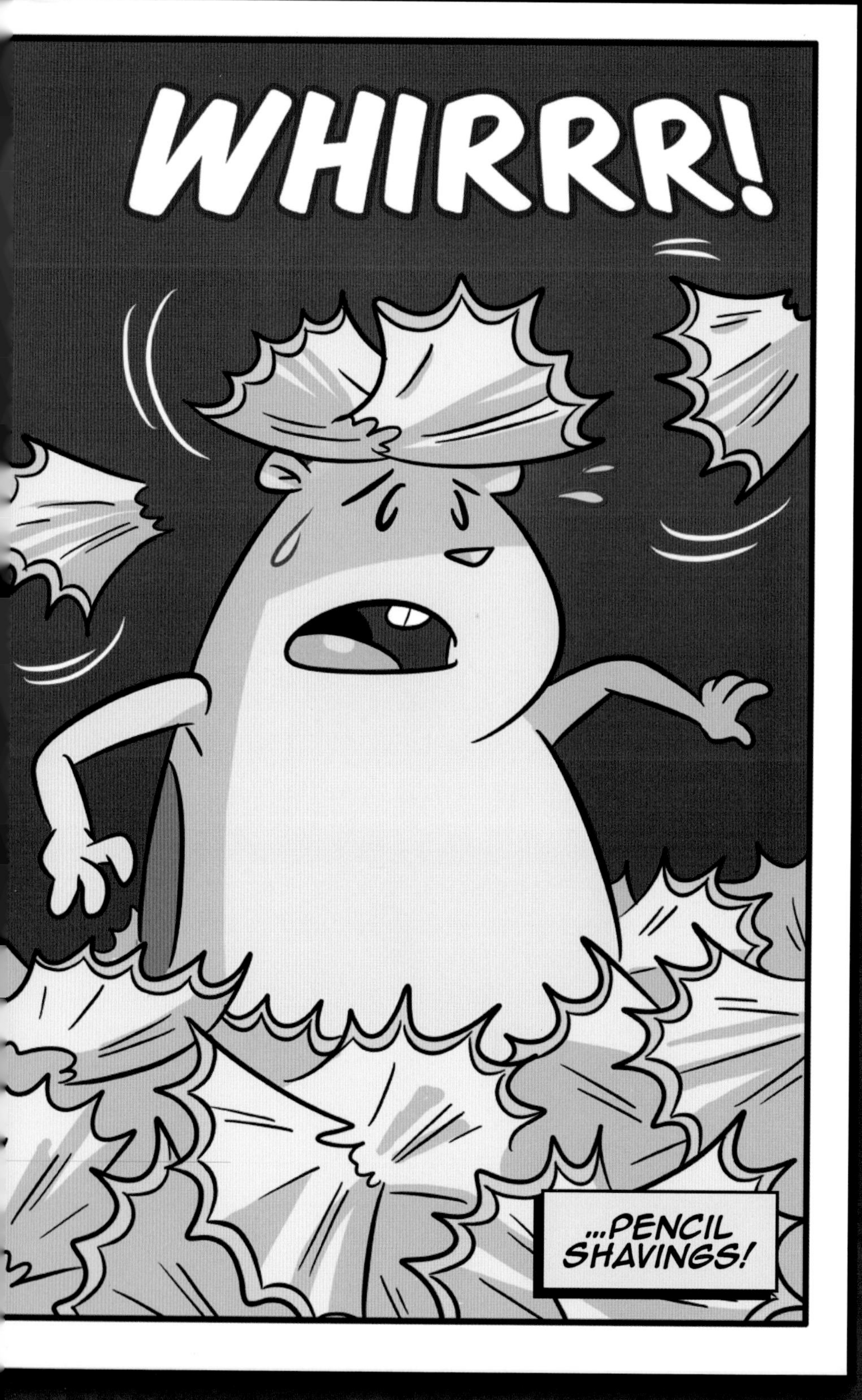
WHIRRR!
...PENCIL SHAVINGS!

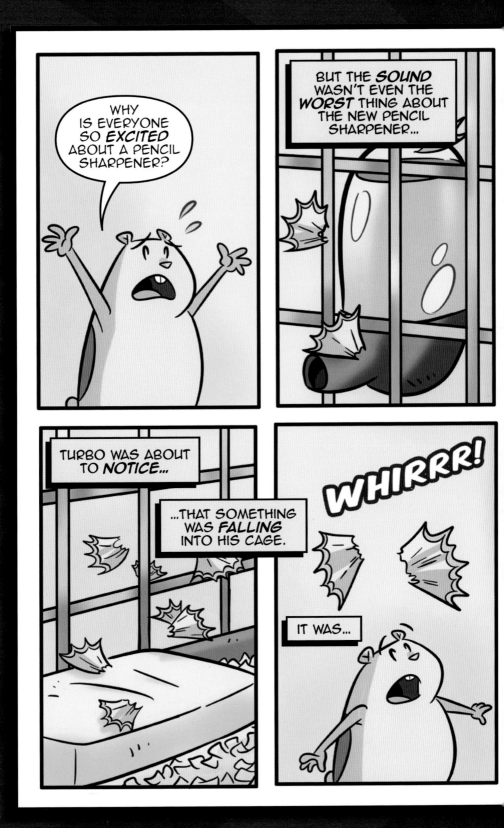